PRAISE FOR AWARD-WINNING AUTHOR BENTLEY LITTLE

The Revelation

"Grabs the reader and yanks him along through an ever-worsening landscape of horrors. . . . It's a terrifying ride with a shattering conclusion."
—Gary Brandner

"*The Revelation* isn't just a thriller, it's a shocker . . . packed with frights and good, gory fun. . . . A must for those who like horror with a bite." —Richard Laymon

"I guarantee, once you start reading this book, you'll be up until dawn with your eyes glued to the pages." —Rick Hautala

The Ignored

"This is Bentley Little's best book yet. Frightening, thought-provoking and impossible to put down."
—Stephen King

"With his artfully plain prose and Quixote-like narrative, Little dissects the deep and disturbing fear of anonymity all Americans feel. . . . What Little has created is nothing less than a nightmarishly brilliant tour de force of modern life in America."
—*Publishers Weekly* (starred review)

"A masterpiece . . . bizarre and frightening. A shocking, unforgettable tour de force from one of horror's top talents." —Barnes & Noble on-line

turn the page for more praise . . .

The Store

"Must reading for Koontz fans. Bentley Little
draws the reader into a ride filled with fear,
danger, and horror."   —Harriet Klausner

The Mailman

"A thinking person's horror novel. *The Mailman*
delivers."   —*Los Angeles Times*

University

"Bentley Little keeps the high-tension jolts coming.
By the time I finished, my nerves were pretty
well fried, and I have a pretty high shock level.
University is unlike anything else in popular fiction."
          —Stephen King

THE
REVELATION

BENTLEY LITTLE

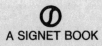

A SIGNET BOOK

SIGNET
Published by New American Library, a division of
Penguin Putnam Inc., 375 Hudson Street,
New York, New York 10014, U.S.A.
Penguin Books Ltd, 80 Strand,
London WC2R 0RL, England
Penguin Books Australia Ltd, 250 Camberwell Road,
Camberwell, Victoria 3124, Australia
Penguin Books Canada Ltd, 10 Alcorn Avenue,
Toronto, Ontario, Canada M4V 3B2
Penguin Books (N.Z.) Ltd, 182–190 Wairau Road,
Auckland 10, New Zealand

Penguin Books Ltd, Registered Offices:
Harmondsworth, Middlesex, England

Published by Signet, an imprint of New American Library,
a division of Penguin Putnam Inc. Originally published
in hardcover by St. Martin's Press.

First Signet Printing, October 1999
10 9 8 7

Ⓟ REGISTERED TRADEMARK—MARCA REGISTRADA

Printed in the United States of America

PUBLISHER'S NOTE
This is a work of fiction. Names, characters, places, and incidents either are
the product of the author's imagination or are used fictitiously, and any resemblance to actual persons, living or dead, events, or locales is entirely
coincidental.

Special thanks to:

My agent, Dominick Abel, for sticking with me for a very long and trying year.

Dean Koontz, an influence who became a friend and ally, for teaching me the ropes and treating me as though I was somebody—when I wasn't.

David Silva, editor of *The Horror Show*, for giving me my first break and for his important and consistent support through the years.

Keith Neilson, teacher and friend, for his ego-boosting belief, solid advice, intelligent criticism, unfailing support, and for guiding this novel through the tricky waters of academia and into the ocean of the real world beyond.

My parents, Lawrence and Roseanne Little, and my brother, Judson Little, for everything else.

PROLOGUE

The shaman stared at the newcomer with thinly veiled scorn. Attired in ceremonial skins that were a slightly altered version of his own, the newcomer was loudly addressing a group of villagers gathered on the far side of the creek. His voice carried clearly on the slight wind that blew from the north. He raised his hands high into the air, his upturned face toward the hot summer sun. Red and blue fire would fall from the skies, he predicted, and soon after, the earth would shake with the footsteps of the dark gods. The assembled villagers gasped and muttered amongst themselves.

The shaman shook his head in disgust and glanced toward the hogan, where his apprentice was supposed to be studying the patterns of color on two hawk feathers. The young boy was outside the open doorway, staring wide-eyed across the creek. When he saw that his master was looking at him, he quickly bent down to examine again the two feathers on the ground.

"Go," the shaman said, not bothering to hide his anger. "Come back when you are ready to learn."

"I am ready—" the boy began.

"Go," the shaman repeated. He watched unmoving as his apprentice grabbed his belongings and scrambled off. The boy headed away from the villagers, in the opposite direction from the creek, but the shaman knew that as soon as he went inside the hogan, the boy would sneak over to hear what the newcomer had to say.

The shaman bent down to pick up the hawk feathers and took them into the hogan. When he emerged again into the sunlight, he saw that Nan-Timocha, the village chief, was standing nearby, staring thoughtfully toward the newcomer. He walked slowly toward the chief, who turned to look at him and nodded. The two men were silent for a moment. "What do you think of this new shaman?" the chief asked finally.

"He is no shaman."

The chief nodded, saying nothing, as though he had expected the answer.

"Why do you allow him to continue his stay in our village?" the shaman asked. "He is frightening the people. They are beginning to believe his wild stories."

"Have you seen his eyes?" the chief asked, staring across the creek. His voice was low, troubled. "They are black. The deepest black I have ever seen."

"You have talked to him?"

The chief nodded. "He has come to me twice, telling me . . ." He shook his head. "I cannot even believe it now."

"Are you going to make him leave?" the shaman asked.

Nan-Timocha met the shaman's gaze. His eyes were vague, unfocused, and there was an unfamiliar emotion etched on his features. "I cannot," he said. "I am afraid of him."

The next night, the fire rained from the skies, blue and red, just as the newcomer had said it would. The shaman remained alone in the ceremonial circle, chanting songs of appeasement to the gods, performing the sacred rituals of protection. He had begun the evening with three assistants, including his apprentice, but all three had run away in fear as the fires fell closer and it was clear that the songs were doing no good.

The shaman fasted the next day, remaining alone in his hogan, offering the appropriate sacrifices, and that evening all was as it should be. But the following night, the earth shook violently, causing jars and pots to rain down on him from their shelved perches as he trembled on the floor in fear of the rampaging feet of the dark gods.

Quiet and subdued, the shaman brought up the rear of the small party that marched down the narrow path to the base of the Mogollon. Overhead, huge black thunderclouds rolled in from the north, casting their shadows on the forest of pines below. To the right, off in the brush, a family of swallows, startled by the presence of the marchers, flew screeching into the air.

The shaman read the signs as they walked. Next to the path, there were three leafless trees in a row and, farther on, a dead squirrel with its legs pointed toward the Mogollon. The omens did not look good.

But the shaman said nothing. After hearing what the newcomer had to say, after seeing the accuracy of the newcomer's prophecies, he now doubted his own techniques and abilities. He walked in silence, cowed in the presence of a man with powers far superior to his own.

Several hours later, the path opened onto a clearing. The sky overhead was dark, and a shifting wind played against them, spraying them with a light mist. The newcomer stopped and motioned for them to remain in place. He took from the small bag he had been carrying a handful of bones and teeth, which he threw down on the dirt. He bent down to examine the positions in which they had fallen and nodded, satisfied.

Nan-Timocha stepped forward, holding the ceremonial headdress he had been carrying since the start of their journey. The newcomer accepted the headdress and placed it on top of his head. He walked into the clearing, the wind whipping his long black hair and tangling it in the feathers. He began chanting the songs of power, petitioning the gods for courage and strength. Suddenly, his voice changed. The cadences became jerkier, less rhythmic. Harsh words poured out in an unknown alien tongue.

Nan-Timocha turned to the shaman. "What is he saying?"

The shaman shook his head. "I do not know the language. I have never heard it before."

From the surrounding bushes came fluid gurgling noises and strange dry rustling sounds. The chief and the two warriors flanking him, Lan-Notlim and Al-Ankura, grasped their weapons tightly, prepared to use them. The shaman stepped backward, holding the sacred beads around his neck.

In the center of the clearing, the newcomer had stopped chanting and was now holding tightly to his own weapon, crouched in a defensive stance.

Though the newcomer had told him what to expect, the shaman had not in his heart believed him. Now he believed. He looked toward the manzanitas, where the noises were now the loudest. The bushes were shaking as though they were alive. He felt the cold sweat of fear break upon his body, his heart pounding wildly in his chest.

The bushes parted.

And as the rain started to fall he began to scream.

PART ONE

ONE

The Coconino Sawmill, Randall's lone industry, loomed over the other buildings in town like an angry parent, its chuted conveyor belts and single-stacked smelter silhouetted blackly against the early morning sun. The mill had been the first structure built in the area, the first encroachment of civilization into this part of the wilderness, and the town had grown up around it, spreading outward. In front of the mill's small cluster of office buildings, next to Main Street, rows of stacked lumber were piled fifteen feet high, ready to be trucked out. In back of the buildings, on the other side of the smelter, next to the river, an equal number of freshly cut logs were piled in pyramidal order, waiting to be converted into boards.

Gordon breathed deeply as he drove past the sawmill on his way to work. He loved the smell of the mill; he never tired of it. Even though it worked at only half-capacity during the summer months, its smell, that deliciously rich odor of pine bark and resin, permeated the air along Main Street from the junction of Old Mesa Road all the way to the post office, supplying somehow a hint of winter to the otherwise overbearing heat of August. In both the fall and winter, of course, the mill warmed the entire town, heat spreading outward from its core as though from a gigantic central heating system, the fresh natural smell of newborn sawdust and burning woodchips drifting as far north as the Rim and as far south as Squaw Creek.

Today the smelter was not operating at all; not a single plume of smoke or flaming speck of sawdust escaped from the black screen that covered the large opening in the top of the stack. He could hear, however, the high-pitched revving whine of the saw blades as they cut logs down to size, and he saw Tim McDowell's blue pickup parked next to the chain link fence that surrounded the sawmill. Nine or ten other cars and trucks were parked nearby.

Gordon passed the sawmill, waving, though he didn't know whether Tim could see him or not, and swung off Main Street onto Cedar, cutting across a corner of the small dirt parking lot Dr. Waterston shared with the Sears Catalog store. The Jeep dipped and bounded over the sharp ruts and washboard surface of the parking lot before leveling off on the paved road. Gordon glanced at his watch. Eight-fifteen. Not bad. He was only fifteen minutes late. He looked to his right. A young boy in short pants—Brad Nicholson's son—was trying to pedal his Big Wheel through the gravel of his driveway out to the street, and Gordon honked his horn, waving. The boy looked up, startled, then grinned and waved back as he recognized the Jeep. Gordon pulled into the vacant lot on the other side of the Pepsi warehouse next door. He hopped out of the car and made his way through a small forest of weeds toward the boy. "Hey Bozo!" he called. "Your dad in yet?"

The boy giggled. "My name's not Bozo. It's Bobby."

Gordon shook his head as though ashamed of himself. "That's right. Bobby. I keep forgetting." He grinned. "Your dad here yet?"

The boy pointed toward the blue metal front of the warehouse. "He's in there. I think he's waiting for you to load up the truck."

"Thanks, pard." Gordon waved good-bye and jogged across the gravel to the warehouse door. It was open, but the lights inside were off. "Brad!" he called, walking in. "You here?"

"I'm out back. Come on through."

Gordon stepped past the couch, chair, and old oak desk that comprised Brad's makeshift office and maneuvered his way through the maze of stacked Pepsi cases toward the rear of the building. He stepped over a stray bottle that had shattered on the concrete floor forming a sticky pond of Pepsi and glass. "How come no lights?" he called out.

"Too damn hot in here. Goddamn metal walls really soak up the heat. I figure if we keep the place dark and shut up it'll stay cool 'til the afternoon."

The aisle of Pepsi cases opened out and Gordon could see Brad's delivery truck backed up to the loading dock. The rear doors were open. Brad had already started loading cases onto the truck, and there appeared to be about a dozen of them stacked against the far side of the van. Gordon signed his timecard on the small folding table next to the loading door and grabbed his hat from its nail on the wall. He put the hat on. "What're we doing today?" he asked, picking up a case. "The boonies?"

Brad nodded, his thick bearded face moving almost imperceptibly. He spat. "Willow Creek, Bear Wash, all of those."

Gordon put his case into the truck. "Is Dan going to be helping us today?"

"No," Brad said.

Gordon let the matter drop. They could have used the help; the small outlying areas didn't take many cases, but there were a lot of them and they were few and far between, and if they wanted to finish by nightfall they almost had to take two trucks. But he had been working for Brad Nicholson for the past four years, and he knew that if Brad said no he meant no. And that was that. Brad wasn't a bad guy, but he did take a little getting used to. He was—what was the word?—unaccommodating. Unyielding. Dan only worked part-time now, down from half-time, and Gordon wondered whether he had quit, whether he had found a better job, whether Brad had fired him or whether he was just ill and taking the day off. He usually helped out on these trips. But Gordon knew that it would be futile to ask Brad anything. He picked up another case of Pepsi.

"Weird fuckin' dream last night," Brad said, changing the subject. He stood there for a moment, pulling on his beard.

"Really?"

"Yeah." Brad picked up a case and laughed. "You're a college boy. Maybe you can tell me what it means."

Gordon put his case down in the truck. "I'll give it a shot."

"Okay. Me and my brother are driving through, like, farmland—"

"I didn't know you had a brother."

"I don't. This is a dream, all right? Okay, so we're driving along, and the road ends. It stops by this farmhouse that's been painted white and turned into a restaurant. We get out of the car and stand there, and a group of men come out through the front door. They're being led by you. You ask us to come into the restaurant and eat breakfast, and we do. It's like a coffeeshop inside. Then this guy I've never seen before comes in and starts talkin' to you. You walk up to us and tell us that we have to help you search for missing children. We walk outside and everybody splits into groups of two, and me and my brother walk across these grassy hills until we come to, like, a canyon. We start walking through this canyon, and all of a sudden we're scared shitless. We hear whispering coming from the rocks. We start to run, and we come to a stand of trees. There're kids swinging in these trees, babies, and they're sitting on these long white swings, laughing to themselves. Only the kids aren't having fun, they're all deformed and crazy. So we run like hell, and then we're back in front of the restaurant. 'Let's get out of here,' I say, and we both hop into the car. I try to start the car, but nothing happens. The car won't start. The battery's dead. This strange guy walks out of the restaurant, and he's carryin' the car's distributor cap in his hands. Behind him, a group of farmers comes out. They're grinnin' at me. And they're carrying pitchforks. And then I woke up." He looked at Gordon.

"All right," Gordon said. "Let's figure this out. You don't really have a brother, but you have one in your dream, right?"

"Right."

"And you're driving through farmland?"

"Right."

"And the restaurant used to be a house?"

"Yeah."

"And the kids' swings were white?"

"Uh huh."

"Okay, and the farmers are carrying pitchforks and you think they're going to harm you somehow?"

"That's right."

"That dream has deep psychological significance," Gordon said. He tried to maintain a serious expression but failed. He grinned hugely. "It means you're a fag."

A half-moon of white teeth appeared suddenly in the midst of Brad's tangled black beard and he laughed. He picked up a bottle cap from the floor of the truck and chucked it at Gordon's head. Gordon ducked, and the cap missed him, clattering onto the concrete floor of the warehouse. "I should've known better than to tell you, you bastard."

"I call 'em as I see 'em."

They both stepped out of the truck and back into the warehouse. Brad picked up a case of Pepsi. He shook his head. "It did scare the hell out of me, though. I thought for sure it was real."

The rains hit in the late afternoon, making the trip up the Rim Road in Brad's truck almost impossible. Besides having three nearly bald tires, which slid at the slightest hint of wetness, the truck had a faulty clutch—something that Brad kept meaning to fix but somehow never got around to doing. They delivered a half-case of Pepsi to the store at Willow Creek, then decided to head back toward town.

Gordon sat silently in the cab as they turned back toward Randall, listening to the faint strum of Willie Nelson's guitar on the radio, barely audible over the static, and staring out at the passing scenery. The rain was thick, almost like winter rain, and only the trees directly adjoining the highway were visible; the others faded impressionistically into gray haze. He could see himself as he sat there, staring out the window. To an outsider, he thought, he would appear lost in contemplation, as though seriously mulling over some deep thought or profound idea. But he knew that nothing was going through his head. He was thinking of himself thinking. That was all.

There was a time, five years ago, even three years ago, when he *would* have been thinking of something—story ideas, plot outlines, clever word associations. Then he had been fresh out of college, recently married, with dreams like millions of other innocents of becoming a writer. Now he was used to—no, *content with*—his life. His job had ceased being a simple form of manual labor that freed his mind for complex thoughts, it had become enough in and of itself. He was fairly happy with his life the way it was. And why not? Hell, he had an intelligent, pretty wife, he had good friends, he lived in a beautiful area. What more could he ask for? So he wasn't contributing to the legacy of humanity, so he didn't have either the talent or the inclination to write the great American novel. So what?

He sighed. Maybe he should start writing again. At least give it a shot. Before he dried up completely. He did have several unfinished short stories and the first forty pages of a novel sitting in the bottom right hand drawer of his desk at home.

"Hey!" Brad poked his shoulder and Gordon looked up. "What's the matter?"

Gordon shook his head. "Fuckin' rain," he said.

Brad grinned hugely and grabbed a can of Pepsi from the ice chest between them, loudly popping it open. "I always liked rain myself. Goddamn heat's what I can't stand. Makes me sweat, makes my balls itch, makes my skin break out, drives me crazy."

Gordon pulled himself away from the window and grabbed his own can of Pepsi. He smiled sarcastically. "That's why you moved to Arizona."

"Northern Arizona," Brad corrected.

"Well why didn't you move to Oregon or Washington if you like rain so much? It rains all the time there."

With the back of his hand, Brad wiped away a thin stream of cola that was dribbling down his beard. "I like the seasons here," he said. "I like the scenery." He laughed loudly. "And this is where Connie's old man wanted to set me up in business."

Gordon laughed too. He knew Brad and Connie did not exactly get along. As Brad often pointed out, theirs had been a marriage of convenience, and he had been only a few steps in front of the shotgun. Still, it hadn't worked out that badly. Connie's father had been granted the Pepsi distribution franchise for the entire Rim area, fully a third of Northern Arizona. He was already rich, having made a killing in the feed and grain market somewhere in Idaho, and he had offered Brad both the franchise and a loan to start the business if he would only marry his daughter. Now Brad was almost as well off as his father-in-law, and he could afford to treat Connie the way he did. "Slut's probably spreading her legs for every man in town," he was fond of saying. Gordon knew Connie and knew what Connie looked like, and he didn't think so, but he himself said nothing.

The truck wandered over the double yellow line as they came barreling down the last hill before town, and a Volkswagen traveling in the opposite direction beeped its horn at them. "Fuck you!" Brad yelled, raising his middle finger.

"I don't think he heard you," Gordon pointed out. "Your window's closed."

"I don't care."

Gordon smiled. "And you *were* going over the line."

Brad snorted. "I don't give a shit. It's the principle of the thing."

They passed a Speed Limit 35 sign almost hidden by bushes and Brad slammed on the brakes. More often than not, Jim Weldon or one of his stooges would be hiding in the dirt pulloff just beyond the sign, waiting for speeders. It was a speed trap, the limit dropping suddenly from 55 to 35 that way, but it was a well-known speed trap and all the locals were aware of it. Only flatlanders and out-of-staters ever got caught. Brad glanced at the pulloff as they passed by. "What do you know," he said. "No cops today." He automatically sped up to 45 and looked over at Gordon. "Listen, do you have to get home right away, or do you have time to stop for gas? Tank's empty and I'd like to get 'er filled up tonight."

"No problem," Gordon said. "I get paid by the hour."

"I'll make it quick."

They drove through Gray's Meadow and pulled into Char Clifton's 76 station on the edge of town. Clifton himself came out as the truck ran over the rubber-coated cable that rang the bell inside the garage. The old man walked slowly, shuffling toward them as they both hopped out of the cab. He looked from Brad to Gordon. "How's it goin'?" he asked, wiping his greasy hands on an equally greasy rag.

"Not bad," Gordon replied.

The station owner spat a wad of chaw that landed just to the left of the truck's right front tire. He squinted up at Gordon as if thinking. He spat again. "Heard the news?" he asked finally.

Gordon looked at Brad, who was inserting the un-leaded gas nozzle into the tank, and shook his head. "What news?"

Clifton grinned, exposing tobacco-yellowed teeth. "You know Father Selway?" he asked. "Out at the Episcopal church?"

"Yeah." Gordon did not go to church, but he knew Father Selway. Everyone did.

"Skipped town," Clifton said simply. "Him and his whole family. Left behind about five thousand dollars in debts."

"Bullshit!" Brad yelled.

"I don't believe it," Gordon said.

"It's a fact."

"What did they do? Just pack up their stuff and go?"

Clifton's eyes shone, and Gordon could tell that he was enjoying this. "That's the weird part. They didn't take nothing at all. All their furniture, clothes, every-thing is still in the house. The front door of the place is still open, even. Only thing gone is their car."

Gordon shook his head. "Then how do you know

they just didn't go off somewhere for a while? Maybe there was a family emergency or something and they had to take off immediately."

"There wasn't."

"How do you know something didn't happen to them?"

"Drive by the church," Clifton said.

"What?"

"Drive by the church."

Brad pulled the nozzle from the gas tank, hung it back on the pump and screwed on the gas cap. He walked over to where Gordon and the station owner were standing. "Why?" he said.

Clifton chuckled. "You'll see."

Brad paid the old man and they got back into the truck. They pulled onto the highway. "You in a hurry to get back or do you want to check out the church?" Brad asked.

"Let's check it out."

They drove into the main part of town, past the Circle K, past the Valley National Bank. They turned right just past the Randall Market. The bumpy and barely paved road curved through a small stand of trees before straightening out near the hospital. A mile or so farther and they reached the Episcopal church.

Brad stopped the truck.

GOD DAMN YOU ALL

The words jumped out—a harsh and jagged red against the placid tan of the brick building. The letters were fully three feet high, covering the north wall of the church, the paint dripping in horror-show icicles. The church's two tall stained-glass windows had been smashed, and multicolored bits of glass littered the gravel parking lot.

GOD DAMN YOUR SOULS

TO HELL PIGFUCKERS

Gordon felt his pulse accelerate as he looked

through the windshield at the desecration. The small peach-fuzz hairs on the back of his neck bristled. His eyes focused on the small shards of colored glass glinting in the sunlight. He had never been an avid churchgoer, but this. . . .

GOD DAMN YOU ALL

He looked again at the message, his eyes following the dripping red paint that obscured the letters on the lower portion of the wall.

And he realized suddenly that it was not paint.

TWO

"Goat's blood," Carl Chmura confirmed, sticking his head through the doorway of the sheriff's office. "The lab just called."

Jim Weldon stopped massaging his tired temples and looked up. "All right, Carl. Thanks." He slowly stood up, grabbing his hat from the rack next to the desk and putting it on. "Wait a minute," he said. "Carl? Call some of the local farmers and ranchers. Check up as far as Turner Draw if you have to. See if any of them have any goats missing."

Carl nodded. "Gotcha."

"Oh, and try Selway's number one more time. Let's give him another chance. I'm going out to the church to see if there's anything we missed. I'll stop by the hospital on my way back and find out if any of the patients saw anything." He grabbed his holster from its hanger on the wall and buckled it on. "Call me if you find something out."

"Will do."

Jim looked around the office, his eyes searching the room as if there was something he had forgotten. He absently patted his pockets. He knew there was something that had slipped his mind, but he couldn't for the life of him remember what it was. He shook his head. This case was really rattling him. Nothing like this had ever happened in his town before—nothing like this had ever happened in any town he'd ever heard of—and he wasn't quite sure what to do. He was just playing everything by ear. He'd already contacted Tim Larson, and Tim was going to clean up the blood and the rest of the mess. And he'd called some glassworkers in Flagstaff who were supposed to come up next week with some new fitted windows. But there was still something he was forgetting.

He sighed heavily and followed his deputy out the door into the hall. He opened the small alarmed gate that separated the back of the building from the front and walked past the front desk toward the sliding double-glass doors that led out to the parking lot.

"Wait a minute! Sheriff!" Rita, sitting by the switchboard, waved him down. "I have the diocese on the line. You wanted to talk to them?"

That was it.

"Yeah. Thanks," he said. He turned back down the hall. "Switch it to my office. I'll take it in there." He walked into his office and picked up the phone, punching the blinking square light of line three. "Hello. Sheriff Weldon here."

"Mr. Weldon? This is Bishop Sinclair. I am returning your call."

"Hello Bishop." Jim's mind quickly ran down his list of options. He could chat casually with the bishop, easing into the news. He could come right out with it, plunge right in. He could pull a Jack Webb, take the official line. He decided to plunge right in. "Has Father Selway been in contact with you at all today?"

"No he hasn't."

"Then you don't know what's happened up here?"

The bishop's voice sounded wary. "No. What happened?"

"The Episcopal church has been vandalized. Some

person or persons unknown smashed all the windows, tore up the landscape—"

"The Episcopal church?"

"That's not all of it." Jim paused for a second, not quite sure how to proceed. "You see, Bishop, someone painted . . . curses . . . all over the front of the building."

"Curses?"

"In goat's blood."

There was a long silence on the other end of the line. "I got a call from Tim Larson this morning," Jim continued. "Tim's the janitor out at the church. Anyway, he told me that the church'd been hit, told me to get over there as soon as I could. I—"

"What kind of curses?" the bishop asked.

"You sure you want to hear this?"

"I'm sure I've heard such words before, Mr. Weldon. I've probably used them myself."

"There were three lines. The top line said, 'God damn you all.' The next line said, 'God damn your souls,' and the bottom line said, 'To hell pigfuckers.' 'God damn you all. God damn your souls to hell pigfuckers.' It covered the whole front of the building."

The bishop said nothing.

Jim cleared his throat. "That's why I was calling you. You see, we don't really know what happened here, and we were wondering if Father Selway had contacted you at all."

The bishop's voice was quiet. "No he hasn't. But he should have. What did he say to you about it? Does he have any idea as to who might have done such a thing?"

Jim cleared his throat again. "Well, that's the thing, Bishop. We don't know where Father Selway is."

"You don't know where he is?"

"No. Tim tried to call him first, before he called me, to tell him what had happened, but no one answered the phone. Then when I went out to the house around a half hour later, no one was there. The whole family was gone. The front door of the house was open, but the place was empty. A team's out there now, investigating the house, but it doesn't appear that anything happened to the family. The Selways' car is gone, and we have reason to suspect that they might have used the car to drive somewhere."

The bishop's voice grew suddenly cold, stern. "What exactly are you trying to say, Mr. Weldon?"

"Nothing, Bishop. Like I said, we don't know what happened. At this point, we'd just like to talk to Father Selway and see if he knows anything about this."

"What are you implying?" His voice was a monotone, but there was a threat in that monotone, a suggestion of rigid enforceable authority.

Jim closed his eyes, beginning to feel a tinge of frustration. There was nothing he hated worse than civilians who tried to throw their weight around, who tried to tell him how to do his job, but he kept his voice even, modulated, official. "I'm not implying anything at all. It's just that—"

"Don't you think something might have happened to the Selway family? They might have been kidnapped."

"We're investigating all possibilities, Bishop. But to be honest, at this stage of the investigation Selway looks more like a suspect than a victim. We found his fingerprints all over the church."

"Of course his fingerprints are all over the church. It's *his* church."

"Bloody fingerprints?"

He could almost feel the bishop's anger through the silence of the line.

"Bishop?"

"Yes?"

Jim cringed at the coldness of the voice. "We just want to talk to Selway right now. That's all. If any charges are to be filed in this matter they will have to be filed by the church."

"You are right there, Mr. Weldon."

Jim looked at his watch. "Look, I'm supposed to be over at the church in a few minutes. Do you think you could give me a call if Father Selway gets in touch with you in any way? Or if you hear anything at all?"

"Of course." There was a half-moment of frozen silence. "And Sheriff?"

"Yes?"

"I will be sending a temporary parish priest to assume Father Selway's duties until such time as this affair is cleared up. I will also be sending someone out to look at the damage. Could you please let the parishioners know that services will be continued?"

"Will do. And I'll call you if anything—"

There was a click as the receiver went dead.

"—comes up." He slammed down the phone, cursing the bishop. "Asshole," he said aloud. Just who did that old bastard think he was? God? He grabbed a pencil from the desktop and walked out of the office, snapping the pencil in two and dropping the pieces into the sand-filled ashtray in the hall. He nodded to Rita as he passed again through the front office. "Anyone calls, you tell them I'll call them back."

"Okay."

Why did this have to happen in his town? he wondered as he walked out to the parking lot. Why couldn't it have happened in Payson or Prescott or Camp Verde? He strode toward the new car at the far end of the lot. This wasn't a small town sort of occurrence. This was something that should have happened in New York or Los Angeles, in one of those big cities with weird cults and gangs.

He unlocked the car, got in and fastened his seatbelt. Turning on the ignition, he jammed the transmission into gear and took off, back tires squealing as he peeled out of the parking lot toward the church.

THREE

Clay Henry had been a rancher all his life, like his father and grandfather before him. But he had never seen anything like this.

Clay grimaced and spat. He could taste the blood. It hung thick and heavy in the air, dank and fetid in the mid-morning heat, penetrating his nostrils, engulfing his senses. He felt as though he were drowning in it. Before him, in the brown and trampled grass of the field, all six of his goats lay slaughtered, their throats ripped open by some crude instrument. Blood was everywhere: on the ground, on the matted hair of the carcasses, on the feathers of the two clucking chickens that had come out to investigate. He could see individual, congealed drops of blood on the long stalks of meadow grass at his feet. From the yawning hole in the throat of the nearest goat there protruded a twisting ropelike entrail that wound along the red-spattered dirt like a deformed and bloated snake. It looked as though whoever had ripped open the goat's throat had afterward stuck his arm into the bleeding opening and reached all the way down into the dying body to pull out its guts. Lengths of intestine hung out of the other five bodies as well.

A chicken pecked idly at a blood-soaked piece of intestine and Clay kicked it, sending it flying. The chicken screamed wildly, uselessly flapping its feathered wings, and ran squawking back to the barn.

Clay ran his tongue over his teeth and gums, tasting again the blood, and spat to clear out his mouth. Already the flies had come. There were hundreds of them, seemingly every fly in the county, and they were swarming over every available spot of blood, flying spastically up at each movement that he made and then settling once more onto the carcasses. The field was quiet save for the flies—even the chickens were silent—and Clay felt . . . not exactly fear, but a strange sort of dread. The same feeling he'd had right before his accident, when he knew in those final seconds that the two cars were going to hit and there was nothing he could do about it. The buzzing grew louder in his ears and he looked down at the mutilated animals. He spat again. He knew he'd have to get this mess cleaned up as quickly as possible, before the carcasses started breeding disease and affecting the rest of the animals, but he thought he should call Jim Weldon first. The sheriff would want to know about this.

A strange mechanical coughing sound suddenly grew out of the buzzing, becoming louder, and Clay looked up. Across the field he could see a cloud of dust rising from the dirt road that led to the house. Someone was coming to see him. He squinted, trying to make out who it was, but he couldn't see from this far away. He listened, and he recognized the loud sputtering engine of Loren Wilbanks' truck. What could Loren want? he wondered. He stood for a moment, watching the dust cloud move toward his house, then, holding onto his bad leg with his right hand, started limping back across the field to where the truck had pulled to a stop.

Loren was waiting on the porch steps when Clay rounded the corner of the old barn. The tall gaunt farmer had been absently and nervously juggling two small pebbles in his hands, staring out across the north field at the broken skeleton of a windmill, but he jumped to his feet as he saw Clay approach, throwing the pebbles into the dirt. He picked up his hat as he rose. "Where'n Christ have you been? I been tryin' to call you all morning."

Clay limped over to the steps and grabbed the wrought iron rail for support. He pulled a red bandana handkerchief from the right front pocket of his overalls and used the handkerchief to wipe the sweat from his forehead. "Someone slaughtered all my goats," he said. "Ripped out their throats."

"That's why I been tryin' to call you. Same thing happened to everybody."

Clay stared at him. "What?"

"All my goats were killed. Ace's, Johnny's, Henry's, everybody's."

"Same way?"

Loren nodded. "Ripped open their throats and pulled out their innards. Looks like it was done with a can opener or something. Goddamn flies everywhere."

"Yeah, same here." Clay sat down on the top step. He looked toward the spot where the six goats lay slaughtered. He couldn't see them from here, their bodies were hidden by the tall grasses and weeds, but he thought he could hear the constant buzzing of the flies. The sound seemed to echo in his head. "I was just going to come in and call Weldon," he said. "See what he could do about it."

Loren looked at him. He waved a fly away from his face with his hat. "No one's called here yet?"

Clay shook his head, puzzled. "They might've. I've been out in the field all morning. Why?"

"Jesus," Loren said. He kicked at the bottom step with his scuffed work boot, staring down. A piece of hardened sod broke off from the side of the step and fell to the ground. "You didn't hear what happened?"

Clay shook his head.

Loren was silent for a moment. "You know the Episcopal church?" he said finally. "That one out there past the hospital?"

Clay shook his head. "You know I never been no churchgoer."

"Well it don't matter. That's the church Verna goes to. All new and modern looking and real nice. What happened is that someone wrote all over the front of the church. 'Damn you all to hell' and shit like that. Wrote it in goat's blood."

"Goat's blood?"

Loren was nodding before Clay had even got the words out. "Yeah. Carl Chmura's been calling all morning. Calling every rancher around. Prob'ly called you too but you weren't in."

"I was out in the field," Clay repeated. He stood up, holding onto his leg, a sharp flash of pain registering on his face as he lurched to his feet. "I better call them then." Holding the rail, he half-walked, half-pulled himself up the last step. He yanked open the ripped and rusted screen door, holding it open for Loren. He looked at the other rancher. "You coming in or you just going to stand there?"

Loren walked up the steps and caught the screen door just before it slammed. Clay was already walking down the long hall to the back of the house.

"You got coffee or anything?" Loren asked.

Clay waved an arm in the general direction of the kitchen. "Didn't have time to make none this morning," he called out. "You go on ahead and make us some. You know where everything is."

Loren walked into the old kitchen. It was spic and span as always, exactly the way Glenda used to keep it. The same anemic, half-dead creeping charlie was struggling for its life on top of the Sears Coldspot refrigerator, the same faded plastic flowers lay arranged in the same brown wicker basket on the red-

and-white checked tablecloth that covered the breakfast table. The ancient gas stove remained brightly polished as always, its few black nicks standing out dully against the gleaming porcelain. Through the greenhouse window above the sink, the mid-morning sun streamed in slatted rays, lighting up the entire room.

Loren walked across the white tiled floor to the row of cupboards that lined the walls above both sides of the sink. He took out a half-empty can of MJB and measured two plastic cupfuls of coffee, pouring them into Clay's drip-pot. He was about to fill the pot with water when he heard a loud crash from the back of the house. He hurriedly dumped out his measuring cup of water, letting the plastic cup fall into the sink, and ran to the hallway. "Clay?" he called. "Clay?"

He strode quickly down the hall, his work boots echoing loudly in the silence of the farmhouse. No noise came from any of the rooms. He glanced into Glenda's old sewing room as he walked by. Nothing. Clay's bedroom. Nothing.

Clay's den.

The rancher lay on the floor amidst debris of fallen books and knocked-over knickknacks. His eyes were wide open and staring, the pupils fixed at oddly askew angles, and there were several thin red marks running lengthwise down his cheeks. His mouth looked as if it had been forced open; his tongue was protruding from between bared teeth. The fingers of Clay's hands were clenched into claws and blood dripped thickly from his two middle fingers.

Loren staggered back as he looked into the den, instantly nauseated by the putrid smell of violence, which was amplified by the heavy close air of the windowless room. He grasped the edge of the doorframe with his hands and swung back against the wall of the hallway, closing his eyes and breathing deeply. The walls of the den had been spattered with blood, and somehow the flies had already found their way in. He could hear their droning maddened buzzing as they feasted on the blood. It sounded unnaturally loud in the silent house.

He stumbled down the hall toward the kitchen. And stopped.

Where had all the blood come from? He had seen only that trace of red on Clay's clawed fingers. There were light marks on the rancher's face, but the rest of his friend's body had appeared to be untouched. He turned around and, taking a huge gulp of air and holding his breath, peered around the corner into the den.

Something small and chuckling, vaguely red and pink, scuttled from the side of Clay's body to a spot under the bed.

Loren felt a trip-hammer of fear interrupt the rhythm of his heart. "Hey!" he called.

The creature belted out from under the bed and in a crazed blur ran into Loren's legs, connecting just below the kneecaps and knocking him down. For a wild disjointed moment he was sprawled on the floor, looking into the dead staring eyes of Clay Henry, seeing his own panicked reflection in the lifeless orbs. Then something small and sharp and painful dug into the back of his skull and he was knocked unconscious.

FOUR

Gordon sat in front of the open window typing, the small plastic desk fan trained directly on his face. Even with the artificially generated breeze he was still perspiring, the sweat coursing down his cheeks in salty rivulets, occasionally dripping from his face to the white erasable typing paper. Brad was right. The heat was miserable. He ran a hand through his damp hair. He was beginning to hate summer, really hate it. Such a thought was un-American, he knew. He was supposed to love the long summer days, to want to play volleyball and other outdoor sports, to go on picnics, to listen to the Beach Boys. But it didn't get dark until nearly nine o'clock at night, and the days were hot, humid, and uncomfortable. He understood that he would be hot unloading cases of Pepsi; that was expected. But here, even wearing shorts and no shirt, he was still sweating like a pig. And when he typed his bare back stuck painfully to the slatted wooden chair.

Of course, the nights and late afternoons had cooled off now that the monsoons had come. But the mornings more than made up for it.

Marina, on the other hand, loved the summer. She always had and probably always would, although God

knew why. He could see her lying on her tinfoil-like
Space Blanket in the clear treeless area in front of the
house, trying to enrich her already ecru tan. He took
a sip of iced tea from the tall glass next to the type-
writer. The recently poured beverage was already
forming a rounded pool of condensation on the walnut
desk top, and he wiped away the puddle with the side
of his arm. Setting the glass back down, he reread the
sentence he'd just typed, thought for a minute, then
ripped the sheet from the machine, crumpling it up
and tossing it into the overflowing wastepaper basket.
On the lawn, Marina rolled over and faced the window, holding her left hand above her eyes like a visor.
"I heard that," she said.

He looked toward her, smiling. "It's too hot to
work."

"You've been saying that all morning."

"It's been true all morning."

She stood up, facing away from him, her back an
intricately patterned mosaic formed by the serrated
material of the Space Blanket. She bent down to pick
up her sunglasses and tanning lotion, and he had a
clear view of her perfectly round ass. He whistled
loudly. Still shielding her eyes from the glare of the
noonday sun, she turned to face him. "If you're not
going to do any work then let's go into town. There
are some things I have to do."

"What things?"

"Things." She stuck her tongue out at him. "And
that's for whistling. Pig."

Gordon watched her fold the blanket into a small
square and, putting it under her arm, trek barefoot
across the rocky dirt toward the side door of the
house. She'd gained weight this summer, he realized.
Not really enough to be noticeable—she still looked
svelte, even in her skimpy bikini—but there was a
small, barely perceptible increase in the size of her
formerly flat stomach. Of course he was a fine one to

talk. He stared down at his spreading paunch. Even
with the increased demand for soft drinks in the summer and the extra work he'd had to do, he still looked
like he had the beginnings of a beer belly. All that
loading strengthened his arms but didn't do a thing
for his stomach. He smiled. Maybe they should both
start to exercise; get the Jane Fonda videotape or
something, do aerobics.

Marina passed by the den, peeking into the open
doorway as she headed down the hall to the bathroom.
"I'm taking a shower!" she called out. "You get
ready too!"

Grimacing, Gordon moved forward, peeling his skin
from the back of the chair, and covered the few pages
of the manuscript he'd completed. He walked next
door to the bedroom, stepping over the small pile of
Marina's clothes on the floor, and walked around the
quilt-covered brass bed in the center of the room.
They'd gotten the bed several years ago at a church
rummage sale, and Marina had spent long weekend
hours scraping the tarnish off the metal and restoring
the bed to its original condition. The antique armoire
next to the bed had been a present from Marina's
mother. Gordon pulled open the drawer at the bottom
of the armoire and pulled out a pair of sneakers. He
searched through the small closet for an appropriate
shirt. After a cursory examination of his wardrobe,
he yanked free from its hanger a loud multicolored
Hawaiian shirt. It was the closest thing to summerwear
he owned. He put on the shirt and sat down on the
bed to tie his shoes.

Although they had been living in Randall for more
than four years now, Gordon had never adjusted to
the complete climate reversals and almost menopausal
shifts in seasons that characterized the meteorology of
Northern Arizona. For some probably psychological
reason, he'd kept telling himself that each year was
an atypical one, that the summers were not usually

this hot, the winters not usually this cold. As a result, his wardrobe consisted of the same moderate weather clothing he'd worn in California. Which meant that he roasted in summer, froze in winter and seldom had anything appropriate to wear.

They'd learned about Randall through Ginny Johnson, one of Marina's coworkers at the high school. One weekend Ginny had run into her old college roommate, and the roommate told her that she had been offered—and had turned down—a full-time teaching position in Randall, Arizona. "It's a beautiful little town," she said. "I'd love to live there, but they just don't pay enough."

"Sounds like just what you're looking for," Ginny told Marina. "The school's looking for someone to teach English *and* typing, the land in the area is cheap, there are four seasons and the town's population is a whopping three thousand. You always said that you and Gordon wanted to get out of Southern California."

"Arizona?" Gordon said when Marina relayed the information.

"It's up near Flagstaff," she explained. Gordon started making disgusted faces, and she playfully slapped his cheek. "Be serious. There are some nice places there."

"In Arizona?"

Nevertheless, they'd driven out to Randall the next weekend. And both of them had fallen instantly in love with the town. It had been a brisk clear autumn day, not a cloud in the ink blue sky, and they'd come in from the southwest, driving the two-lane from Prescott. Their first view of the town looked like a Currier and Ives painting, or the falsely pastoral picture on an artfully retouched postcard. They were driving over a ridge. Below them, the town was nestled into a long narrow valley. The only building clearly visible from this vantage point was the sawmill. Around the mill,

smoking chimneys and A-framed roofs peeked out
from between leafless oaks, multihued aspens, and
green ponderosa pines. Here and there glimpses of
blue—brooks or streams or ponds—could be seen between the green foliage. To the north, overlooking the
entire region, dominating the scenery, stood the
Rim—a huge majestic forested mesa that stretched
spectacularly from horizon to horizon.

At his first sight of the town, Gordon had begun
grinning widely, the excitement showing in his face.
He pulled off to the side of the road, getting out of
the car and grabbing his Canon. He snapped several
shots of the unbelievable view, finishing off the roll,
and took a deep breath of air, inhaling the intertwined
fragrance of living forest and burning firewood. He
stared down at the panorama below him. "This is it,"
he said. "This is our town."

Marina coughed loudly from inside the car: a melo-
dramatic stage "ahem." She looked out at him. "Don't
you think you should ask my opinion before making
blanket pronouncements about 'our' town?"

He swung around in surprise. "You don't like it?"

She got out of the car and walked to the edge of
the cliff, looking around her at the scenery. She pretended to think for a moment. "It's . . . all right," she
said finally in her most affected voice. She looked
toward him, eyebrows raised.

Then the smile broke through.

Marina had interviewed for the teaching position
the next week and had been accepted. They'd bought
the place two months later, after several weekend
house-hunting trips to the area. Gordon had originally
wanted to buy a converted farmhouse—he had dreams
of living a cinematic small town existence, complete
with a cow for milk and a couple chickens for eggs—
but the only farmhouses for sale were way out of their
price range. Even with the bank loan and money bor-
rowed from both their parents they were only able to

afford someplace small. Still, their new home *was* by itself, outside the town limits, backed up against untouched National Forest land. An old one-story woodframed structure, it was set in the middle of a halfacre of thickly wooded property. The previous owners had built a small animal pen next to the tool shed out back and had cleared a large area on the side of the house for gardening. Gordon was delighted. The old owners had also added several large picture windows to the house, allowing for unobstructed views of both the Rim and the surrounding woods.

That first year, they too had made a lot of changes: converting the breakfast nook in the kitchen to a small solarium, furnishing the house with Marina's antiques, painting the peeling walls white, adding on to the storage shed so they would have a place to store firewood. Yes, the winter had been colder than Gordon had expected, and the summer hotter. And the entire cycle had repeated itself the following year. But he really did love living here. It was everything he'd hoped for. He loved the house, loved the forest, and loved Randall. Hell, he even liked his menial job.

Marina emerged from the bathroom dressed and ready to go. She walked into the bedroom and stopped just inside the door, staring at him, her eyes moving visibly upward from his grubby sneakers to his torn cutoffs before finally settling on his obnoxious Hawaiian shirt. "You're not planning on going like that?" she asked.

"This is all I've got."

"What about that new light-blue short-sleeve shirt I bought you?"

"It's dirty."

She shook her head. "If we see anyone, I'm pretending like I don't know you."

He grinned. "Want me to walk ten paces behind you? Just in case?"

"You think I'm joking?"

He grabbed his wallet and keys from the dresser and was about to start out the door.

"Wait," she said, as if remembering something. "Maybe you'd better change after all. I forgot I have to stop in and see Dr. Waterston."

"What for?"

"Oh, nothing."

"He's open on Saturday?"

Marina nodded.

He scanned her face, looking for telltale signs of sickness. "What's wrong?"

"I told you. Nothing. I'm just going in for a checkup."

"Why didn't I hear about this checkup before?"

"Because it's not important. Just get dressed so we can go." Annoyance had entered her voice, and she walked over to the closet, pulling out a pair of Levi's and throwing them on the bed. "Wear these," she said. He put on the pants as she rummaged through the closet for a shirt. She finally picked out a plain, light green, cotton dress shirt. "Here. Just roll up the sleeves."

He bowed down before her. "Yes, master. Will there be anything else?"

She laughed. "No. You can keep your shoes."

He put on his clothes.

FIVE

Gordon sat in the small air-conditioned waiting room for what seemed like an eternity, glancing periodically at the stulted wall clock that hung above the door. The clock's oversized hands moved in a cruelly slow parody of time, ticking off minutes that registered as seconds, hours that clocked in as minutes. He already knew by heart the minute brushstrokes that made up the three watercolor prints on the waiting room walls, and now he simply stared into space. Every so often he would pick up one of the magazines on the low glass coffeetable in front of him—*Flying*, *Computer Science*, or perhaps *Modern Medicine*—and scan the glossy pages for some item of interest. He had exhausted the magazines and was just about to start on *The Children's Living Bible* when he heard Marina's muffled voice through the thick clouded glass partition that separated the receptionist's desk from the waiting room. He put the book down and looked up. There was a blur of colored movement behind the frosted glass.

Marina's face was an embarrassed mixture of conflicting emotions as she came bustling through the waiting room door shoving a folded slip of prescription paper into her purse. Fear and joy, anxiety and excitement all vied for time on her features. She looked around the empty room for a second, as if not seeing him, then fixed him with an unsure smile. Her face was red. "I'm pregnant," she said.

Gordon blinked in startled incomprehension, not sure he had heard her right. "What?" he said.

"I'm pregnant."

He shook his head, still not believing what he heard. What was this? What the hell was going on here? She had just gone in for a routine checkup. Dr. Waterston had just wanted to look her over, make sure everything was functioning properly. How the hell had he found out that she was pregnant?

How *could* she be pregnant?

She tried to smile, an attempt that only partially succeeded. She was opening and closing the snap clasp of her purse nervously. "We have to talk," she said.

He nodded dumbly, still stunned, still unable or unwilling to believe her news.

She walked over to him and took his hand, glancing around the empty waiting room. "I—"

"Out in the car," he said. "I don't want to talk about it here."

Outside, the afternoon storm clouds had appeared over the Rim, their blackness blocking the entire northern half of the sky. The two tall pine trees next to the doctor's office stood out against the dark background, their upper branches still illuminated by the afternoon sun, creating a strangely artificial highlighting effect. Across the street, the sawmill's black metal stack was also still in sunlight. They walked across the empty gravel to the Jeep, parked next to the Sears Catalog store. Gordon unlocked Marina's door. "Why didn't you tell me about this earlier?"

"I wasn't sure about it. I didn't want to worry you."

"You didn't want to worry me? You didn't want to worry me?" His voice rose in pitch, the anger showing in his face. "You think it's better to spring it on me like this?" He laughed shortly. "Jesus. You could've at least prepared me." He walked around the front of the car to the driver's side.

"I'm not even sure I'm going to keep it," she said quietly.

He looked up. "What?"

"I said, 'I'm not sure I'm going to keep it.' "

He stared at her for a moment, and she could see the pain registering on his face. His brown eyes, usually so clear, looked troubled. They met hers and looked quickly away. He opened his door, getting in, and Marina climbed into the Jeep from her side, closing the door carefully. Gordon started the car's engine.

"I thought you wanted to talk," she said.

"I do." He put the car into reverse. "But I don't feel like doing it here in the parking lot." He pulled onto Main Street. A blue pickup truck—Tim McDowell's pickup—drove past them going the opposite direction and honked, a hand appearing over the cab, waving. Gordon stuck his own arm out of the Jeep's window and waved tiredly back. He sighed loudly. "Jesus," he said. He was silent for a minute. "All right. Start from the beginning."

Marina smiled feebly. "Well, about a month ago . . ."

He didn't laugh. His face, instead, was strained, almost angry. "What happened? Didn't your pills work?"

"Obviously not."

The Jeep sped past Char Clifton's 76 station on the way out of town. Gordon shook his head. "Isn't the percentage of failures about point-one percent?"

"Something like that."

He looked at her suspiciously. "You have been taking them, haven't you?"

"That's not even worth answering." Her voice was cold.

His eyes met hers. "Okay," he said. "I'm sorry."

"You should be." Now it was her voice that was angry. "I'm the one who didn't want kids in the first place, remember? I'm the one who'd have to carry the baby for almost a year and then be its constant slave for another two. I'm the one who'd have to feed it and take care of it."

"Okay. I'm sorry."

They drove for a while in silence.

"So tell me what happened."

Marina sighed. "I didn't get my period when I was supposed to. I waited a week, then another few days, then I called Dr. Waterston. I thought about telling you, but . . . I wasn't sure. I didn't want to worry you. So I decided to keep quiet until I knew for certain. He gave me the test a few days ago." She stared out the window, watching the green blur of the passing scenery as the Jeep zoomed down the winding road through the forest. A hazy prestorm sunlight filtered in prison slats through the trees.

"And?" Gordon prompted.

She turned to face him. "And?"

"Come on."

She sighed again and her voice, when she spoke, was low, mumbling, as though she were talking to herself rather than him. "I was praying to God I wasn't pregnant. I knew something like this would happen."

"Yes?"

She shook her head, her eyes half-closed. She looked tired, and she pushed a stray wisp of hair back from her eyes. "You know about Julie Campbell's baby, right?"

He nodded, frowning. In June, Julie Campbell had gone into labor a full five months early; the doctors still did not understand why. The premature birth, in the back of the maternity ward at Randall General

Hospital, had been little more than an abortion. The stillborn fetus had been only a little bigger than a fist, its body and facial features not yet fully formed.

"And Joni Cooper's baby last year?"

Joni Cooper's baby had also been stillborn and premature.

He nodded again.

"And Susan Stratford's?"

"So what are you trying to tell me? That you're afraid to have a baby?" His voice softened. "Look, delivering a baby is a smooth procedure. Those three were just a fluke. We'll go down to Phoenix and have a real doctor look at you. In a real hospital. They have tests for these kinds of things. We'll find out beforehand if the baby will be retarded, deformed, what the chances are for a premature birth or a stillbirth. Hell, we'll even find out whether it's going to be a boy or a girl."

"We'll try the tests," she said. "But . . ." She paused, trying to think. She closed her eyes, massaging the lids with the thumb and forefinger of her right hand. She opened her eyes and looked at Gordon. "They're probably not flukes. Dr. Waterston thinks they're connected."

His gaze snapped toward her.

She pointed out the windshield. "Keep your eyes on the road."

"What the hell are you talking about?"

"He doesn't know what it is. He doesn't know if it's anything. But think about it. All three of them— Julie, Joni, and Susan—live north of town, like we do. All of them are under thirty-five, like we are. All of them get their water from the Geronimo Wells pump—"

"The fucking water!"

"We don't know if it's—"

"I should've known it!"

"Known what? There's nothing to know. Dr. Waterston just pointed out all the things that Julie, Joni, and Susan have in common. It may be nothing; it may not."

"It may be nothing?"

"Look, they might be coincidences. Dr. Waterston just thinks, possibly, that it might be something else, and he wanted to warn me. Just in case."

"It *might possibly* be something else? Three dead babies in the space of one year? In a town this small?"

"You were the one who said they were probably flukes."

"I was wrong, okay? I was wrong." They had driven past Tonto Wash and were coming up on the small dirt side road that led to their house. Gordon was silent for a few moments. His face, when she looked at it, was working silently in a confusion of anger and frustration. His brow was furrowed, his jaw clenched. He slammed on the brakes of the speeding Jeep, slowing down, and turned onto the dirt road. "There has to be some kind of investigation into this," he said. "I'm calling the EPA, the county government, the state government, everyone I can think of. Goddamn it, there are going to be some lawsuits."

"Lawsuits against who?"

"Against . . ." He faltered. "Against whoever it is that's causing this." He pulled up in front of their house and cut the Jeep's engine. He sat silently for a minute, staring out at the line of trees next to the car. He breathed deeply, audibly. When he spoke again his voice was quiet. "What do you want to do?"

"Well, I think we should go to Phoenix like you suggested, and have some tests run." She put her hand on his. "Then we can start talking about the normal questions: Do we want a baby? Can we afford a baby? All that."

"The normal questions." Gordon smiled sadly. "Jesus."

The sky was completely black now, all traces of the

hot morning sun erased. A drop of water fell on the
windshield. And another. And another. Marina motioned toward the house. "We'd better get in. It's
starting to rain."

Gordon said nothing.

She stared at him for a moment, then shifted her
attention to the rain-splattered windshield. Several
drops exploded on the glass, causing a network of minuscule waterfalls to cascade down the window to the
cracked rubber of the windshield wipers where the
water formed two small pools. Out of the corner of
her eye, she saw Gordon shift in his seat, heard him
pick up the set of keys from the seat between them.
He opened his door, got out, and made a dash for the
house. She waited a few moments, until he had unlocked the front door of the house, and then followed
him. By the time she reached the porch, it was raining
heavily, huge hail-sized drops pelting the broad leaves
of the oak tree next to the door and causing the loose
gravel of the drive to skitter about with noisy click-
clacks.

Inside, the house had retained the morning heat
despite the cold rain outside. It seemed stuffy, uncomfortable, and Marina went around the house
opening all of the windows to let in the cool water-
freshened air. Gordon put his keys on the kitchen
counter then moved to the front doorway, where
he stood looking out through the screen. The thick
monsoon clouds formed a wet ceiling above the forest, blocking out even a partial view of the Rim.
"Damn," he said.

Marina finished opening the windows in the back of
the house and returned to the living room. "What?"
she said.

Gordon tried to smile for her sake. "I said 'At least
it's cool.'"

She stood next to him and put her arm around his
waist, snuggling into the crook under his arm. She

looked with him out the screen door toward the forest. Her eyes brimmed with tears, but she did not allow him to see them. The tears flowed freely down her cheeks. "Yes," she said softly. "At least it's cool."

SIX

Jim Weldon slept for ten hours straight—a record for him—and for the first time in almost a month his sleep remained undisturbed by nightmares. He was exhausted; his body and brain were just too damned tired to allow him to dream, and he lay on the bed unmoving from four in the morning until two in the afternoon.

He had never had a day like this before.

The morning had dawned clear and hot like any other, and he'd gotten to the office by eight. He'd expected a few minor complaints, maybe some drunks or speeders, then an afternoon of paper shuffling and serious rest. But Tim Larson had called less than an hour later with news of the vandalized Episcopal church, and by noon the investigation had spread to include the mysterious disappearance of the Selway family and the series of goat mutilations, which apparently stretched all the way from the Green River Ranch south of town to Bill Heard's place up on the Rim. The bodies of Loren Wilbanks and Clay Henry, or what was left of their bodies (connected somehow with the goat mutilations?), had been discovered by a neighboring rancher late in the afternoon, and by the time they had dusted for prints, taken the pictures, examined the house and carted off the bodies six hours later, the other five churches in Randall had been vandalized. Although the desecration of these churches had to have taken place between six and ten p.m., none of the nearby residents had seen or heard a thing, and they'd had to spend another four hours sifting through the piles of broken glass and combing every inch of each church, trying to gather what clues they could. Judson Weiss and Pete King were working night shift, and when Jim's brain finally became too tired to function properly, he left everything in their hands and went home to get some much needed sleep.

He'd been up for almost twenty-four hours.

Jim had prayed before falling asleep that somehow, miraculously, Judson and Pete would solve everything in his absence and that the two murders, the disappearances, the vandalism, and the livestock mutilations would all be neatly tied up into one package and written into a typed, double-spaced report that would be placed on his desk for him to read and sign.

No such luck.

A call to the station upon waking revealed that no progress had been made in any of the cases. There were still no leads and nothing to go on.

He hung up the phone, feeling a headache coming on. A bad one. He massaged his temples with his fingers, feeling the rhythmic pounding of blood beneath the thin layer of skin. He just wasn't cut out for this shit. This was for the big-city cops and the motion-picture sheriffs, not him. Already he felt way out of his league, and he wondered vaguely if he shouldn't call for some help on this.

But who would he call?

He pulled on a robe and lumbered into the bathroom, his bare feet sticking to the green tile floor as he walked. He pulled back the shower curtain and turned on the water in the shower, adjusting the two

faucets by feel. Why the hell had he been born in
Randall instead of one of the hundreds of other small
towns scattered throughout Northern Arizona? Why
wasn't he sheriff in Sedona or Heber? He climbed
into the shower, wincing as the water hit his skin. This
was going to make national news for sure—if not television then at least the wire services. People were
going to be watching him closely. He'd better not fuck
it up.

A note on the refrigerator said that Justin and Suzonne were at the movies with Ralph Pittman and his
mother. A second note, held up by a Tweety Bird
magnet, told him that Annette was at the grocery
store. Jim left his own note in reply and grabbed a
donut before taking off. He said in the note that he'd
be back for dinner, but he knew that was probably
just wishful thinking. In all likelihood he'd be coming
home late. He had a feeling there were going to be a
lot of missed meals over the next couple of weeks.

The child was waiting in his office when he arrived.

The sight threw him for a second, but he did not
let the surprise register on his face. He threw his hat
on the rack next to his desk, as always, and sat down.
Carl Chmura was sitting next to the boy on the low
vinyl couch against the far wall, and he stood up when
Jim entered the room. "Howdy, Sheriff."

"What's up, Carl?"

The deputy walked across the carpeted floor toward
the sheriff and nodded his head toward the boy. "This
kid here came in around noon today, maybe a little
earlier. Said he had something important to tell you.
He wouldn't talk to anyone else. I told him you probably wouldn't be coming in for a while, but he wanted
to wait. Said it was real important."

Jim looked at the boy. He was small and pale and
couldn't have been more than eleven or twelve. He
looked as though he had not been out of the house

all summer. He was wearing an ill-fitting shirt that looked like it had probably been his father's or grandfather's and a pair of ripped Levi's faded almost white. His hair was thin and greasy and too long, and it curled around his shoulders in matted tangles. He was clenching and unclenching his hands nervously.

But it was the boy's face that captured his attention. His face was filled with fear.

Jim stood up and smiled kindly at the boy, not wishing to frighten or intimidate him. "What's your name, son?"

"Don Wilson." The boy's voice was timid and uncertain.

Jim motioned Carl to the door with his eyes. "Thanks a lot, Carl. I'll call you if I need you." The deputy nodded, understanding, and closed the door behind him as he left.

Jim sat on the corner edge of the desk facing the boy. He put on his all-purpose concerned-father expression and bent forward, placing his hands on his knees. "So, Don," he said. "What did you want to talk to me about?"

The boy's frightened face looked first toward the door then toward the window—in human approximation of a cornered rabbit checking out its options for escape. He looked immediately sorry that he'd come, and Jim thought for a second he was going to bolt. The sheriff smiled understandingly. "It's okay, Don," he said. "You can talk to me."

"I know where the Selways are!" the boy blurted out. "I know how to find their bodies!"

Jim's smile of patient understanding froze on his face. He stared at the pale scared youth before him, his mouth suddenly dry, his hands holding on to his knees with a viselike grip. Adrenaline flushed into his system.

Their bodies.

Jim snapped his head toward the door, his sheriff's instinct taking over. "Carl!" he called. "Carl!"

The deputy rushed in instantly. His head did a one-eighty as he quickly scanned the room. His eyes stopped on Jim, baffled, but Jim had already turned back toward the boy. "Why the hell didn't you say something about this earlier? Why didn't you tell Deputy Chmura?"

The boy was still cowering, and under the sheriff's verbal onslaught he appeared to almost visibly shrink, but he held his ground. "I can only tell *you*," he said. His voice was scared, shaky.

"Where are they?" Jim demanded.

The boy looked from the sheriff to the deputy and shook his head.

"All right!" Jim yelled. "Carl, get out of here for a minute!" The deputy retreated, confused, and closed the door behind him. Jim swiveled his gaze back to the boy. "Okay. Where the hell are they?"

The boy licked his lips. "I had this dream a few nights ago—"

"Where the hell are they?"

"Let me finish my story!" The boy looked as though he was about to cry. His shaking hands were balled into fists, and frustration and fear were battling it out for supremacy on his face. A hank of hair fell across his forehead and he angrily flipped it back.

Jim took a deep breath and nodded. It wasn't the kid's fault; the boy was doing the best he could. "All right," the sheriff said quietly. "Tell me what happened."

The boy looked at him for a moment, not sure he wanted to tell him. "I had this dream a few nights ago," he said finally. "And I saw the Selways being murdered."

A dream?

Jim felt his heart begin to pound in his ears, but he forced himself to remain calm. "By who?" he asked.

Don looked at the floor, his feet shuffling nervously, crossing and crisscrossing his legs. He did not look up. "I . . . I can't tell you," he said.

"Yes you can."

"No, I can't. You won't believe me."

"Yes I will." His voice softened. "Tell me," he said.

The boy looked up at him. "Monsters," he said. "It was too dark to see what they looked like, but they were monsters." He looked at Jim, to make sure he wouldn't laugh.

But Jim did not feel like laughing.

"There were a whole bunch of them," the boy continued, again staring at the ground. "They broke into the Selways' house and took them off to the dump." His legs were doing nervous figure eights on the carpet. "They . . . they killed the little baby first. They tore her apart and ate her. Then they tore the other kids apart, ripping open their skin. There were hundreds of them. Then they . . . they . . . ripped off Mrs. Selway's head while she stood there and made Father Selway watch." He looked up at Jim, his eyes shiny with remembered terror. "Her body just sort of crumpled to the ground, like in slow motion, and I could see all the veins and muscles and things popping out of her neck and squirming around. Blood was everywhere. It was squirting up like a fountain."

"Which dump was this at?"

"The one off the control road. By Geronimo Wells."

Jim nodded. "Go on."

The boy's eyes focused on a point far away, in his mind. "They . . . the monsters . . . played with Mrs. Selway's head for a while, throwing it around and kicking it. Her eyes opened and closed as it flew through the air. There were a lot of them around, but I still couldn't see them. They were in the shadows. But I could see Mrs. Selway's head real good. And I could see Father Selway perfectly. He was just standing there, staring. Then one of them reached over and turned Father Selway toward the fire."

"What fire?" Jim asked.

"The one where they burn all the wood and paper."

"It was night?"

"Yeah. They made him look at the fire and said . . ." Don looked down, his hands now trembling badly. He clamped his hands between his legs to hold them still. His face, framed by the long greasy hair, was taut and serious, the muscles pulled tight. "They said, 'Worship your new God' or 'Bow down before your new God' or something like that. And then . . . something . . . started to come out of the fire. It was huge. It was big and black and looked like it had two horns." He looked at Jim. "It looked like the devil."

Jim reached over and put his hand on the boy's shoulder. "Was that all?" he asked.

"No." Don shook his head. "All of a sudden, the fire went out and Father Selway and the devil were gone and the other monsters shoved Mrs. Selway's body into a big hole. Then they threw her head in a little hole and threw the kids in another hole and covered them all up."

"Where? What part of the dump?"

"Under the garbage, by the big tree next to the cliff. Right next to a tractor."

Jim jumped up. "Carl!" he called. The deputy pushed the door immediately open. "Get the posse together. We're going to search for the Selways' bodies."

"But I thought—"

"Never mind what you thought. Get everyone together. Tell them we'll meet out at the Geronimo Wells landfill. Now!"

Carl ran down the hall toward the switchboard out front, his boots clicking loudly on the tile.

Jim turned back toward the boy. He looked even smaller and paler than he had before. His hands, between his legs, were clasped together, and sweat was running in twin lines down both sides of his face from beneath his hair. Jim looked at the boy and tried to smile reassuringly. He didn't know why he believed the kid, but he did. Jesus, he thought. His mind really was going. Not just scared of his own dreams, but believing others' as well. "Why did you wait 'til now to tell us?" he asked Don.

"I thought it was just a nightmare. I didn't know it was real. I didn't know anything had happened." His lower lip started to tremble. His hand intercepted a tear sneaking down his cheek. "I just found out that the Selways were missing this morning. I didn't know."

Jim patted the boy's shoulder. "It's okay, son." The boy wiped away another tear. "But how come you wouldn't tell anyone except me?"

"You were in the dream. I knew you'd understand. I knew you'd know I didn't do it. I knew you'd know I wasn't really there, I didn't really see anything."

A bolt of fear—wild, irrational—shot through Jim's body, causing his heart to trip-hammer crazily. A wave of cold washed over him. He stared at the boy. He had never seen this kid before in his life; he did not look even vaguely familiar.

But he had automatically believed his story.

And, he realized, something about the boy's dream seemed naggingly, disturbingly true. It had seemed right. As if this were knowledge he'd already had but just could not bring to consciousness. As if the boy had simply put known facts together in a new way; a way he understood intuitively, on a gut level, but could not reason out.

The boy was right, he knew. He *had* been in that dream somehow, although he could remember none of it.

He turned back to Don. His voice was not as as-

sured as he would have liked, but he forced himself
to speak anyway. "What was I doing in your dream?"

"You were just standing there watching. Like me."
The boy licked his lips, "Like everyone else."

The cold intensified. "Who else?"

"I don't know. You were the only one I recognized.
But I'd know them if I saw them."

Carl poked his head in the door. "Car's ready, Sheriff. I called the posse and they're going to meet us
there."

Jim put on his hat and grabbed his holster. "Okay."
He strapped on the belt and looked at Don. "You
coming?"

"Do I have to?"

Jim shook his head.

"Then no, I'd rather not."

"Okay." He looked into the boy's face and saw underneath the childish features a maturity; maturity that
had been forced upon him and for which he was not
exactly ready but which he was able to cope with. The
kid had handled himself well, he thought. Better than
a lot of adults would have under similar circumstances.
He wished this could be the end of it, the boy could
just go home and forget about everything, letting the
sheriff's office handle the situation, his civic duty done.
But there was a lot more to come. It would be tough
on the kid. "We have some more talking to do," he
said. "Leave your name and address with Rita out at
the front desk. I'll get in touch with you later."

Don stood up, wiping sweaty palms on his faded
jeans. "Do you have to tell my parents about it?"

Jim thought for a moment. Tell his parents what?
That they'd decided to look for bodies at the dump
because of their son's nightmares? That Don had had
some type of psychic experience?

"No," he said. "I don't have to tell your parents if
you don't want me to."

The boy looked relieved.

Jim lightly punched Don's arm. "I'll see you later," he said. "I have to go." He strode quickly down the hall and out the front doors, waving without looking back. Carl was waiting in a patrol car, the engine running. Jim got into the car, flipped on the roof lights and told his deputy to take off.

The car pulled onto the highway, tires squealing. "What happened?" Carl asked. "What'd the kid tell you?"

"He told me where the bodies are buried."

Carl whistled. "Did he actually see anything?"

Jim stared out the windshield as they sped north through town. "Yes," he said. "Yes he did."

The sky was covered with blackened monsoon clouds by the time they turned off on the control road, twenty minutes later. The dark thunderheads were backlit periodically by the strobe flashes of lightning, although there was no rain yet. "Goddamn it," the sheriff said. "Does it have to rain every fucking day? We're going to be out there digging in a downpour."

They had to go a little slower here than they had on the highway. The control road was narrow, barely one lane, and the campers, hikers, hunters, and fishermen who drove their pickups down the dirt road usually assumed no one would be coming toward them. They invariably sped around the hairpin turns as though they were the only ones on the road. Usually they would be. The control road, winding as it did through the forest along the base of the Rim, was so rough and rutted that it was absolute hell for anyone without a four-wheel-drive vehicle.

The convoy encountered no other traffic on their trip to Geronimo Wells, however, and they pulled into the landfill just as the rain started. Jim got out of the car and walked back to tell the other members of the posse that they could either wait in their cars and trucks for the rain to stop—which might take several hours—or they could start digging now. "Me and Carl are going to dig," he said. "The sooner we get this done, the sooner we can get out of here."

He looked around the landfill as Carl took the shovels out of the trunk. The dump did not look as familiar to him as it should have. He had been out here before, of course, and he knew that scrap metal was dropped off near the large pile just to the north of the cars, that wood went on the pile of combustibles to the left of that, and that regular garbage was dumped over the small dirt cliff just beyond the woodpile and buried. But it looked like only a dump to him; it did not look like the scene of ritualistic killings. He had no intuitive flashes about the landfill, no psychic revelations. He did not even feel any bad vibrations. The dump seemed to him the same as it always had. He had nothing to go on but the kid's testimony.

The other members of the posse got out of their vehicles and took their own picks and shovels from their trunks and the beds of their trucks. They stood in a huddled group in the drizzling rain, looking toward the sheriff.

Jim jumped onto the hood of the brown sheriff's car and held up his hands. "All right!" he said. "Listen up! We're going to split into two groups. Six of us are going to dig through the garbage by that big tree over there." He pointed toward a tall pine tree by the sandy cliff. A tractor was parked next to the tree, just as Don had said it would be. "Three of you will dig through the woodpile there."

"The boys 'n' I'll take the woodpile," Scott Hamilton said, gesturing toward his two sons. All three of them were still wearing around their necks the protective goggles required for all mill workers.

"You know what you're supposed to be looking for?" Jim asked.

The three nodded grimly.

"All right then. Let's get to work. Everyone else,

come with me." He jumped down from the car and led the rest of the posse past the woodpile to the garbage area. He let his shovel fall into the rain-softened ground. "Start digging anywhere," he said. "We don't know the exact spot where we're supposed to be looking. Just make sure you all stay near the tractor."

The six men spread out along the garbage pile. Jim and Carl moved to the edge of the cliff. It was starting to drizzle harder now, and the ground was soft and spongy beneath their feet. Jim's clothes were already soaked clear through, and he took off his hat and dumped the water from the brim. He put the hat back on and started digging.

It was Kyle Heathrow who, almost half an hour later, called out: "Sheriff! C'mere! I think I've found something!"

Jim stepped through the wet pile of garbage, his feet sinking almost to the ankles, toward the spot where Kyle was digging. It was pouring, the rain coming down in torrents, and all of the diggers looked like drowned dogs. He stopped and stood next to Kyle, staring down into the newly dug hole. A woman's face looked up at him, eyes open, a bloodless gash across the cheek where Kyle's shovel had made contact.

Mrs. Selway.

Jim looked away, forcing himself to look at a plastic garbage sack. He licked his lips, suddenly dry despite the rain. "Okay!" he yelled. "Over here! We're going to dig around this area!"

The others slogged their way through the wet garbage and stared into the hole. Rain had already washed some of the mud from Mrs. Selway's face, making it look strangely alive. Drops of moisture caught on the long eyelashes, and a puddle had formed within the open mouth. None of the men said a word as they turned away.

Carl went to the car to get a body bag.

Jim stared upward, into the falling rain. The water that had collected on the brim of his hat went cascading down the back of his neck but he hardly noticed. He realized suddenly that he did not know Mrs. Selway's first name.

He looked again at the ground, at the wet and muddy garbage, and picked up his shovel. He started digging.

SEVEN

Gordon spent the evening making phone calls. As Marina lay on the overstuffed couch in the living room trying to watch a snow- and static-tinged *Goldfinger* on the only TV station they could get—an ABC affiliate out of Flagstaff—Gordon dialed St. Luke's Hospital in Phoenix and made Marina an appointment with the resident obstetrician, Dr. Kaplan, for one o'clock Monday afternoon. Marina had refused to make the call herself, and Gordon had agreed to do it for her. He understood how she felt.

After hanging up, he called Brad and told him that he needed to take Monday off. Monday was their busiest day because most of the local stores ran out of Pepsi over the weekend; and since they still had some of the outlying areas to do he assumed he'd have to fight Brad tooth and nail for the day off. But Brad was uncharacteristically understanding, and he told Gordon that he'd get Dan to take his place for the day. Gordon promised to be in extra early on Tuesday.

Next was a call to Dr. Waterston. Gordon told the doctor his fears and outlined his plans. Dr. Waterston agreed wholeheartedly with his decision to take Marina to Phoenix. "Best thing you could do," he said.

After some initial, abstract conversation on the subject of babies and births, they got down to specifics.

"I really have no facts to go on," Dr. Waterston said. "This is all conjecture. But as I explained to your wife, there are similarities between Julie Campbell, Joni Cooper, and Susan Stratford that I find are just too close for comfort." He paused. "Similarities your wife shares with them."

"That's what Marina told me."

"Like I said, I have no proof. But I have sent a sample of water taken from the Geronimo Wells pump station to a lab in Phoenix for analysis."

"The water!" Gordon said. "That's exactly what I thought."

"I'm not saying that's what it is. I could be way off base, here. But you know there's a county landfill just a half a mile or so east of the pump station, off the control road, and some of that might be seeping into the groundwater system. There's been no toxic waste buried there so far as I know, but something could be leaking down. From where I sit, it sure as hell looks like it."

"Have you told anyone?"

Dr. Waterston laughed shortly. "Have I told anyone? I've told the mayor, the town council, the county board of supervisors, the state water control board, even the local chapter of the AMA."

"Nothing happened?"

"Zippity shit; pardon my French. They all promised to look into it, of course, but I never heard from any of them. That was a good three months ago. I call each of the organizations at least once a week, just to bug them into getting off their dead asses, but I just get shunted around from secretary to secretary." He laughed again, and his voice became absurdly, mockingly officious; the voice of a petty bureaucrat. "With the exception of the mayor's office and the town council, of course. They're looking into it, examining all possibilities, but they are conducting a secret investigation and can't tell me about it yet." He snorted. "What a crock."

"When are you supposed to hear back from the lab?"

"Any day now, I'll let you know when I do."

Gordon nodded into the telephone, though he knew the doctor couldn't see him. "Thanks," he said. "I'll let *you* know what happens Monday."

"Damn right you will. Just because Marina's going to have her tests and analysis done in Phoenix doesn't mean I'm not still her doctor. She has an appointment for next week and she's going to keep it."

Gordon smiled. "All right. Call you Monday, Doc."

"I'll be waiting."

He hung up the receiver and went out to the living room to check on Marina. The room was dark save for the blue light of the TV, and it took him a moment to find her, stretched out on the couch. "Hey," he said. "You all right?"

She waved him away. "Shhh. This is an important part." On the screen, James Bond came barreling through a chain link fence in his car while an old lady shot at him with a machine gun. The old lady grimaced as the gun kicked back. Marina laughed. "I love that part. That old woman cracks me up."

"Your appointment's for Monday at one," Gordon said.

Marina did not answer. She appeared to be raptly watching the movie, but Gordon knew that she had heard him. She just didn't want to talk about it.

He retreated back into the den and leafed through the phone book until he found the number he wanted. He dialed Keith Beck at the newspaper. He wasn't sure the editor would be there this late on a Saturday night, but Beck had an unlisted home phone and he had no other choice. The phone was answered on the first ring.

"Hello?"

Gordon felt a little uncertain talking to the editor about their problem. He did not know a whole hell of a lot, and he could substantiate even less, but he told Beck what he could about the infants and the editor promised to look into it. He said it might take a few weeks, though, what with the rodeo coming up and the desecrated churches and . . .

"Church-es?" Gordon interrupted. "Plural?"

"You haven't heard?"

"No." Gordon thought of the bloody letters he'd seen on Father Selway's defiled church and he felt a subtle chill caress his spine. It seemed suddenly darker in the room, and he flipped on a desk lamp. "What happened?"

The editor laughed, the laugh turning into a phlegmy smoker's cough. "Read the paper next Wednesday."

"Come on."

"Okay. What have you heard so far? What do you know?"

"I saw the Episcopal church, and Char Clifton told us Father Selway was missing."

"Well the same thing happened to the rest of the churches. All of them. Windows broken, obscene graffiti, the whole bit. That's why I'm still here, in fact. Jim Weldon gave me a buzz about an hour ago and gave me all the details. Thought I'd like to know. Right now, I'm just trying to figure out how to write about the obscenities. Should I use those cartoon punctuation symbols for the words? Should I use the first letter of each word, followed by an appropriate number of blank spaces? Or should I just refer to them as 'profanities' or 'obscenities'?"

Gordon ignored the editor's tunnel-visioned account

of the situation. "What about the other clergymen? Have they disappeared?"

"No. But that's really all I can tell you," Beck admitted. "The sheriff is supposed to call me back. The way it's going now, it looks like I'll be here 'til dawn."

"I'll let you go, then. Thanks."

"No problem. And I'll look into that baby situation as soon as I can. I'll get back to you if I find anything out."

Gordon made his final call of the evening to his parents in California. After he'd told them of Marina's pregnancy they wanted to talk to Marina herself, and he yelled for her to pick up the other phone. The four-way long distance conversation was very sober and very tearful, and it continued on until well past midnight. Finally his parents hung up, promising to call again Monday night. On his father's request, he dialed the operator and had the charges reversed.

Outside, the rain had long since stopped and the world was completely quiet. Looking out the window, Gordon could see the short line of stars that formed the handle of the Big Dipper standing out sharply against a background of galaxies and nebulas in the now clear night sky. Closer in, the pine trees stood tall and straight, completely unmoving in the breeze-less air. He closed the drapes and walked down the hall to the bedroom, slipping naked into bed, where Marina joined him a few minutes later. Although it was late and they were tired, they made love, more for the closeness and intimacy it afforded than the pleasure, and it was nearly two o'clock before both of them finally fell asleep, curled next to each other under the thin sheet.

Neither of them heard the soft scuttling noises that whispered through the house soon after.

And neither of them noticed in the morning that the furniture in the living room had been subtly, slightly moved.

EIGHT

Jim Weldon turned on the fluorescent office lights and shuffled across the carpet to his desk, sitting tiredly down. He leaned back in his chair, closing his eyes tightly and pressing against the lids with the palms of his hands. It had been one hellacious day. They had found the rest of Mrs. Selway's body and the bodies of the children in various stages of dismemberment by nightfall, and all of the corpses had been loaded onto Scott Hamilton's truck for the trip back to town. Jim had ridden with Scott and a few other men to the mortuary and had called the county coroner, while Carl had remained at the dump with the rest of the posse, trying to find the body of Father Selway. Jim had stopped briefly at the newspaper to let Keith Beck know what was happening, then had hurried back out to the dump. Father Selway's body had not been recovered. They had continued searching for another hour and a half with no luck and had finally given it up for the night.

Jim did not think they would ever find the body.

He took his hands from his eyes and let his chair fall forward.

"Supervisor Jones called."

He stared at the three-word note sitting on top of his desk and swore to himself. Jesus fuck. Leslie Jones. The last thing he needed today was to talk to that bitch. She'd probably found out from the coroner that the Selways' bodies had been recovered and wanted to chew him out for not finding them sooner, or for not giving them adequate protection while they were alive, or for . . . something. She always had some bug up her ass. He crumpled up the paper and tossed it on the floor, shaking his head. Luckily, it was a weekend and her office was closed. He didn't have her home phone number, so he couldn't return her call until Monday.

He picked up the other messages that had been left on his desk and glanced through them. Beck had called from the newspaper and wanted him to call back as soon as possible. Reverend Paulson from the Presbyterian church had stopped by, but he'd come back tomorrow when things weren't so busy. Annette had called to say that she'd heard what had happened and would hold dinner for him.

Don Wilson had called.

Jim tossed the remaining messages aside and dialed the number written on the small square of pink memo paper. It was late, he knew, but he couldn't afford to take any chances. A woman's voice answered. "Hello."

"Hello," he said. "Is Don Wilson there?"

The woman's voice sounded suddenly suspicious. "Who is this?"

"Sheriff Weldon. I'd like to speak to Don if I could."

The suspicion changed audibly to anger; an anger directed at her son. The woman's voice grew tense, and Jim could almost see the jaw muscles clenching. "What's he done now?"

"Nothing." Jim had promised the boy that he wouldn't tell his parents anything, but he did not want his silence on the subject to get the boy into trouble. He thought quickly. "I'm calling about the antilitter campaign we're starting," he said smoothly. "We're getting a group of volunteers together to pick up cans along the highway next Saturday, and I was told Don might be interested." He knew it was a lame excuse, but it was the best he could do on the spur of the moment.

The woman's voice sounded incredulous. "Don?"

"Could you just put him on the line please, Mrs. Wilson?"

"Okay," the woman said. "Just a second."

There was a moment of silence, then the boy came to the phone. His voice sounded tired, and Jim thought he had probably been sleeping. "Yeah?"

"Don, this is Sheriff Weldon."

"Oh." The boy's voice was suddenly alert and wide awake.

"We found the bodies. Just like you said."

"I know."

Jim cleared his throat. "I got a note here that you called. You wanted to talk to me?"

"Yes."

The boy's answers were unnaturally short, and his voice sounded not quite relaxed. Jim had a feeling that the boy's mother was standing there in the same room, listening. "Can you talk now?" he asked.

"No."

"Is your mother there? Is that why?"

"Yes."

"Okay," Jim said. "But I'd like you to come down to the office tomorrow. I want to talk to you about all this."

"All right."

"How does ten o'clock sound?"

"Fine."

"Okay. I'll see you then." Jim was about to say good-bye and hang up when he thought of something else. "One thing more. Father Selway? We found no trace of him. His body wasn't there."

Don's voice was still calm and controlled in front of his mother, but Jim could hear an edgy undercurrent of fear in it. "I know," he said.

"Is that what you wanted to talk to me about?"

"Sort of." Don's voice grew suddenly into a whisper. He spoke quickly, and Jim knew that his mother had left the room for a moment. "I had another dream," he said. "It was—" The whisper cut off in midsentence, and the boy's voice resumed its normal tone. "Later."

"You'll tell me later?"

"Yes."

"Okay, Don. I'll see you tomorrow then. Ten o'clock. My office."

"Fine. Good-bye, Sheriff."

"Good-bye." Jim hung up the phone feeling slightly edgy himself. He knew he was an adult, and a sheriff, and he was supposed to have gotten rid of his childhood fears years ago, but he was frightened nonetheless. The window of his office looked completely dark, he could see nothing but his own reflection in it, and he was reminded of a particularly horrible nightmare he had had last week. He stood up, suddenly spooked, knowing that both Judson and Pete were keeping watch in the front of the building and that he was all alone back here. He saw again the mutilated bodies of those two farmers, and the face of Mrs. Selway in the mud, rain dripping down her dead lips. He walked quickly across the office toward the door.

There was a quiet swishing noise in the hall outside.

Jim stood perfectly still, unmoving, every muscle in his body on alert. He listened carefully, head cocked, but all he could hear at first was the rapid beating of his own heart. Then the swishing sound came again, darting down the hall toward the rear of the building. He drew his gun, knowing that nothing human could have made that sound, but hoping to God that he was wrong. He counted to five, then threw open the door.

The lights in the hallway were off, and he barely saw the dark shadow skitter around the corner at the far end of the corridor. He ran forward, gun in hand. The hall was cold, unnaturally so, much colder than even the air-conditioning system could have gotten it, and the air smelled faintly of sewage or rotting vegetables. He ran around the corner . . . and into Judson Weiss.

The deputy went sprawling, his wildly flailing arms knocking over a freestanding ashtray and sending a spray of white sand flying across the tile floor. "Jesus!" he yelled. He slid backward for a few seconds, then regained his balance and used his hands to push himself to his feet. He noticed Jim's drawn gun and instantly became alert. He reached for his own firearm. "What is it?"

Jim was trying to regain his own balance; though he had not fallen, the collision had sent him backward into the wall. "Did you see anything run by here?" he asked.

"What?"

"Something—" He stopped, knowing that what he was about to say sounded stupid, but having to say it anyway. "—something small and dark that made sort of a . . . whisk-broom sound?"

Judson stared at him. "Like what? A rat?" His voice was puzzled.

Jim ran a hand through his hair. "Did you see *anything* run by here?"

"No sir."

"All right." Jim put the gun back in his holster. He knew how he probably sounded, and he was aware of the deputy's worried glance. He smiled to show he was all right. "I'm just tired, I guess. I thought I saw something run by my door. I don't know what the hell I thought it was." He picked up the spilled ashtray and refastened its bowl-shaped top. "Maybe I oughtta get home and get some sleep."

Judson nodded. "Maybe so. Me and Pete'll be here tonight. We'll call you if anything comes up."

"Yeah," Jim said. "Maybe I will head home. After that autopsy report is delivered none of us are going to get any sleep around here."

"Don't guess we will."

Jim pointed toward the spray of sand on the floor tile. "Think you could clean that up there?"

"Sure."

He patted Judson on the back. "Sorry I bumped into you."

"No problem, Sheriff."

Jim went back to his office to get his keys. He knew he probably *was* too tired. He seemed to be losing his grip. He wanted Judson to think nothing was wrong, but something was very much wrong. He had no proof, nothing to substantiate his fears, but he had a gut feeling that whatever was going on in Randall was not caused by anything human. He knew, though, that despite his inner unfounded suspicions he would have to investigate everything using proper police procedure—procedure that automatically assumed that all circumstances were the result of normal criminals operating in normal criminal ways. Maybe that was for the best. It wouldn't do to have a sheriff who based his actions on dreams, who saw things that weren't there.

But Don had been right about the Selways.

Jim sighed. He knew it was irrational, but it was almost inconceivable to him that so many things could be going on at once and not be connected somehow, particularly in a quiet small town like Randall, a town where the annual crime rate hovered just above zero. The way he saw it, in fact, they *were* connected. Several farmers' goats had been slaughtered, and the goats' blood had been used to desecrate the town's churches. Two of the farmers whose goats had been killed had themselves been murdered. And Father Selway, whose church had been the first hit, had been murdered.

No, not murdered. His *family* had been murdered. He was still only missing.

Jim closed his eyes. He could feel a headache coming on. He knew he was thinking irrationally, not reasoning correctly, and he knew he should probably tell someone his fears, his suspicions. Judson or Pete, Carl. But he could not bring himself to do it. This was something he could not share. He grabbed his keys and his hat. He nodded as he walked past Pete, who was manning the switchboard for the night, and made his way out to the parking lot. He couldn't help looking at the bushes surrounding the parking lot for any sign of movement, and he stopped to listen before he opened the car door.

But there was no movement and no sound, and he drove home still troubled.

NINE

The church bells rang out in staggered order, calling people to their respective Sunday services, their different tones and pitches blending, harmonizing, to create one lovely melded semimelody. From his office, Jim could hear the bells of five of the town's six churches, and he could pick out the individual sounds of three of them. He looked out the window, staring at the fluffy white clouds above the Rim; the clouds that would turn into raging thunderheads by midafternoon. All but one of the bells quit pealing. Their ringing tones faded, quieted, died out. Only the bell to the Episcopal church continued. Three extra rings. Then it, too, was silenced.

Jim stared in the direction of the Episcopal church, though he could see nothing but trees. He wondered who was taking Father Selway's place in the pulpit today. He thought of the horrible attitude of the bishop and he grimaced. He was half-considering popping over to the church for a quick look, just to see what was happening, when he heard the unmistakable sound of the fire department's siren. He cocked his head, listening. The truck seemed to be heading down Main Street, away from Old Mesa Road. He skirted around his desk and turned up the scanner on the shelf above the rifle case.

". . . Ash Lane." There was a sharp crackle of static. "Fire reported at the residence of John Wilson," a woman's voice stated. "Twelve thirty-four South Ash Lane."

Wilson!

Jim ran down the hall to the front office. "Rita!" he called. "Do you have the address of that kid who was here yesterday? Don Wilson?"

The dispatcher looked startled. "Yes, but I think I put it on your desk."

"Never mind! Do you remember whether he lived on Ash?"

"I think he did . . ."

Jim was out the door and running, fumbling the keys out of his pocket as he sprinted across the small parking lot. He hit the lights and the siren and spun out onto the street. He grabbed the radio microphone from its spot on the dash. He clicked the radio tuner to the fire emergency channel. "Weldon!" he shouted into the mike. "Get me an update on that fire!"

The woman's voice came over the car's speaker. "Sheriff?" It was Natalie Ernst, Chief Ernst's daughter-in-law.

"How bad's the damage Natalie?"

"The truck's there right now. The neighbor who called said the house just sort of exploded about ten minutes ago."

Ten minutes ago. He hadn't heard a thing. "What about the family?"

"Someone got out, but we're not sure who."

"Was it a kid?"

There was a short hesitation. "I don't think so."

Jim turned the car onto Old Mesa Road. The four travelers on the street pulled over as they heard his siren. He let the radio mike hang. "Sheriff?" Natalie said. "Sheriff?" He flipped the radio off and turned onto Ash. Ahead, he could see the square yellow bulk of the town's new fire engine blocking the road. Smoke was billowing out from the house in front of the fire engine, partially obscuring the scene. A tangle of hoses, like gigantic anacondas, snaked across the partially paved road into the thickest part of the smoke. A helmeted, uniformed man, probably Ernst, was standing in the middle of the street shouting orders and gesturing authoritatively.

Jim slammed on the brakes and hopped out of the car. He ran straight for the fire chief. "How's the kid?" he yelled.

Ernst looked at him, his face already blackened by soot. "What kid?"

The neighbors were out now, standing in front of their houses in huddled groups, a bizarre mixture of Sunday-suited churchgoers and sleep-garbed stay-at-homes. They were milling around nervously, looking this way and that, talking among themselves in hushed tones. Jim walked up to the nearest group. He nodded toward a well-dressed elderly man. "Do you know the Wilsons?" he asked.

The man shrugged. "Not too well."

"Any of you?"

"I used to baby-sit Don," one lady offered. She clutched the top of her pink terry cloth robe to her neck, trying to hide her semi-nakedness.

"Have you seen Don this morning?"

The lady shook her head. "I just got out here a few minutes ago. I didn't know anything was happening till I heard the sirens pull up."

Jim strode over to another man, standing by himself, staring into the smoke. "You seen anything?"

The man shook his head. "I heard the woman got out. That's all I know."

"Did you see her?"

The man pointed toward an adjoining lawn, where

several people were milling about. "I think she's over there. They're waiting for the ambulance to come."

Jim started toward the house next door, but he could see the sheeted figure on the grass between several legs before he even reached the spot. His heart sank as he pushed two people out of the way and looked down on the moaning remains of Don Wilson's mother, her arms, little more than stumps, trying unsuccessfully to shield her charred and blackened face from heat that was no longer there. The sounds that came out of her mouth were barely human, and discolored blood seeped out from beneath peeling folds of burned skin.

He turned away and walked back across the street to where Ernst was adjusting a hose on the fire truck. Orange flames were now leaping out of the smoke. "Chief!" he called.

Ernst waved him away with one short motion of his hand. "You're in the way, Weldon," he said abruptly. "I'll be glad to talk to you, but not right now. We've got a fire to put out."

Jim stepped back and watched as Ernst and another man ran into the smoke toward the house carrying a hose. He heard several voices shouting orders.

He stood alone in the middle of the street, staring numbly. Don was dead, he knew. The boy had never even made it out of the house. He had probably died in his sleep from smoke inhalation. Or else he had fried trying to escape. Jim thought he saw shapes moving through the smoke. It looked like the fire was coming under control. This was no accident, this fire. Someone—something—had wanted Don dead, had known that the boy had come to him and wanted to get him out of the way. He stepped over a puddle, walking back to his car. He was going to make sure that Ernst followed through with an investigation of this fire. A full arson investigation. The fire had been deliberately started, and he wanted some answers.

He stood for a moment staring at the remains of the Wilson house, now visible through the thinning smoke, and remembered the small scared boy sitting in his office, nervously clenching and unclenching his hands, flipping his too-long hair off his dirty forehead. He had not really known the boy, but he had liked him. He'd seemed like a good kid.

He thought unreasonably of his own son Justin. He saw him the victim of a deliberately set fire or some other form of murder made to look like an accident and he shivered. Maybe he should send Annette and the kids down to Phoenix to stay with his brother for a few days. Or a few weeks. Or however long it took for this thing to blow over.

He got into the car and backed slowly out, lights and siren off. Glancing in the rearview mirror at the chaotic street, at the incendiary destruction, he felt as though something had been taken out of him, as though he were empty. He had not realized until now how much he had been depending on that boy to see him through this crisis, to provide him with more dream-inspired clues, to help him, somehow, solve all of these interrelated cases. He had been expecting the boy to be with him every step of the way, to lead him. Now he was alone. He was on his own and he would have to use his own deductive powers and abilities to put an end to all this.

And he had nothing whatsoever to go on.

He drove slowly back toward the sheriff's office.

TEN

The trip to Phoenix was uneventful. Neither Gordon nor Marina felt like speaking, and they drove down Black Canyon Highway without talking, listening only to the sound of the tires on the washboard road and to the cheerily artificial conversation of the morning deejays on the radio. They left early, so there was no traffic, and they stared silently out at the craggy cliffs, massive gorges, and thick forests of the Coconino as they traveled, both lost in their own thoughts.

They reached the Valley well before noon and spent the morning looking through the myriad expensive Fifth Avenue shops in Scottsdale, talking obviously and self-consciously about third-party events entirely unrelated to the upcoming ordeal.

After a quick and quiet lunch at a fake French out-door cafe, they drove into Phoenix. To the hospital.

Gordon stared up at the peeling white paint and run-down exterior of the hospital's administration building. He couldn't see the top floor of the structure through his car windshield, but he did notice that several of the third-story windows were broken. Obscene graffiti was spray-painted on the lower portion of the street wall, and the first floor windows were barred with chain link fence. He had never been to St. Luke's before, and the hospital did not look as he had expected. He looked over at Marina, suddenly apprehensive. "I didn't know the place was this old," he said.

She smiled reassuringly. "Don't worry about it. It's a good hospital." She pointed past the administration building to where a giant complex of new concrete buildings arose. "Besides, that's where we're going. This is just the original hospital. I don't think they even use it anymore."

She was right. Gordon pulled into the parking lot and followed the white arrows painted on the asphalt to the new wing, where he found a spot near the entrance, adjacent to a handicapped space. They got out of the Jeep and walked through the sliding glass doors into the air-conditioned hospital lobby. Marina sat down on a cushiony chair and picked up a magazine while Gordon strode purposefully across the carpeted floor to the front desk. A woman wearing a telephone headset was staring intently down at a series of file cards. Gordon cleared his throat to let her know of his presence. "Excuse me," he said.

The woman looked up. "May I help you?"

"Yes, my wife is here to see Dr. Kaplan."

The woman opened a large notebook. "Does she have an appointment?"

"For one o'clock."

"Name?"

"Lewis. Marina Lewis."

The woman's finger ran down the notebook page to a line halfway down and then stopped. "Just a minute." She punched a key on the switchboard in front of her and spoke into the mouthpiece of her headset. "Dr. Kaplan? Mrs. Lewis is here to see you." She paused. "Yes." Another pause. "Okay. Thank you, doctor." She looked up at Gordon. "Dr. Kaplan is ready for her. A nurse will be coming out with a wheelchair to take her into the exam room."

Gordon walked back across the lobby to where Marina sat reading her magazine. Her overstuffed straight-backed chair was pushed flush against a wall of crisscrossing unfinished wood. Above her head hung a framed Dan Namingha print. She was staring down at the pages of the magazine and did not notice when he walked up. He cleared his throat loudly, pompously.

She looked up at him, smiling. "So?"

"So a nurse is coming to bring you back to Dr. Kaplan." He grinned. "You're going in style."

She sighed disgustedly. "Wheelchair?"

Gordon laughed. "You got it." He sat down in the chair next to her and gently lifted the magazine from her lap, putting it back on the small table on the other side of her. He took her hands in his, looking into her large brown eyes. "Are you going to be all right?"

She nodded. "Do you want to come back there with me?"

"I don't think they'll let me. Besides, I have to fill out the insurance forms and everything. I'll just wait here for you."

Marina smiled lightly, mischievously. "You're just afraid to go back there."

He smiled back. "You're right."

"What a wuss."

A thin old nurse, wearing a traditional white hat and uniform, came through the set of swinging double doors next to the front desk, pushing an empty wheelchair. She looked down at the clipboard she was carrying. "Mrs. Lewis?" she called, scanning the lobby.

"That's you," Gordon said. He stood up and walked with her to the wheelchair. They stared silently at each other for a moment, each painfully aware of what the other was thinking, feeling, and she hugged him tightly before sitting down. "Don't worry," he said. "Everything's going to be okay."

She smiled, but her smile was less genuine than before and there seemed to be a hint of sadness in it. She held up her crossed fingers. "Let's hope so."

The nurse wheeled her through the double doors and into the depths of the hospital.

The smile fled Gordon's face immediately after the doors swung shut, and he walked slowly back to the front desk feeling tired and emotionally fatigued. God, he hoped everything was going to be all right. A gut-level feeling told him that Marina's test results were going to be bad and his brain told him logically that he should prepare for the worst, but part of him *wanted* to believe the best and was *hoping* for the best.

He received a sheaf of duplicate forms and a pen from the woman at the desk and sat wearily down in the nearest chair. He twisted his neck in a slow semi-circle to relieve some of the stress and closed his eyes for a few seconds. Then he glanced over the papers and began filling out the top form.

"And the Lord said unto woman, 'I will greatly multiply your pain in childbearing; in pain you shall bring forth children.' "

At the sound of the deep oratorical voice, Gordon jerked his gaze up from the forms in his lap. Standing before him, he saw a tall, business-suited man carrying what looked like a small black-bound Bible in his right hand, next to his chest. A bundle of thin pamphlets was clutched in his free-dangling left hand. The man's graying hair was short and neatly combed, parted on the side, and his face was almost pleasant. His eyes were two piercingly black orbs that burned with the fiery intensity of fanaticism. His tie clip, Gordon noticed, was in the shape of a cross.

"Genesis 3:16," the man said.

"I'm not interested," Gordon said shortly. He looked down, turning again to his paperwork, hoping the man would go away. But instead the stranger sat down in the chair next to him. Gordon continued writing, trying to ignore the man. He was acutely aware

of the man's presence, and he knew without looking
that those burning black eyes were boring into him.
After a minute or so, he glanced up. Sure enough, the
man was staring. "What do you want?" Gordon asked.

"My name is Brother Elias," the man said. "I want
to help you."

"I don't need any help," Gordon said. He turned
back to his insurance forms.

"Yes you do. Your wife is going to have a baby.
And there will be troubles."

Gordon jerked his head up, shocked and, against
his more rational impulses, a little frightened. "What
do you mean?" he said. "Who the hell are you?"

Brother Elias smiled distractedly. He fingered his
tie clip. "Do you realize," he said, "that if Christ had
been killed with a knife instead of on the cross we
would today be worshiping a knife? This tie clasp
would be a knife." He made an expansive motion in
the air. "Sculpted knives would hang on the fronts of
our churches."

The man was crazy, Gordon realized. He did not
know whether Brother Elias was an ex-hippie who had
turned to Christ, bringing his fried brain along with
him, or whether he was a fallen fundamentalist, but
he knew that the man was not one of your ordinary
everyday Bible-thumpers. Gordon picked up the pen
from his lap, grabbed his forms and stood up, preparing to move to another seat.

Brother Elias stood up as well.

"I know what has befallen you and your loved ones,
and I want to help you," Brother Elias said. "You are
suffering the consequences of the wicked." He knelt
on the lobby carpet and reached up to grab Gordon's
hand. "Sit here and pray with me and we will put
it right."

Gordon pulled away, shaking his head, staring in
disbelief at the kneeling man. "No."

" 'The field is the world, and the good seed means

the sons of the kingdom. The weeds are the sons of the evil one. And the enemy who sowed them is the devil. The harvest is the close of the age.' Matthew 13:39."

Gordon looked around the lobby to see if anyone else had caught this, to see if anyone else was watching. But the few people sitting in the overstuffed chairs were either staring out the smoked glass of the window onto the parking lot or looking at the carpet, contemplating their own miseries and misfortunes. No one was paying any attention to Brother Elias.

Brother Elias bowed his head. "Praise Jesus!" he said. "Praise the Lord!"

Gordon stared. Why the hell had this guy decided to pick on him?

Brother Elias looked up. "If Christ had been hung instead of crucified, we would today be worshiping a noose."

Gordon walked over to the front desk. He tapped his hand on the white countertop to get the headsetted woman's attention. "Excuse me, miss," he said. "But is this man supposed to be here?" He pointed toward Brother Elias, still kneeling on the floor of the lobby praying.

The woman took one look at the business-suited preacher, at the Bible and the stack of pamphlets on the carpet next to him, and pressed a red key on her switchboard. "Security?" she said. "The reverend is back again. Would you please escort him out of the hospital? . . . Thank you." She looked up at Gordon and nodded.

Gordon returned to his seat, but this time Brother Elias did not follow him. "Pray," the preacher said, walking voluntarily toward the glass doors of the front entrance. He looked back at Gordon. "Pray for your wife. Pray for your daughter. 'For I have come to set a man against his father and a daughter against her mother.' " His black orbs bored into Gordon's for a moment, then he was gone, walking out of the building just as two uniformed security guards entered the lobby from another door.

Gordon picked up his pen and the sheaf of insurance forms.

On top of the stack of papers was a small cheaply printed pamphlet. The large bold letters on the cover of the pamphlet said: "SATAN is using YOU! HE is here NOW!"

He did not even bother to read the leaflet. He crumpled the paper up and deposited it in the ashtray of the table next to him.

He got to work on the insurance forms.

It was nearly four o'clock when Marina finally emerged from behind the swinging double doors, a different nurse wheeling her out. Gordon, who had been situated in a chair by the front window, staring at the doors and waiting for Marina's return, stood up immediately and went over to her. She looked tired, but she was smiling, and she stood up from the chair as soon as she saw him. "Good news," she said.

"Really?" He could not believe it. He had been preparing himself for the worst, and her announcement took him by surprise.

"I think so. The preliminary tests look good. But it'll be tomorrow before we know for sure." She smiled at him, her eyes twinkling. "Better start thinking up girls' names."

"Are you sure?"

"No, I lied."

"I mean, it really looks promising?"

She laughed. "It looks that way."

He hugged her, squeezing her close. They kissed. "Let's celebrate," he said, pulling back. "Let's go out somewhere to eat. Somewhere expensive."

Marina shook her head. "I'd rather not. I don't really feel all that well. Some of those tests, you know . . ." She shook her head and rolled her eyes in an expression of unbelievability, leaving the sentence unfinished. "Let's just get home."

"Are you sure you wouldn't rather stay overnight in the Valley and drive back up tomorrow?"

"You have to work tomorrow."

"I'll call in sick. Brad won't care."

She looked at him as if he'd just said something outrageous. "You're joking, right?"

He smiled. "All right."

"Besides, we need to save all the money we can. We're going to be proud parents."

He thought of her earlier ideas about an abortion and wanted to ask her what her thoughts were now, but he decided against it. "I get the hint," he said, smiling. He offered her his arm and she took it. "We'd better get started if we want to get back before dark."

They walked out of the lobby into the parking lot. Although it was late afternoon, the temperature was still well over a hundred and the sun was high in the clear blue, cloudless sky. There were no monsoons to relieve the heat in Phoenix. They got into the Jeep, leaning back into their seats slowly. The vinyl upholstery of the car felt hot even through their clothing. Gordon rolled down his window and turned the air conditioner on full blast, trying to drive out the hellishly heated air. He was already sweating.

"Thank God we don't live here," Marina said.

"That's a fact."

They pulled onto Washington Avenue, heading west toward Black Canyon Highway.

A few minutes later, they passed Brother Elias, calmly standing by the side of the road in his business suit, hitchhiking. The preacher smiled directly at Gordon and waved as they drove by—*How did he know my car? Gordon wondered*—but Gordon continued driving and stared straight ahead, ignoring him. He thought he could feel those intense black eyes cutting

through the glare of the windshield and boring into
him. Marina did not notice a thing.

On the way out of Phoenix, they stopped at a Dairy
Queen where they each got a sundae for the long
trip home.

ELEVEN

Old Mrs. Perry was going to have a baby.

Phil Johnson, director of the Randall Rest Home, shook his head and tossed a twisted paperclip into the wastebasket as he reread the doctor's report. It was inconceivable. The woman was well over eighty and just this side of senile. On her best days she was barely coherent. On her worst days she was little more than a blubbering overgrown infant.

Sighing, he stood up and folded the report, placing it in the top drawer along with several file folders. He flipped off the desk lamp and walked down the sterile white-lighted hallway to Mrs. Perry's darkened room. Slowly, quietly, he pushed open the door and looked in, staring down at her sleeping form. Her cadaverous chest rose and fell visibly with each rasping breath. Her back, propped up by a series of pillows, only accentuated her rising belly. His eyes shifted to her face. A thin line of mucus stretched from her small nose across the wrinkled mustached skin to her dried cracked lips. Even in sleep, he noted, her expression was not peaceful. Her brows were furrowed; her mouth curved down in a painful grimace.

He shook his head again. How could she be pregnant?

Who the hell would sleep with her?

The question was never very far from his thoughts. Who *would* sleep with her? What kind of sicko would want to have sex with an eighty-year-old woman?

And how in God's name had she gotten pregnant? She was long past menopause. It should have been physically impossible for her to conceive.

But Dr. Waterston had checked her over thoroughly. Several times. That rising midsection was not caused by overeating, malnutrition, some disease, or any of the other countless possibilities he had first considered. It was caused by the growth of the living fetus inside of her.

Phil quietly left the room, closing the door behind him, and started down the hall to the coffee machine in the kitchen. It was his fault things had gone this far. He should have noticed earlier, he should have kept a closer watch on her, he should have. . . .

But there were other patients in the rest home who also required constant supervision. Too many of them. And he was so hopelessly understaffed that it was a miracle there were not more problems.

Now it was too late for an abortion. In his report, Dr. Waterston said that such a procedure would almost certainly be fatal for the mother as well as the fetus at this stage of the pregnancy. Mrs. Perry's age and precarious physical health made it not only more dangerous but genuinely lethal.

Phil walked into the kitchen, got a Styrofoam cup from the half-unwrapped bag on the counter and poured himself some coffee. The room was dark, and he did not bother to turn on a light. A diffused refracted light entered the kitchen through the open hallway door, and the edges of the room were bathed in shadow. He shuddered as he looked into the darkness and thought of what the poor baby would probably look like.

Years ago, as a medic in the army, he had assisted with the birth of an infant to a similarly overaged woman in a small town in Italy. It had not been a pretty sight. The baby had emerged horribly disfigured, almost indistinguishable from the bloody afterbirth, and had died almost instantly. He had had nightmares about it for years afterward.

He downed half a cup of the lukewarm black coffee and poured himself some more. He looked up at the broken wall clock above the refrigerator, illuminated by a shaft of moonlight coming through the partially open kitchen curtains. The clock said two-thirty. He mentally subtracted an hour, then added ten minutes. One-forty. Another four hours and twenty minutes until Mrs. Stowe needed her medication. He could catch a little sleep.

He finished off the coffee then passed through the back of the kitchen to his bedroom. He set the small alarm on the nightstand for six A.M. and sat down on the edge of the bed. He started to take off his shoes.

The scream rent the air of the rest home like a harsh and high-pitched siren.

He jumped up, startled, scared. The scream came again; a hideously inhuman shriek of pure physical pain. He ran into the hallway. The instinctive fear left his body as quickly as it had come and was replaced by a trained sense of professional duty. The scream had come from Mrs. Perry's room, and he rushed over to her door, flinging it open.

The old woman sat straight up in her bed, her face contorted with agony. Unchecked tears ran down her wrinkled cheeks, and her mouth was wide open, screaming continuously without stopping for breath.

"What's wrong?" Phil called. "What is it?" But he knew she could not answer him, and he ran up to her, pulling the covers from her body.

He stared in shock.

The white sheet of the old woman's bed was covered with blood, which was seeping outward from the space between her legs in a rapidly spreading semicircle.

She was going to have the baby.

Phil pushed her back onto the stack of piled pillows, trying not to panic, telling her all the while to relax, things were going to be all right. Other people had gathered in the doorway by this time, and he yelled for someone to call Dr. Waterston. John Jacobs, a retired air force pilot and the most physically fit of the nursing home's residents, ran off to follow the order.

"It's going to be okay," Phil said, turning back to the old woman on the bed. "Don't worry." But he was not at all sure. It looked like she had lost a lot of blood, and that did not seem natural. More blood was still flowing from between her legs. Taking a deep breath, he held her bony chest down with one hand while he attempted to part her thighs with the other.

The baby was already halfway out.

Phil gasped. The baby's head was already protruding from the opening, flopping deadly back and forth on a too-small neck. It looked as though the neck had been broken by Mrs. Perry's panicked movements. Holding his breath, looking away, trying to keep down his own feelings of panic and terror, he reached between her legs and gently grabbed the baby's head. It was soft, slimy, slippery—like a piece of pulsating raw liver. He felt a rush of horrified disgust in the pit of his stomach, but he held on. He started to pull.

The baby squirted out in one sickening pop.

"Towel!" he yelled. "Somebody get me a towel!"

A woman handed him a blanket, and he wrapped the baby up in the material, wiping off the blood. He bent down and pressed his ear to the newborn's tiny chest, but he could hear no breathing, no heartbeat. The infant was not moving. Instinctively, he flopped the baby over onto its back and started pressing down on its midsection, trying to get its heart started, trying to get it to breathe. When that didn't work he covered the baby's mouth with his own and attempted mouth-to-mouth resuscitation. He could taste the sickeningly acrid blood on his tongue, and the taste, combined with the strongly rancid smell, almost made him retch. But he fought down his gag reflexes and kept on.

A few minutes later, tired and out of breath, he pulled his mouth away from the baby's and once again pressed his ear to the infant's chest.

Nothing.

He pounded hard on the infant's skeletal ribcage, trying to jar the heart into action, and again started the mouth-to-mouth.

It was no use, though. And he knew it was no use.

The infant was dead.

After a few more seemingly endless moments of frantically trying to revive the dead baby, Phil gave up. He pulled back, wiping the sweat from his eyes, and looked at the small child. It was a girl. Or would have been a girl. Her face, as he had feared, as he had known, was monstrously malformed. There was only one eye—open and staring—and no nose. The mouth spread almost vertically up the side of the right cheek. Her arms and legs were twisted almost beyond recognition.

He covered the infant with the blanket and stood up. Jill had come in while he'd been trying to revive the baby. She was standing at the foot of the bed, half-dressed but fully awake, a concerned-social-worker expression on her face. He told her to stay with Mrs. Perry until Dr. Waterston came. "The rest of you," he said, gesturing toward the gathered patients, "go back to bed. We'll get everything sorted out by morning, and we'll have a group meeting at ten in the dayroom and talk. I'll answer all of your questions then."

The patients reluctantly shuffled off to their individual bedrooms, talking in low shocked tones amongst themselves, while Phil carried the dead infant to the infirmary. He placed the blanketed baby on the steel counter that ran along the south wall of the room, making sure she was completely covered, and went back down the hall to help Jill with Mrs. Perry.

The doctor arrived fifteen minutes later.

"What the hell happened?" he asked, stepping quickly through the open doorway.

"Mrs. Perry had her baby," Phil said.

Dr. Waterston strode down the hall toward Mrs. Perry's bedroom. "She wasn't supposed to have that baby for another month!"

Phil shrugged, not sure of what to say.

"Why didn't you call me earlier?" the doctor demanded. "When she was in labor?"

"She wasn't," Phil said. "I mean, I looked in on her, checking to make sure she was okay, and she was sleeping soundly. Five minutes later, she started screaming, and when I rushed in there she was covered with blood."

"What did you do?"

"She was sitting up. I made her lie back down, then I spread her legs and looked. The baby's head was already halfway out."

"That's impossible."

"That's what happened. It looked like the baby's neck was broken."

They walked into Mrs. Perry's room, and the doctor took a needle and syringe from the white bag he was carrying. He rubbed a swab of alcohol on the old lady's arm and injected her. The drug took effect almost immediately, and Mrs. Perry's sweaty, agonized, tear-stained face relaxed into unconsciousness.

Dr. Waterston examined the mother, checked her heart, her breathing, looked at her pupils, thoroughly studied her dilated vagina, then turned to Phil. "Let's look at the infant."

Phil led the doctor down the hall to the infirmary without speaking. He opened the infirmary door, turned on the light . . . and saw that the baby was gone.

"What the—"

He ran over to the spot where he'd laid the dead infant. The bloodied blanket was thrown onto the floor next to the counter, but there was no sign of the baby. The doctor strode up behind him. "Is this where you left the infant?"

Phil nodded. "I don't know who would . . . I can't understand why anyone would want to . . ." He swallowed hard as he thought of the newborn girl's deformed face and horribly twisted limbs. He looked at the doctor. "It must have been one of the patients." He started going over a mental list of the more emotionally unbalanced residents of the nursing home. "It had to be one of the patients."

The doctor was bending over, looking down at the linoleum floor. "Maybe," he said quietly. "Maybe not." He stood up and pointed at the top of the steel counter, at the small pool of blood left by the baby.

Claw marks were clearly outlined in the blood.

And the faint imprint of tiny feet could be seen on the floor next to the discarded blanket.

TWELVE

"It woulda scared the shit out of me, too." Brad loaded the last case of Pepsi onto the truck and pulled down the metal door, closing it. "I'd sue the bastards if I were you."

Gordon shook his head. "I wouldn't know who to sue. Besides, there's nothing really to sue over. The tests said Marina's okay. Even if she was exposed to something there's no way we could prove it." He picked up his hat from the table and put it on. He jumped off the concrete rim of the loading dock and got into the passenger seat of the cab. Brad finished locking up the warehouse, then came around to the front of the truck and got in. Gordon lifted up the visor of his hat and scratched his head. "As if that wasn't enough, I had a real mother of a nightmare last night."

"That's understandable."

"I can't remember all of it exactly, but it had something to do with my cousins and a huge monster spider."

Brad grinned at him. "You know what that means, don't you? It means you're a fag."

Gordon laughed.

The truck pulled out of the warehouse driveway onto Cedar, then turned from Cedar onto Main. The turn was sharp, and the left rear tires dipped into the ditch as they rounded the corner. Gordon braced himself for the sound of tires popping—a sound he knew was inevitable—but the truck, against all odds, made the turn safely on to the paved street. He looked at Brad and smiled. "I thought for sure we'd eat it that time."

"Are you kidding? Take a lot more than that to cripple this baby." Brad pounded the steering wheel affectionately and the horn bleated. A small car, a Toyota, passing them in the left lane, heard the sound and honked back. Brad leaned on the horn, sending out a long sustained blast, and stuck his middle finger out the window. "We weren't even honking at you! Asshole!"

The truck turned onto the highway and headed toward the south end of town. Today they would be covering the gas stations, liquor stores and fast food places within Randall. And, as always, they would work from south to north, then from east to west, big streets to little streets.

Brad pulled into the Whiting Bros. gas station at the southern tip of town. "You say that's what happened to Julie Campbell's baby, huh? Something to do with the water?"

Gordon shrugged. "Near as we can figure."

Brad shook his head. "Fuckers." The truck pulled to a stop in front of the ornamental wooden hitching post before the door to the gas station office, and he yanked hard on the emergency brake. The Whiting Bros. station was on the downward end of the hill sloping into town, but it was still on a considerable slant, and once before, when he had forgotten to put on the brake, the truck had started rolling on them. He always made sure the emergency brake was on now. "I used to go out with Julie's sister," he said, getting out of the cab.

"June?" Gordon raised his eyebrows. "I didn't know that."

"Well, it was a long time ago. Before me and Connie met." He grabbed the back door handle and stood for a moment without opening it, staring at the red, white, and blue Pepsi logo painted on the metal. "Took her to my senior prom. Fucked her brains out in the car afterward. First piece of ass I ever got. I still have the picture somewhere."

"Of you fucking her brains out?" Gordon grinned. "That must be a sight to see."

"No, dickmeat. Our prom picture."

"Whatever happened to June? I've heard Julie talk about her, but I don't think I've ever seen her. Is she still around here somewhere?"

Brad pulled up on the door handle, pushing it upward toward the roof of the truck. "Married some redneck, I think. Some construction worker up in Prescott or something." He looked at Gordon, and the expression on his face said that the topic was closed. "They always take at least a case of regular Pepsi here. You bring that on in, and I'll see what else these jokers need."

Gordon watched Brad's back as he walked into the gas station office. So Brad still had a soft spot for Julie Campbell's sister. He'd have to tell Marina about that one. She'd get a big kick out of it.

He grabbed a case of Pepsi and, grunting, carried it into the gas station office.

After delivering cases of Pepsi, Diet Pepsi, and Pepsi Light to the other gas stations on the south end of town and to Marty's Liquor, they drove back to the warehouse, loaded up again and then headed back onto the highway to finish the job. Brad pulled to a stop in front of Char Clifton's station. He looked at

Gordon. "Is your insurance going to cover the cost of the doctors?"

"I'll probably have to fight like hell for it, but I was looking over our policy last night and it should cover most of it. Of course there is a two-hundred-dollar deductible. I'll have to scrape that together somehow."

Brad pulled on his beard and nodded. "Tell you what," he said. "I'm going to give you a hundred-dollar bonus this month. To help out."

Gordon stared at him in surprise. "Really?"

Brad opened the door and got out, not looking at him. "Yeah. What the hell. This is our busy season. We've made quite a bit this summer from all the tourists coming up to the lakes and all. And you've done a damn good job. Done the work of two men this summer."

"I don't know what to say."

"Don't say nothing," Brad growled. "Just grab a goddamn case and bring it in." He stomped hard on the rubber cable that rang the gas station's bell and started walking toward the office, taking out his order pad. "Shit. Maybe I can get some kind of raise for you too. To help out with the expenses. Kids cost a lot these days."

Gordon just stared at him.

He heard about Mrs. Perry's baby in Pete's Diner.

It was a fifth- or sixth-hand retelling of the story by one customer to another, but at the sound of the words "baby" and "born dead" Gordon had put down his load and stopped to listen. The two customers were seated at the counter, drinking coffee and eating french fries soaked in ketchup. The man who was telling the story looked like a regular, one of those retired men who hang out at diners and coffeeshops to talk to others like themselves. He was nearly bald and wearing jeans and a faded work shirt. A straw cowboy hat occupied the vinyl seat next to him. The other man was around Gordon's age and was wearing a greasy mechanic's uniform.

Brad, too, stopped work for a few moments to hear the story, following Gordon's lead.

"She was damn near ninety or ninety-five," the old man said. "They're not even sure how she got pregnant. But there she was. Woke up the whole damn place with her screaming, and by the time anyone got there she'd already had the baby. Guy who told me about it said the thing crawled out on its own."

"But I thought it was born dead," the other man said.

"Oh it was. And it was all deformed, too. Didn't hardly look human at all. They put it in another room while they checked over the old lady, and when they came back it was gone. Disappeared."

"Do they know who stole it?"

The storyteller nodded. "They found some footprints." His voice dropped. "But they weren't human."

"Really?"

"The cloven hoof of the Beast." The old man took a sip of his coffee. "Brian—he's the one that told me about it—he said he's thinking of writing to the *National Enquirer* or something and telling them about it. They'd probably be interested in something like this."

The mechanic nodded. "Make mucho bucks off it, too."

"Damn straight."

Gordon didn't believe the last half of the story, but he had no doubt that the first part was true. Even the most outrageous exaggerations usually had some basis in fact. He looked at Brad, then stepped toward the two men. The thought that yet another deformed and stillborn infant had been born in Randall troubled him. He cleared his throat loudly. "Excuse me," he said. "I couldn't help overhearing your story."

The old man nodded. "Yeah, it's something."

"I'd like to know when and where this happened. Could you tell me what you know about it, where you heard about it?"

The man put a ketchup-soaked french fry in his mouth and followed it with a swallow of coffee. "I heard about it from Brian Stevens. It happened at the Randall Rest Home last night." He held up his empty cup and signaled to the waitress for more coffee.

"Last night?"

"Yeah. Brian's wife is in the nursing home. She saw it with her own eyes."

"The woman was ancient," Brad said, tapping Gordon's shoulder. "What do you expect? You think she's going to have a healthy blue-eyed bundle of joy when she's ninety goddamn years old?"

Brad was right. Such a situation could be attributed to age. Women who had children past the age of forty often had retarded babies or babies with birth defects, and that was certainly possible here. Still, the story bothered him. He knew nothing save what he'd heard from this old man—and three-fourths of that he attributed to exaggeration—but he had a hunch, a gut feeling, that the baby's problems had been unrelated to the age of the mother.

"Come on," Brad said, picking up his case. "Let's get back to work."

"Yeah, sure," he said. He nodded toward the two men at the counter. "Thanks."

"No problem." The old man opened a packet of sugar and poured half of it into his coffee, throwing the rest into a dirty amber ashtray. "Glad to be of service."

Gordon followed Brad back out to the truck. Behind him, he heard the mechanic mention the Beast. "I don't like this," he said. "I don't like it at all."

"I don't blame you." Brad grunted as he pulled a case of Diet Pepsi from the truck. "But I wouldn't worry about it too much if I was you. The doctors took all those tests and they said everything's going to be okay." He smiled. "Whatever it was didn't seem to affect your baby maker none."

Gordon shook his head. "I just don't like it." He pulled down another case of Pepsi and carried it into the diner.

THIRTEEN

The kitten was . . . cute. It was the only word to describe her, much as Marina hated to admit it. Cute. Even surrounded by unkempt derelict cats in a hideous wire cage at the rear of the Humane Society building, the kitten's spirit was still undaunted; it shone through the dismal surroundings like a beacon. The kitten's light gray fur was clean and fluffy and stuck out on the sides of her flattened face like a mane. Greenish yellow owl eyes, wide and perfectly round, peered bravely, curiously forth from amidst the hair. A red mouth, filled with tiny baby teeth, emitted barely audible but heartrending peeps. Marina cautiously stuck a finger through the bars of the cage and the little kitten bounced happily toward her on fat little feet. The kitten reached up with her two front paws and grabbed onto the finger. She bit the tip affectionately. The bite tickled, and Marina pulled her finger back, laughing. She turned to the Humane Society attendant. "I'll take her," she said.

The man shrugged noncommittally. "Cost you ten dollars, including shots."

"That's fine." Marina smiled as she stuck her finger

once again through the wire cage. The kitten grabbed onto the finger and started biting.

She filled out the proper forms and paid the money at the front desk, trying to think of names for her new pet. She definitely didn't want to name the kitten something like Coco or Princess or any of the other sickeningly saccharine names favored by old ladies or young girls. And names like Missy or Queenie that ended in an "ee" sound were definitely out. Perhaps Alfalfa would be good, after the Little Rascals' character. Or Horton, after Dr. Seuss' elephant. Or Francois, after Truffaut.

The attendant brought the kitten out and asked Marina if she would like a box for the trip home, but she said she'd rather hold the kitty instead. The man handed her the peeping ball of gray fur, and she cradled her new pet in her arms like a baby. The kitten lightly bit her finger and purred.

Dracula. That would be a good name.

No, Vlad. After Vlad the Impaler, the original Dracula. She looked down at the gray furry face. "Hi Vlad," she said.

The kitten looked up at her and bit her finger.

Vlad spent the trip home exploring the car. She crawled under the seats, hopped on the dashboard and spent quite a while doing God-knew-what in the very back of the Jeep. Marina tried to drive and keep an eye on the kitten at the same time. She didn't want her to get stuck under the seat or try to jump out or something.

Once home, she grabbed the kitten, who was rummaging around in a box of emergency car parts, and took her immediately into the house. She put her down on the hardwood floor of the kitchen. Vlad looked around suspiciously at first but quickly lost her fear. She trotted off to explore the living room, padding across the floor on her fat little feet.

Marina spent the afternoon following Vlad around the house, keeping the kitten away from restricted areas such as the couches by picking her up, saying "No" and putting her down someplace else. She poured her new pet a saucer of milk but discovered that she had forgotten to buy any kind of cat food. She opened a can of Star-Kist tuna and made a note to have Gordon get some real cat food.

She made a makeshift litter box from an old Pepsi carton and filled it with dirt from the garden.

At a little after three, she put Vlad back in the car and drove into town to pick up Gordon. She parked in front of the warehouse, held the kitten in her lap and waited. A few minutes later, Gordon pulled open the door of the Jeep, sat down and sighed. "Damn I'm tired. My arms hurt like hell."

Marina said nothing.

He looked at her. "What are you waiting for? Let's go." His eyes found the small bundle of fur in her lap. "Got a new pussy, huh?"

She hit his shoulder with her fist. "How can you be so crude?"

He smiled. "Must be from hanging around Brad all day. You'd be that way too if you had to spend all your time with him." He held out his hands. "Let me see the little guy." Marina handed him the kitten and he held the animal's face next to his. "Cute little thing, isn't he?"

"It's not a he, it's a she. And her name is Vlad."

"Vlad? That's a boy's name. Why are you calling her that?"

"Put your finger next to her face."

Gordon held out an index finger and Vlad grabbed it with two paws and began biting. Gordon laughed. "That's great." He put the kitten down on his lap and rubbed her fur, playing with her. The kitten leapt and attacked. He held his hand over the kitten's face, and she tried to bite his palm. "You're a little fighter, aren't you? Aren't you?"

Vlad bit.

They drove toward home.

FOURTEEN

The white Dodge Dart, its bumpers and windows covered with a thin layer of fine reddish dust, sped down the forest service road toward Aspen Lake. The windows of the car were up, the air-conditioning on, and the stereo was cranked up almost to the pain level. Matt McDowell, bouncing around on the ripped upholstery of the back seat, leaned forward, sticking his head between his two friends in the front. "How much farther?" he yelled.

Jack Harrison shook his head, unable to hear above the noise of the stereo.

"I said, how much farther is it?" Matt screamed.

"Another ten minutes or so!" Jack screamed back. "It's pretty far in!"

Matt sat back in his seat and looked out the window at the passing scenery. Although he had heard about Aspen Lake since his nursery school days, he had never been there. The most inaccessible lake on the Rim, it could be reached only by taking a narrow untended forest service road; what used to be an old logging trail. His father had never been willing to drive the road—he said he didn't want to ruin his truck— so they had always gone to Crestwood and Sherman lakes instead. And since Matt was still too young to drive, he'd never had any way to get there. Until now. Until Jack and Wayne had invited him to come along with them on an overnight fishing trip; their last of the summer.

An antlered buck, standing stock-still near a puddle of muddy water at the side of the road, looked up suddenly as they approached then bounded away into the trees. Matt watched it disappear into the forest. He had never been on a camping trip alone before, without an adult, and he was a little nervous. He was conscious of the fact that the last sign of civilization they'd passed had been a small bait and tackle store back on the main highway, a good thirty miles behind them. If something should happen, if one of them got bitten by a rattlesnake or broke his leg or choked on his food or something worse, they wouldn't be able to get help. The store was a forty-five-minute drive away from the lake on this road, and it probably wasn't even open at night. Way out here, they could scream all they wanted and no one would hear them. Since this was a weeknight and not a weekend, there probably wouldn't even be any other campers around. And of course there was no phone and no electricity.

No electricity.

That was what he was really worried about, though he wouldn't admit it to Jack or Wayne. There was no electricity out here. No lights. When the sun went down, it would be dark. Completely dark. They'd have a campfire for a while, but they'd have to make sure it was extinguished before they went to sleep so it wouldn't start a forest fire.

They'd be all alone.

In total darkness.

Matt felt a rush of goose bumps cascade down his arms just thinking about it. He turned around and looked through the dusty rear window at the sky. It was clearing already, the storm clouds moving off the

Rim toward Randall, but Matt knew from what everyone told him that it often rained at night on the Rim, that a second storm, a storm that would never reach the town, often unleashed its fury on campers around the lakes.

And he'd only brought his sleeping bag. He had no tent.

He might have to sleep in the car.

Jack turned the stereo down for a second, heavy metal guitars fading into a drone that offered a perfect counterpoint to the humming of the rebuilt engine. "We're almost there," he said.

Matt leaned forward and looked through the front windshield. Around them, the pine trees were thinning out, being subtly replaced by white-trunked aspens. The ground, previously a dusty red gravel covered with a layer of brown pine needles, was becoming green, grassy. Before them, through the round thickly clustered leaves of the aspens, he could see the shimmering blue of the lake. "Where are we going to camp?" he started to ask.

But Jack had turned the stereo up again and couldn't hear him.

They camped on the south side of the lake underneath a small outcropping of rock that Jack said would protect them if it rained. They were not directly on the shore of the lake but were separated from the water by a clump of boulders and several trees. The car was parked off the edge of the road, several yards up an incline from the camp.

Although the lake had supposedly been stocked the day before, none of them got even a bite in their attempts to fish, and after trying several spots and several different types of bait, they decided to give it up. The rods, reels, and tackle boxes were dropped next to the car, and Jack opened the car door and turned on the stereo. He popped in an old Black Sabbath tape, and the opening strains of "Iron Man" blared through the door speakers, assaulting the silence.

They walked back down the dirt path to the campsite.

Matt sat on a fallen log, staring out at the lake and listening to the music. Jack read a car magazine. Wayne lay on his back on a rock, looking up at the passing clouds, then jumped off and began pacing around the cleared campsite. "I'm bored," he said.

Jack laughed, "Fine. You can pick up wood. We need to get some if we're going to have any kind of fire tonight."

"Fuck that."

"Suit yourself." Jack went back to his magazine. "But it's going to get awfully cold tonight. And *I'm* not collecting wood."

"I'll do it," Matt said.

Wayne looked from Matt to Jack, smiling, "He'll do it."

Jack shrugged. "Fine."

Matt slid off the log and brushed off the back of his pants. His fingers felt something sticky on the material, and they came away with small smears of sap on their tips. "Damn," he said.

Wayne looked at him. "Sap?"

Matt nodded.

"Those pants are gone. There's no way you can get sap out. I've ruined more pants that way."

Matt looked at Jack. "What do I use to carry the wood?"

"Your hands," Jack said.

Matt started up the hill. He passed the car on the road and continued climbing. There were a few small twigs on the ground, but no branches big enough for burning. He headed toward the top of the ridge in search of other, more promising trees.

Overhead, the sky was clouding up again. The dark

gray clouds were moving visibly, propelled by airborne winds, billowing, growing thicker. Matt didn't have a watch, but the sun was already starting to go down and his stomach was making whirring sounds of hunger, so it was probably around four or five o'clock. Soon it would be dark.

Above him, on the top of the hill, he thought he saw something move. "Hello!" he said loudly. He didn't know if it was human or animal, but it didn't hurt to be on the safe side. He wasn't wearing hunter's orange, and he didn't want to be accidentally mistaken for a deer or a bear and shot by some nearsighted hunter. "Hello!" he yelled again.

He reached the top of the ridge and used his hands to pull himself up the last steep little cliff.

The crest of the hill was flat, like a mesa. Most of the trees here had either been cut or had fallen over and there was plenty of good firewood for the gathering. Matt looked around him. Ahead, other hills and other valleys alternated in an endless progression atop the Rim. To the sides, his hill continued, the trees getting thicker and thicker until they finally obscured his view completely. He picked up a nice sized branch, long dead and completely dry, then dropped it. This would probably be his first and only trip up this hill; he would have to be careful about the wood he chose. His picks would have to last them all night.

He looked around for the hunter, but he couldn't see anyone. Perhaps it hadn't been a hunter after all. It might not have even been human. Perhaps he had seen a deer or an elk or some other large animal.

Or a bear.

No, it couldn't have been a bear. It wasn't possible. He looked around tentatively, carefully. If it had been a bear he had scared it off.

He quickly started picking up branches. •

Out of the corner of his eye he saw something move.

The wood dropped from his hands and he whirled around in panic. There was nothing there. The top of the hill was empty.

He was starting to spook himself. He walked to the edge of the ridge and looked down. He could see the water of the lake shimmering through the round clustered leaves of the aspens, but he could see neither the car nor the camp. "Jack!" he called. "Wayne!"

There was no answer.

A cold breeze came up suddenly, swirling the leaves and blowing Matt's hair. He shivered, and goose bumps ran down his arms. He turned around and began once again to gather up wood. There was a name for things seen out of the corner of a person's eyes, he knew. He had read about it in his parents' *People's Almanac* one day. Some cultures thought they were ghosts, but there was really some scientific explanation for them.

Out of the corner of his eye he saw something move again.

He grabbed one last chunk of wood, headed toward the edge of the hill, and tripped.

He fell sprawling, the wood flying out of his hands, his chin hitting the rough rock of the ground. His jaw was snapped forcibly shut and pain erupted through the nerve endings of his teeth. A sharp twig cut into his hand. A knee of his jeans ripped.

Matt sat up, twisting around to see what he had tripped over. The wind was blowing hard now, tugging at his sleeves, and a few splashes of rain hit his face. He kicked at a clump of wildflowers next to his foot.

The leaves of the plant parted to reveal a small stone cross.

He jumped up, heart pounding, but fell immediately back down. His ankle was hurt, twisted, probably broken. He couldn't stand on it. He looked carefully at the rest of the hilltop. All across the flat ridge he could see tiny crosses hidden by weeds and wildflowers and piles of dead wood. He was surrounded by them.

A twig cracked behind him. "Jack!" he yelled. "Wayne! Jack!"

Another twig cracked. Closer.

"Jack!" he screamed.

But his voice was carried away by the wind and by the hard rain that had started to fall on the forest.

FIFTEEN

Annette Weldon stared down at the sleeping form of her husband as he tossed and turned next to her in the bed, rolling over onto his stomach then rolling back and throwing his arm over his face. His expression was troubled, his brows furrowed into a sleep-bound frown. His mouth worked agonizingly, opening and closing as if to scream, but no sound came out. She reached over and put her hand on the top of his head, letting her fingers run through the rough straw-like hair as she attempted to soothe him. She wanted to wake him up, but he got little enough sleep as it was and she didn't want him to waste any more.

Suddenly he sat bolt upright in bed, his eyes popping wide open, and screamed.

Annette screamed too, in shock. His glazed and staring eyes turned on her, then settled back into normalcy as his brain registered the fact that he was awake. He closed his eyes and opened them, blinking hard. When he saw how scared she was, he reached out to put a hand on her shoulder and tried to smile. "Just a nightmare," he said.

"You never have anything *but* nightmares anymore."

"I know." He idly caressed her upper arm. "It's all

these damn murders and all this . . . weird shit. It's
really starting to get to me."

She stared at him and there was concern in her eyes.
"You're going to get an ulcer."

"I know it." He sighed heavily and settled back
down on the bed. "Maybe I should turn it over to the
state police." He looked at her. "I've been checking
into it, you know. The state police does handle things
like this if the local operations aren't equipped to handle it. And I don't think we're equipped. I'm tempted
to just turn the whole damn thing over to them and
admit that I'm baffled."

"You still don't have any leads? On any of these
cases?"

He turned his face toward her on the pillow. She
was still sitting up, looking down at him, and there
was such a look of sympathetic understanding in her
eyes, such kindness in the rounded corners of her
mouth, that he thought about telling her his thoughts.
His real thoughts. His crazy theories. But no, he
couldn't do that. She wouldn't understand. She would
want to understand, she would *try* to understand, but
she would not be able to. Hell, who could? "No," he
said. "We don't have any leads."

She lay down next to him and nestled close, laying
an arm over his hairy chest, letting her hand rest in
the crook of his arm. He put his hand on hers and
they lay there like that for a while.

"Did you ever think that all of this might be connected?" she asked finally.

He had been about to fall back asleep. His eyes
were closed and his mind drifted in that netherworld
between sleep and wakefulness. But at the sound of
her words he jerked awake, eyes opening, startled.
"What did you say?"

"Did you ever think that all these cases are connected? I mean, it's common sense. I thought one of

you would have noticed by now. All those goats killed and their blood all over the churches."

"Well, we did put that together."

"And two of the farmers killed? And one of the preachers? It's obvious."

"We're not completely dense," he said defensively. He sat up against the headboard then looked at her indulgently, playing the condescending cop role, trying to remain outwardly calm though he was beginning to feel very excited. "We know they're connected. We just don't know how. Do you have any ideas?"

"Not really. It just seems to me that it's probably a group of devil worshipers or witches or a cult of some kind."

Close but no cigar. Their minds were not quite meeting. Still, they were thinking along the same lines. He was tempted to tell her about Don's dream, about his own dream, about Don's death, about the . . . thing . . . he had seen and heard outside his office. Maybe she would understand. Maybe she wouldn't think he was that crazy. But as he looked at her he realized just how far off the deep end his ideas sounded. Her thoughts may have been courting his territory, but they made a hell of a lot more sense than his irrational theories of—what? Supernatural forces? Monsters?

"You've been watching too many movies," he said.

She frowned. "You just admitted that you're stumped. My idea might be stupid, but it can't hurt to check it out."

"That's true."

"It's not as if you have a million other things to follow up on."

"All right," he said. "I'll look into it."

"Thank you." She settled back into his arms. They were silent for a few moments. "What was your dream about, anyway?"

He shook his head. "Nothing."

"Are you sure you don't want to talk about it?"

"I'm sure."

Fifteen minutes later Annette was asleep, her mouth open, snoring softly. Carefully, slowly, so as not to disturb her, Jim crept out from under the covers and walked on tiptoe down the hall to the family room. He was awake already; he might as well call the office and see if Judson or Pete had come up with anything. He picked up the phone and automatically dialed the number. Pete answered. "Hello. Sheriff's Office. Pete King speaking."

Jim smiled at the young deputy's formal Jack Webb voice. "What's up?"

"Oh, hi Sheriff." His voice relaxed for a moment then grew tense. "Is there anything wrong?"

"No. I was just up and I figured I'd call, see what's happening."

"Not much, really." There was a pause. "Something did come over the wire, though. I thought you might be interested so I put it on your desk. Two churches in Phoenix were vandalized the same way ours were, blood smeared all over them, words written and everything."

Jim's eyebrows shot up in surprise. "Really?"

"Yeah. I thought maybe the person who did it up here had moved on down to Phoenix, so I put the wire copy on your desk. I figured you'd want to check on it."

"Definitely. Thanks, Pete." Jim finished the conversation with a list of office questions he knew by rote, but he did not pay attention to the answers. So the same thing had happened in Phoenix. This really made it a candidate for the state police. Identical crimes in two jurisdictions were automatically investigated by the state men anyway. He felt relieved that he would be getting some help on this, that he could give up some of the responsibility he had been shouldering single-handedly up until now, but he felt guilty about abandoning his own investigation, about not following up on his own train of thought, not acting on what he knew to be the real facts, or the truth behind the facts. He felt, in some way, as though he was deserting Don, as though the boy had died needlessly, uselessly.

But all deaths are needless, he reasoned. All deaths are useless.

But he was pushing everything under the carpet, whitewashing it, not trying to find out the real reasons behind all this.

Don would be ashamed of him.

He was a coward.

"Is that all, Sheriff?" Pete's voice sounded anxious to get off the line.

"Yeah," Jim said. "That's it. I'll see you in the morning." He hung up the phone and stared out the family-room window at the darkened house on the acre lot across the street. He imagined he could hear the river, though it flowed through the opposite end of town. So what if Don Wilson wouldn't approve of his actions? He didn't even know the boy. He only met him the one time and talked to him once after that over the phone. What did he owe him?

He walked slowly down the hall and peeked into Justin's and Suzonne's rooms before going back to bed, checking on them to make sure they were all right. He crawled carefully into bed next to Annette and lay awake for a while, staring at the dark ceiling, listening, thinking.

Finally he fell asleep.

He had nightmares.

SIXTEEN

Father Donald Andrews took the small teapot off the stove and poured half a cup of Earl Grey into his ceramic mug. The old Erroll Garner record playing on the stereo in the living room suddenly got stuck, the same three notes repeating over and over again, and the reverend put his tea down on the counter, rushing out into the other room. He lifted the stereo's dust cover and pressed down on the needle with his forefinger. The song skipped over the rough section and Erroll resumed playing "Afternoon of an Elf." He went back into the kitchen to get his tea.

When the bishop had ordered him to take over the congregation in Randall until Father Selway returned or a new reverend was permanently assigned, Andrews had jumped at the chance. For a relative novice, who had until now assisted other priests, the opportunity to preside over an entire congregation, even for only a short while, was a major coup. And when the bishop had offered to let him stay in Selway's house, he had gratefully accepted. The church owned the home and would allow him to stay rent free, thus saving him money on lodgings.

But he had been here for four days now and, truth

to tell, he did not like the house. Father Selway had disappeared and his entire family had been murdered—that in itself was enough to start someone thinking unpleasant thoughts in the dead of night. But aside from that, *below* all that, there was something wrong. The house gave off—what did they used to call it in the sixties?—bad vibes.

It was not a friendly house.

Andrews carried his cup into the living room and turned the record up a little louder before settling down into his chair, hoping to drown out the subtle creaks and cracks made nightly by the old house. The reverend was by no means an easily frightened man, but he had joined the church precisely because he had known, had realized, that there was such a thing as good and such a thing as evil, that these were not nebulous concepts dreamed up by philosophers and religious prophets but were actual concrete realities, facts of life.

And this house was not good.

Andrews considered himself "sensitive" to auras, to feelings, to "vibes." Perhaps he was a trifle psychic. He wasn't sure. But he had always had bad feelings about certain spots and certain people and good feelings about others. Once, as a college student traveling through Germany, he had been unable to enter a restaurant. The restaurant was a popular spot on a guided tour, but the wave of nausea, fear, and revulsion that had swept through him upon nearing its door had been too strong to allow him to enter. He had learned later that hundreds of gypsies had been murdered in the building in the first wave of killings prior to the outbreak of World War II.

The feeling here in Father Selway's house was not quite as strong as it had been in the restaurant, but it was similar.

Andrews shifted uncomfortably in his chair. Only one light was on in the room—a freestanding lamp between his chair and the couch—and the rest of the room seemed suddenly bathed in shadow, considerably darker than it had been a few moments ago. He had to stop thinking about things like this. He forced his mind to concentrate on something else. The sermon he was going to give Sunday. He picked up the black-bound Bible from the small walnut table next to him and opened it to the page he had marked before dinner; a chapter in Job. Out of the corner of his eye he thought he saw something move, and he looked up. The light was still on in the kitchen and he could see nothing there, but the hallway was completely dark. No lights were on in the back of the house at all.

He heard a strange shuffling noise from somewhere back in the hallway.

Andrews jumped slightly, startled, spilling his tea on the Bible lying in his lap. The already thin and translucent pages became instantly transparent, backward letters from the next several pages soaking through the words on the open page, blending to form one unreadable black mass.

Black Mass.

Stop it, he told himself.

He was an adult now, not a little child afraid of the dark. And he was a priest, a man of the cloth, a man with the power of the church and the Lord behind him.

Then why were his muscles tensed? Why was he staring into the dark hallway as if looking for signs of movement? Why was he straining to hear strange sounds over the rhythmic cadences of Erroll Garner's piano?

Andrews closed the Bible, folded his hands atop the smooth black surface, shut his eyes and began to pray. "Our Father . . ." His mouth formed the words, but his voice was silent.

The record ended and there was a sound of tearing

paper from one of the back rooms of the house. He could hear it clearly in the sudden stillness.

Adult or no adult, priest or no priest, he wanted to run. His instinct was to throw open the front door, and dash into the street, jump into his car parked next to the curb, take off and spend the night in a nice, clean, modern hotel with well-lit rooms and a peopled lobby. And his instincts were usually good.

He had not been this scared in years.

That's why he had to stay.

Andrews pulled lightly on the chain around his neck and fingered the gold crucifix that hung on the end of the chain. He closed his eyes and again said the Lord's Prayer. When he reached "Deliver us from evil," he said it aloud.

He opened his eyes and sniffed. There was the smell of something burning—*charred flesh?*—in the air.

No, it couldn't be. He was overreacting, making himself hysterical. His brain was overloading on imagination. He wasn't approaching this logically, rationally.

But there was a definite burning smell.

What was it? Sulfur? Cinders? The fiery pits of hell?

Nothing. It was nothing. He was just imagining—

The smoke alarm went off.

He jumped from his chair this time. The alarm was loud, a piercing shriek that cut through the quiet like a sledgehammer through ice cream and which would have blotted out even the loudest noise.

Now he was no longer worried about the house's vibes or the strange noises in the dark. Here was something real—a fire. He ran toward the hallway, no longer afraid. He flipped on the hall light as he dashed past it. The smell was horrible, almost an emetic, and it was getting stronger. The air was beginning to cloud up with a thick brown smoglike smoke.

He turned on the light to Father Selway's study and stood for a second in the doorway, trying to see through the thick smoke. His eyes were watering, and when he rubbed them they began to itch. The smoke was definitely coming from within this room, but he could feel no heat and see no flames. The fire had to be small, still controllable. He ran back to the kitchen and grabbed a big metal cooking pot from the cupboard beneath the sink, turning both the hot and cold water on full blast to fill the pot. He left the water on and sprinted back down the hall.

A bad electrical connection had probably started something on fire. A scrap of paper, perhaps. Or a portion of the rug.

He ran into the room. There was a small single flame visible through the clouded air and he quickly poured the water onto it. He ran back to the kitchen for more water.

Three trips later, the fire was out. Andrews, coughing heavily, lurched through the study and opened both windows. He would have to tell the bishop about this. It wasn't serious enough for him to notify the fire department, but the bishop would want to know what happened. He staggered out into the hall and took a deep breath of fresh air, but that only caused a coughing spasm, and he dropped to his knees, almost throwing up. The coughing spell passed, and he stood up. His throat felt raw and sore. The smoke had cleared from the study for the most part, and the reverend looked into the room.

The study was a shambles. All of Father Selway's books, which had been neatly stacked on bookcases against the far wall, had been thrown on the floor and were rudely scattered around the edges of the room. It was a miracle that they had not caught fire. In the center of the room, the front and back covers of Father Selway's oversized display Bible, which had been exhibited on a special stand next to his desk, lay skeletally empty, all the pages torn out. The pages themselves had been torn and crumpled and put into a pile. That was what had been burning.

Andrews stared at the desecrated room in shock. Who had done this? And why? And how? He had been in the house all evening and had heard nothing until five or ten minutes ago, and even that had been barely noticeable.

He blinked back the tears caused by residual smoke and rubbed his eyes lightly. They watered more. He left his eyes alone and stared at the room. By all rights, the place should have gone up like a torch. Why had there been so little fire damage? He walked toward the desk and picked up one of the remaining pages of the display Bible. It was wet from the water and charred around the edges. It felt slimy to the touch. He held it up close to his face, in order to see it better, then dropped it, gagging.

It was covered with excrement.

He looked down at his feet. All of the pages, and all of the other books, had been smeared somehow with human excrement.

On top of Father Selway's desk was a cross made out of molded feces.

Andrews fell to his knees and vomited. Convulsively. Uncontrollably. He tried to pray, but his mind could not shift its focus from his involuntarily heaving stomach.

From outside somewhere, through one of the open windows, came something that sounded like a whining high-pitched laugh.

SEVENTEEN

The morning did not dawn clear and hot like any other. Instead, it was overcast, a low ceiling of continuous cloud blocking out the sun and weaving through the ragged line of tall trees at the top of the Rim. Although it was not drizzling, there was a light mist in the air, and when Gordon peeked through the partially parted bedroom curtains his view was blurred by the running moisture on the plate glass. He reached over and pulled open the wood-framed window, expecting a blast of humid hothouse air, but the light breeze that splattered the thin mist through the screen was cool and comfortable.

When Marina woke up, she leaned her chin on Gordon's right shoulder, her cheek next to his, and snuggled close against his back. She stared with him out the window, yawning. "Well this is a pleasant surprise."

He let the two halves of the drapes fall back together. The breeze blew them slightly inward. "The weatherman was wrong again." He fell back on the bed and rubbed the sleep from his eyes with the palms of his hands.

"So what else is new?"

Gordon stopped rubbing his eyes and stared up at the ceiling for a minute. "Sandra," he said.

"What?"

"We can name the baby Sandra."

Marina looked at him for a moment then sat up in bed. He looked so calm, so happy lying there that she hated to disturb his mood, but they had to talk this out, they had to discuss the baby sometime. She'd been wanting to bring it up for three days now, and this was a perfect opportunity. She licked her sleep-dried lips, unsure of how to start. "We have to talk," she said.

Her seriousness must have imparted itself to Gordon because he sat up on his elbows and looked at her, his eyes expectant, troubled. "I know," he said quietly.

She put her hands on his, feeling the rough hair on his bony knuckles. His hands felt larger than they should, different, and she had to subdue an instinct to pull her own hands away. Her fingers began tracing an outline of his hand. "I'm still scared."

"I know you are. I am too."

"It's . . . not right. We don't deserve this." She felt confused. Alternately hurt and angry. She knew words could not convey her feelings—she was not articulate enough to be able to voice such subtle, disparate, and deeply conflicting emotions—and it frustrated her. She felt as if she might cry, but she knew that would do no good.

Gordon brought her hand to his lips and kissed it gently. "I know," he said.

This was not exactly what she had wanted to talk about, this was not how the conversation was supposed to go. But she couldn't help herself. The emotions flooded over her, the rage, the frustration, an excess of feelings threatening any moment to burst out through the psychological safety valve of tears. "Goddamn it. Why did this have to happen to us? . . .

Why does this sort of . . . shit . . . have to happen at all? To anyone?"

Gordon did not have an answer. He did not even have a good substitute, an adequate reassurance. He simply kissed her hand again, murmuring sympathetically, empathetically, hoping it was enough, knowing it was not.

"It's . . . so . . . fucking . . . unfair."

The sobs came. Tears rolled down her cheeks, silently at first. She closed her eyes tightly, but tears snuck out of them anyway, and her mouth, which had been ready to utter another protest, another complaint, suddenly turned to rubber. She began to cry aloud. Primally. Unashamedly.

He pulled her to him. He kissed her wet cheeks, tasting the clean saltiness of her tears. His hands ran softly through her thick hair, combing it back. His mouth found hers and they kissed, their tongues touching hesitantly at first then actively entwining. The sobs stopped, slowly, and Gordon's hand slid gently under her nightie, between her legs. She was already wet and offered no resistance.

Soon he was inside her and they were making love. Slowly. Languorously.

They came simultaneously.

Neither of them spoke for a while afterward, and he stayed on top of her until he fell out. He rolled next to her on the bed and tried to kiss her, but his lips instead became entangled in her hair. She giggled in spite of herself.

Gordon smiled. "Cheered up?"

"Against my will."

"It works every time."

Marina bit her lower lip and put a finger lightly on his mouth. "We might have killed the symptoms, but the problem's still there. We still have to talk."

He nodded. "Shoot."

"What are we going to do?"

Her voice was completely serious once again, and Gordon sat up, looking into her eyes, trying to gauge her feelings, trying to determine in which direction she was leaning. "I don't know," he said.

"I know the tests that were supposed to be positive were positive and the tests that were supposed to be negative were negative, but I'm still worried. What if they're wrong? What do we do then?"

"There's nothing we can do."

"I'm not sure it's worth the risk. I don't know if I want to take that chance. I'm not sure I'm willing to go through with it because I'm not sure I could handle it if anything went wrong."

He put his hand in back of her head and leaned toward her, looking into her eyes. "It's going to have to be your decision. And I'll be behind you no matter what you decide. But I think we should see it through. The doctors said everything's okay. There's probably a small margin of error there, but not much." He smiled at her. "I think it would be nice to have a little miniature Marina running around here."

She smiled back at him. "Somehow I knew that you were going to be in favor of going through with it."

"What do you think?"

She ran her tongue across her teeth and shrugged noncommittally. "I don't know."

"You're not leaning one way or the other?"

"Well, maybe I am. But—"

"You'd better decide pretty quick, you know."

"I know. But I'll have to quit school, we'll have to get by on just your salary . . ."

"You mean this is because you're worried about money?"

"No, of course not. But we have to take everything into account, and so far the bad points seem to outweigh the good."

"Which way are you leaning?"

She tried to look at him seriously, full in the face,

but she could not keep the smile from her lips. "I'd kind of like a little Marina running around the house, too."

"Then it's settled."

"Not quite. I still want to think it over a bit." She held up a hand. "I know, I know. I'd better think fast." She kissed his nose. "I will."

Gordon kissed her back, then put his head down on her stomach, as if listening. "Hey," he said, sitting back up. "What about sex? How much longer can we keep on doing it?"

Marina laughed, and her laugh sounded happy, free of troubles. "I should've known you'd worry about that."

"I'm not—"

"We can do it as long as we want."

"It won't hurt the baby?"

She thought for a moment. "Well, maybe we'll have to try a few new positions. You probably shouldn't be on top all of the time."

"*All* of the time?"

She smiled. "Pretty close."

He looked at her haughtily. "Maybe we should give it up for the next eight months or so. Just to be on the safe side. After all, you do have two other holes."

"Oh no," she said.

He laughed and kissed her. "So how do you feel about Sandra?"

"I was thinking more along the lines of Olga or Helga. Perhaps Bertha."

"If it was going to be a boy you would've planned on Percy?"

"Or Otis," she agreed.

Gordon leaned back against the brass headboard, his head fitting neatly between two brass bars. "You laugh now, but we're really going to have to start thinking about names soon." He cleared his throat. "If you decide to keep the baby," he added.

Marina swung her legs over the side of the bed. "We *will* have to start thinking about names," she said.

"We will? For sure?"

She nodded. "We will."

"That was quick."

"I'm a quick thinker." She walked over to the Queen Anne chair in the middle of the room and took her flowered bathrobe from its seat, putting it on. She pulled her hair from inside of the robe and let it hang outside the collar. She walked out of the bedroom.

Gordon heard her enter the bathroom and a few moments later heard the toilet flush. She walked into the kitchen . . . and came screaming back down the hall.

"Marina!" Gordon jumped out of bed and almost collided with her as she ran through the bedroom door. He grabbed her shoulders. "What happened?" he demanded. "What's wrong?"

She was sobbing so hysterically that he could not make out what she was saying. He pushed past her into the hall and hurried into the kitchen. Where he stopped.

The makeshift cat box Marina had fashioned from a Pepsi carton was overturned, its dirt spilled all over the tile floor. The kitten's food and water dishes had also been emptied onto the kitchen floor.

And everything was covered with cat blood.

Red blood had been smeared all over the yellow refrigerator like paint. Smears of blood and black guts were trailed across the table top. A gray paw stuck out of the garbage disposal in the sink.

The kitten itself, or what was left of her, was lying in the middle of the floor directly in front of the stove. The body—little more than gutted skin and fur—was spread-eagled on the floor and pinned in place with steak knives. The head, severed from the body, lay like an unused gray tennis ball, dead greenish yellow eyes staring up toward the roof.

Gordon's eyes quickly scanned the room. The windows were shut and locked, as was the door. He ran into the living room, but the front door was also closed and bolted.

How?

What?

He opened the front door and looked outside. The mist had dissipated somewhat, but the air still felt damp. A forerunner of autumn; a taste of the coming fall. His eyes searched the gravel driveway, but he could see nothing unusual. He closed the door and returned to the bedroom where Marina, still crying, lay huddled under the blankets. He knelt next to her. "It's all right," he said, hugging her close. "It's okay."

But he was not sure himself that everything was OK. He suddenly felt an unfounded irrational fear for the baby.

PART TWO

PART TWO

ONE

The hitchhiker stood next to the off-ramp of Black Canyon Highway on the road to Randall. He had been standing there for several hours and was sweating profusely in the wet heat of late summer, but the stains under his arms and on his back were covered by his expensive jacket. As always, his tie was securely knotted. Next to him, on the ground, was a blue Samsonite suitcase containing his clothes, toothbrush, and personal effects. On top of the suitcase rested a photo album and a parcel filled with religious tracts. In his hand was a copy of the Revised Standard Version of the Bible.

A Dodge pickup truck, the first in nearly an hour, pulled off the highway and the hitchhiker dutifully stuck out his thumb. The driver passed him by without a glance.

Another truck, following close upon the heels of the first, passed him by as well, then pulled to a stop a few yards ahead. He looked at the truck and the driver honked, waving him on. The hitchhiker picked up his parcel and suitcase and jogged up to the dirty dented vehicle, pulling open the passenger door. He smiled at the driver, a burly bearded man wearing a red tank top and a yellow Cat hat. "Thank you, sir."

The driver nodded and flicked a newspaper from the seat to the floor of the truck to make room for the hitchhiker's suitcase. "What's your name?"

"Call me Brother Elias."

"Brother Elias?" The driver snorted. "What the hell kind of name is that?"

"I am a preacher of the Lord's living gospel, a testament to his glory, and this is the name by which I am known to his followers." He got into the truck and slammed shut the door.

The driver put the truck into gear and pulled back onto the road. "A preacher, huh? I knew you weren't no ordinary hitcher. I could tell by the way you're dressed. To be honest with you, that's the only reason I picked you up. I don't usually stop for anybody unless I know them or I see their car's broken down. Can't tell what kind of people are out there these days. Never can tell who you're picking up. Some of these guys'd just as soon kill you as look at you." He offered Brother Elias a thick calloused hand. "Name's Tim McDowell. I work over at the sawmill in Randall. Just got through collecting orders from Hargreve." He looked at the preacher. "You ever been to Hargreve? Little town out in the Coconino. Hardly more'n fifty people in it and you can't get there except on this little one-lane dirt road that curves down the side of a cliff to the valley. It's a real bitch." He looked immediately embarrassed, and he smiled sheepishly at Brother Elias. "Sorry." He drove for a few miles in silence, but when the preacher didn't say anything he cleared his throat. "So, what brings you out this way?"

Brother Elias stared straight ahead, his eyes fastened on the road. "The Lord's work."

Tim nodded, smiling, and lapsed back into silence. He should've known better than to pick up a hitcher. Any hitcher. Even the ones who looked normal and respectable were weird these days. He snuck a glance out of the corner of his eye at Brother Elias. The preacher was staring straight out the windshield, his hands folded over the Bible in his lap, his face a complete blank. Tim shook his head. It was his own fault; he had picked this clown up. But it was his duty to be friendly. He drove silently for a few miles then turned to the preacher. "So you just travel around? Hitching? Seems like it'd be easier to have your own church and stay in one place to me."

"I go where I am needed," said Brother Elias.

"And where're you headed now? You going to Randall?"

Brother Elias nodded.

"You think Randall needs saving?"

Brother Elias nodded again.

"Seems like there're a lot of worse places than Randall to me. Los Angeles, for one. Damn place is full of hippies, punks, queers, you name it." He cleared his throat, embarrassed. "Sorry again. So how do you pick where you're going? How come you decided Randall was the next place needed to be saved?"

"I have seen the coming evil," said Brother Elias. "I have seen it in a vision. The Lord has shown me the foulness of Satan's corruption and the face of his evil. He has shown me the means by which the adversary will triumph in this new Babylon. 'And he called out with a mighty voice, "Fallen, fallen is Babylon the great! It has become a dwelling place of demons, a haunt of every foul spirit." ' Revelation 18:2.

"The Lord has sent me to combat this evil with his holy word and the teachings of Jesus Christ our Lord and Savior."

Tim did not respond to the preacher. He said nothing. Instead, he looked ahead to where the two-lane road curved through a wooded canyon and inwardly cursed himself for picking up the man. Brother Elias was crazy. Not playing with a full deck, deuce high,

as his daddy used to say. This should teach him not
to pick up hitchers. No matter how they looked. He
hazarded another glance at the preacher and saw that
he was again staring straight out the window, his face
a blank. Tim shivered and gave the truck more gas,
pushing it up to sixty-five.

They passed through the canyon and sped past the
small dirt road that led to the ranger station. There
was nothing but flat forest the rest of the way into
Randall, and Tim turned on the radio to make the
drive a little more pleasant and to ease the strain of
silence that he felt. He looked toward the preacher as
he tuned in the clearest station, but Brother Elias'
face remained impassive. Since he did not seem to
object to the noise, Tim left the radio on. A few minutes later, the preacher closed his eyes.

They were almost on the outskirts of town when
Brother Elias jerked wide awake. He looked at Tim.
"You have a son," he said. It was not a question but
a statement of fact.

"Yes," Tim admitted.

"Drop me off at the police station," Brother Elias
said.

"We don't have a police station. We have a sheriff's office."

"Drop me off at the sheriff's office."

Tim drove through the main part of town and pulled
in at the sheriff's office. He watched as the preacher
picked up his suitcase and small brown parcel from
the seat between them. "Why did you say I had a
son?" he asked.

The preacher opened the passenger door and
stepped out.

Viv came running out of the sheriff's office, her face
red and wet with tears.

Tim stared at his wife as she dashed across the small
parking lot. He jumped out of the truck and hurried

toward her, leaving the keys in the ignition. "What is it?" he demanded. "What happened?"

She threw her arms around him and held tight, burying her face in his shoulder, sobbing uncontrollably. Her face was hot and wet against his skin. He hugged her, his hands pressing against the soft flesh of her back. Above her head, he could see Carl Chmura striding slowly but purposefully out of the sheriff's office. The deputy was staring at the ground as he crossed the parking lot, avoiding Tim's eyes. Tim felt a sudden rush of panic—*Matt!*—and looked quickly from Carl Chmura's averted face to his own white knuckled hands grasping Viv's back.

No, he thought, please God don't let it be Matt.

"Tim—" the deputy began.

"Is it Matt? Tell me, Carl."

The deputy nodded. "He never came home this morning. Neither did Jack or Wayne. Your wife reported Matt missing around ten o'clock this morning. I tried to get ahold of you, but you'd already left. I called the store up in Hargreve, but I guess they didn't find you in time."

"What happened to Matt?" He was starting to feel numb, disconnected, as though his brain was preparing itself for the inevitable shock.

"We don't know," the deputy admitted. "We have a search team out there looking for the boys right now. Your wife said they went camping at Aspen Lake—"

"That's right."

"—so we sent a posse." He looked at Tim. "There was quite a big storm on the Rim last night."

"What the hell's that supposed to mean?"

The deputy shrugged. "Can't tell. There was a lot of lightning, lot of rain, lot of wind. If we're lucky, they just got lost; they were out hiking when the storm hit and somehow got turned around in their directions.

If we're not lucky . . ." The deputy left the sentence unfinished.

"Maybe their car just broke down—"

"We found the car. And all their gear. They started to make a camp down by the lake itself."

"We should never have let him go!" Viv screamed, looking up at him. "I told you he shouldn't have gone!" Her face was contorted with shock and pain and fear.

"Maybe you'd best take her home," the deputy said quietly. "We'll call you if anything turns up."

"I'm going up there," Tim said. "I'm going to look for my son."

"Take me home," Viv sobbed, looking up at him and clutching the shoulders of his tank top. "Please take me home. I want to go home."

"Take her home," Chmura said gently.

"I'll be back," Tim said, leading his wife toward the truck. "I'm going up there." He opened the passenger door and helped his wife in. Closing the door, he ran around to the driver's side and jumped up on the seat, knocking a small illustrated pamphlet onto the floor. He bent down to pick up the pamphlet.

"Do you know where your children are right now?" the headline screamed up at him. "They could be caught in the clutches of Satan."

He tore the pamphlet in half and tossed it out the window, and the rear tires of the truck scattered the pieces as he sped out of the parking lot toward home.

TWO

Gordon parked the Jeep in front of the closed chain link gate of the dump and got out, leaving the headlights on. The high beams stabbed forcefully into the moonless dark but failed to illuminate more than a straight narrow stretch of the landfill. Around the edges of the light, the blackness closed in thicker, as if gathering for an assault of its own.

Gordon raised his arms and linked his fingers through the square holes in the metal fence, pressing his face against the chain link. He could smell the powerful odors of unburied garbage, rotting food, burning trash. The dump had been here almost as long as Randall, he knew. There were literally tons of garbage buried beneath this land. A lot of it was natural, organic, but a lot of it wasn't. There were various synthetic products, the used goods of an increasingly disposable society, discarded carburetor cleaner, old oil from oil changes, old transmission fluid. God knew what all was down there.

Dr. Waterston was right. It could be leaking into the wells below, into the water supply.

He peered into the dimness, trying to make out specifics of the several-acre landfill. This was where the

Selways' bodies had been found, he knew. He'd read it in the paper. They'd found the kids' bodies all torn up and ripped apart, barely recognizable. Mrs. Selway's head had been removed from her body and buried separately. Gordon shivered, feeling a tremor of fear pass through him, a shiver of dread.

A white figure inside the dump passed through the diffused headlights of the Jeep.

Gordon's heart jumped in his chest, his blood pounding. His fingers squeezed against the strong metal wires of the fence. "Hey!" he forced himself to call bravely. "What are you doing in there?"

There was no answer. He continued to stare into the landfill, his eyes searching through the blackness for some sign of movement.

The figure passed again through the headlights, this time closer.

Gordon backed away from the fence, not daring to look away but terrified of what he might see. The figure had been burned, badly burned, a charred husk of a person in a glowing white T-shirt. It had beckoned to him, wanting him to join it.

He bumped against the Jeep and felt behind him for the reassuring solidity of the vehicle's metal hood. He guided himself by touch around to the driver's door, still keeping his eyes on the spot where he'd seen the terrible figure.

He started to climb into the Jeep. And then he saw the boy sitting in his seat.

He leaped back.

"It's okay," the boy said, trying to smile. He was a kid of twelve or thirteen, wearing strangely ill-fitting pants and a white T-shirt. His greasy hair was long, and it curled onto his shoulders. Although he was trying to appear brave, confident, at ease, Gordon could tell that the boy was nervous, scared. "There's nothing to be afraid of," the boy said.

Gordon backed away from the Jeep. "Who are you?" he demanded.

"Your friend," the boy said. He climbed out of the Jeep and approached Gordon, hand extended. "I have something to show you."

The boy's voice was tremulous, nervous, but there was an undercurrent of iron resolve in it, as though he knew he had to say something but was afraid to say it. Gordon shook his head, backing away. He was backing into the darkness of the forest, he knew, away from the modern comfort of the Jeep and its headlights, but he did not care. The natural darkness behind him seemed infinitely preferable to the unnatural boy in front of him.

"I have something to show you," the boy repeated. One hand pulled a wisp of hair from his forehead. "Don't run away."

He turned away from the boy . . . and he was standing in a large semicircle with several people from town. The fire before them was so large and so hot that the shimmering heat waves radiating outward obscured the faces of the other people, but he knew they were from town instinctively.

The fire raged and crackled, flames shooting upward higher and higher until they were well above the tops of even the tallest pines. From somewhere within the blaze came cries and moans, sounds of pain and agony, and Gordon could see that what he had mistaken for blackened kindling at the base of the fire was moving, wiggling, writhing. A charred hand reached upward, then disintegrated into ashes.

The person next to him grabbed his hand. The hand felt cold, dead, and Gordon looked down to see the boy, holding hard onto his hand, his face set in an expression of grim determination.

And then he and the boy were alone in a small meadow surrounded by pines and aspens. The wind was blowing hard, and though there was a full moon,

the storm clouds passing continuously over its face
gave a fluid shifting quality to the bluish light surrounding them. Far off in the forest, a wolf or coyote
howled mournfully.

"This is what I wanted to show you," the boy said,
letting go of his hand.

Gordon looked down at the ground, at the tiny
white crosses sticking up from between clumps of
overgrown weeds. He was scared, filled suddenly with
an icy terror he had never before experienced. He
looked next to him, at the boy, but the boy was gone.
He was all alone in this hateful place, and he closed
his eyes, hoping it, too, would disappear, but when he
reopened them, all remained as it was. The wind blew
hard, tinkling the round leaves of the aspens, sending
small leaves and branches skittering across the rough
ground. The white crosses, some standing straight, others falling over at various angles, seemed to glow with
an unnatural luminescence.

A large cloud passed over the moon, sending the
small meadow into total darkness. And then the weeds
before the tiny crosses were parting. The hard rocky
soil beneath was pushed upward as if something under
the ground was trying to break free.

The wind blew harder, carrying away his terrified
screams. He felt a soft hand on his leg and he looked
down . . . to see Marina's fingers on top of the crumpled sheet that covered his body. He was sitting up in
bed, his skin wet with a cold sweat, the sheets sticking
to his body. He looked over at Marina. She was staring at him with concern, worry wrinkling her pretty
features.

"Are you okay?" she asked.

He nodded, still unable to speak. He could feel his
heart pounding, taking its own time about slowing
back to normal. He reached over and grabbed her
hand, squeezing lightly.

Marina looked him over carefully. "You've been having quite a few nightmares lately," she said.

He nodded. "I know." He closed his eyes, leaning back on the pillow. "That was a really bad one."

"Is there something wrong, something you want to talk about? If there's something the matter, we should talk it out. I don't want you keeping it all bottled up inside."

"It's everything," he said, shaking his head. "All of the pressures, I guess. The baby. What Dr. Waterston told us about. The kitten. The money situation." He pulled her close to him. "It's not anything I can't handle. I don't even feel that stressed out during the day."

"But at night you have nightmares."

"At night," he agreed, "I have nightmares."

They lay there for a few moments, saying nothing, enjoying the closeness. Marina listened to the sound of a dog barking somewhere close to town. "Maybe," she began, turning toward him.

But he was already asleep, starting to snore, and she turned back over, staring up at the ceiling.

Soon she, too, was asleep.

THREE

"Jesus Christ! Is the whole damn world going crazy?" Jim ran an exasperated hand through his sweat-soaked hair and replaced his hat. He slumped in his chair. "All right," he sighed. "Send him in."

Rita nodded and moved out into the hallway. She looked toward the front desk and beckoned. Jim heard the sound of familiar shoes clomping down the hall. He sat up in his seat and tried to make his expression appear interested and concerned, but it was too much effort and he gave it up.

Gordon walked past the receptionist, who was holding open the door, and into the room. The sheriff motioned for him to sit down. "What's new today, Mr. Lewis?" he asked tiredly. Rita closed the door behind her.

"I was going to ask you the same question."

The sheriff smiled. "Not a damn thing," he said.

"Look, sheriff—"

"No. You look. I have several murder investigations going on at this moment, several missing person cases and hundreds of thousands of dollars in damages from vandalism that I have to explain. Your kitty cat is not real high on my list of priorities right now."

"Yeah. It's small stuff. People break into houses and mutilate kittens all the time." Gordon stood up. "Look, Sheriff. My wife is terrified, and I'm not sleeping too well myself. Some fucking weirdo is walking around loose out there and you try to make it sound as though a group of kids was playing a harmless prank. I'm getting pretty damn tired of your—"

"You stop right there," Jim told him. He stood up and pointed a finger in Gordon's face. "Don't you say another word." He glared at Gordon, and the younger man looked embarrassedly away. Jim shook his head. "Look, I apologize, all right? I didn't mean to dismiss your problem or make it seem unimportant. It's just that there's been a lot on my mind lately. There really *are* some weirdos out there, and I'm doing my best to keep things under control. A lot of strange things have been happening in this town."

"I know," Gordon said. "One of them happened at my house." He sat back down.

Jim smiled, the tension eased. He walked over to the window and looked outside. Somewhere on the Rim, search parties were trying to find Jack Harrison, Wayne Fisk, and Matt McDowell. Closer in, the mill was working at only partial power. Many of the workers, Tim McDowell included, were out searching. Jim turned toward Gordon. "You know Tim McDowell?"

Gordon nodded. "Yeah. We're good friends. He called me as soon as he found out. I was out searching with him yesterday afternoon." He kicked at a scrap of paper on the floor. "It's hard to believe."

Jim snorted. "You don't know the half of it. I could tell you things . . ." He trailed off. "Hell, I feel like one of those movie sheriffs surveying the wreckage of his town after the big disaster and saying, 'This used to be a nice place to live.' " He laughed shortly. "Except I have this horrible feeling that the big disaster hasn't happened yet."

"Me too," Gordon said quietly.

"You too?" The sheriff turned to look at him. "What do you mean, you too? You have no idea what's going on here."

"Then tell me."

Jim stared at him for a moment, as if thinking, then shook his head. "No." He moved over to the desk and leaned against it, taking off his hat and setting it on a pile of papers. "Look, why don't you just go home. I'll call you if anything comes up."

Gordon looked at him suspiciously.

"I will." Jim smiled, holding up three pressed-together fingers. "Sheriff's honor."

"Okay," Gordon said, standing up. "I have a lot of work to do anyway. My wife wants me to put new dead bolts on all the doors and see if I can do something about the windows. Call me if you find anything out or if you have any more questions about what happened." He yawned. "Sorry," he said, smiling apologetically. "Between this and the dreams I've been having, I haven't been getting much sleep."

Jim's bland farewell smile faded. He had been about to open the door for Gordon, but his hand remained unmoving on the round brass doorknob. "Dreams?" he said.

"Yeah. Nightmares." Gordon looked at him quizically. "What does that have to do with anything?"

"Are these normal nightmares?"

"I don't know what you mean by normal—"

"Do you have them often?"

Gordon nodded. "Fairly often."

"When did you start having them? Did it all start recently? Say, a month or so ago?"

Gordon looked at him. He started to back slowly toward the desk. "What is all this?" he asked. "What do you know?"

An hour later, the two men were speeding down Old Mesa Road past the abandoned hulking building that had once been the town's bowling alley. "I want you to talk to the priest," Jim said. "Tell him what you told me. I'll tell him what I know, too. I've kind of hinted around about things, but I haven't come out and told him what I really think." He turned onto a side street. "I met Father Andrews a few days ago when his place was vandalized. He's a very intelligent man. He knows a hell of a lot about ESP and parapsychology and all that. I think he can help us out a lot."

"His place was vandalized, too?"

"Much worse than yours. The whole library was destroyed; books torn up, pages covered with shit." He looked at Gordon. "I mean real shit. Human excrement. The whole thing set on fire—"

"Was this his house or Father Selway's?" Gordon asked suddenly.

"Selway's."

"You think maybe they're connected?"

The sheriff nodded grimly. "I'm sure of it."

The car pulled up in front of a one-story wood-frame structure set back from the road. An old black Plymouth was parked in the dirt driveway. The sheriff stopped the car and got out. Gordon got out as well and followed him up the path toward the front door.

They were almost to the door when a clean-shaven man with short blond hair, wearing jeans and an old work shirt, peeked around the corner of the house. "I thought I heard someone pull up," he said. He waved at Jim with a dirty trowel. "I'm back here, trying to put together some sort of garden."

The two walked around the edge of the house. The priest was standing next to a large rectangular patch of cleared ground that covered almost the entire side yard. The soil here had been recently tilled, and a pile of dried weeds and manzanita bushes was pushed against the wall of the house. A few tentative rows had been started in the dirt at the far end of the rectangle. The priest dropped his trowel next to a

stack of seed packets and wiped his hands on his jeans
before offering one to Gordon. "Father Donald Andrews," he said. "First Episcopal Church."

Gordon shook the priest's hand. "Gordon Lewis,"
he said. "Pepsi deliveryman."

The priest laughed. He shook hands with the sheriff.
"What can I do for you gentlemen?"

Jim looked at Gordon, then back at the priest. "We
have to talk. There are some things I'd like to tell
you."

Father Andrews' face became serious as he listened
to the sheriff's tone of voice. "Is this along the lines
of what we were discussing the other day?"

Jim nodded.

"I thought so. I had a feeling you were keeping
something back; though I hoped I was wrong." He
picked up his stack of seeds and started walking
toward the rear of the house. "Come on. We can
talk inside."

Jim and Gordon sat on opposite ends of the couch
in the living room while Father Andrews washed up
and put on a pot of tea. The priest emerged from the
kitchen a few moments later and sat down in the large
overstuffed chair opposite the couch. He looked at the
sheriff. "So what is all this about?"

"Dreams," Jim said.

"What?"

"You know about psychic experiences, Father.
You've studied them, and you may have had a few
yourself."

The priest nodded.

"I think that's what's happening here. Gordon and
I have both been having some pretty strange dreams
lately. Nightmares. For all I know, a lot of other people have been having them too." He paused. "A boy
named Don Wilson had these kinds of dreams also."
He leaned forward in his seat. "But that boy *saw*
things in his dreams. Real things. He saw the Selway

family being murdered, and he told us where to find their bodies."

The priest's eyebrows shot up in surprise.

"He's dead," Jim said, anticipating the priest's next question. "He'd had a new dream, an important dream that he said he had to tell me about, but he was killed before he could explain it to me."

"What happened?" Gordon asked.

"His house burned down. Officially, he died of smoke inhalation." Jim shook his head. "I mean, he *did* die of smoke inhalation. But it was intentional. He was murdered. Do you understand? It was a very convenient fire."

Father Andrews frowned. "What? Some sort of cult?"

"That's just what my wife thought. But no, I don't think that's what it is. I know this sounds crazy, but just bear with me." The tea kettle started whistling in the kitchen and the sheriff looked at Father Andrews questioningly, but the priest shook his head. Jim looked from the priest to Gordon and back again. "In his dream, the boy said he saw the Selway family tortured and killed by monsters. He said the creatures ate the baby, ripped apart the other children and tore off Mrs. Selway's head. *We found the half-eaten remains of the baby, the eviscerated kids, and the mother and her head exactly where Don told us we would.*" The sheriff looked at Gordon. "None of this leaves the room, understand?"

Gordon nodded silently, his face pale.

"But that wasn't all. Don told us that after the creatures killed Selway's family, they made Selway himself kneel before a fire, telling him to bow down before his new God. Something huge came out of the flames, something with horns that Don said looked like the devil, and Selway walked into the fire." He paused. "We never found Selway's remains. Don told us we wouldn't."

"That's quite a story," Father Andrews said. "But you expect me to believe it all?"

"What don't you believe?"

"Where do you want me to start?" He looked at the sheriff and sighed. "Okay, first, the conception of the devil as an entity with horns and a tail and a pitchfork comes from artists and fiction writers. It has no theological basis in fact—"

"Are you telling me that the Bible gives detailed descriptions of each and every demon mentioned and that none of them have horns?"

"Well, no," the priest admitted. "There are very few physical descriptions."

"Okay then."

"But psychic dream correlations are very seldom literal. There's hardly ever a specific one-to-one correspondence between the details of a premonition and what actually occurs—"

The sheriff held up a hand. "Look, humor me. Suppose the boy saw what actually happened? What then?"

"I'm—"

"Take into account the fact that several churches have been vandalized and painted with goat's blood, that goats from neighboring farms have been slaughtered, that two of the farmers themselves have been killed, that similar things have happened around the state. Throw in your own experience, the disappearance of some teenage boys and some small stuff like Gordon's cat. What have you got?"

The priest looked at him. "Do you want my official answer as a member of the Episcopal church, or do you want my own personal answer?"

"Your personal answer. Your honest answer."

"I don't know," Father Andrews admitted. "But you're starting to scare me."

FOUR

Marina was standing in the front doorway when Gordon hopped out of the car. She walked down the porch steps to meet him. "What took you so long?"

He shook his head. "Nothing." He kissed her lightly on the lips.

"Did you find anything out from the sheriff?"

"No. Nothing new."

"That bastard. I'll be damned if I'll vote for him again. He hasn't done a single thing to find out what happened."

"He's trying," Gordon said.

She stepped back from him, her brows furrowed. She crossed her arms. "What did he do? Give you some sob story about how overworked he is?"

Gordon smiled. "No."

"Well then why are you sticking up for him?"

"A lot of things have been happening around here. He's busy."

"That doesn't help Vlad." Marina turned away with an angry toss of her head and walked back up the porch steps.

Gordon followed. "Look, I don't want to argue about this right now." He hefted the small brown paper sack in his hand, making a clanking jingling noise, and she turned around to look. "I bought some locks," he said.

She stared at him levelly. "That's something."

"I'm going to put them on so we don't have to worry about anyone else breaking in."

She nodded, softening but still not smiling. "You do that. I'll start making dinner."

For the next hour he lost himself in the menial job of installing locks on the windows. He was all the way around to the kitchen window when Marina called him in for dinner. He waved at her, telling her he'd be through in a minute, and hastily put in the last screw before going inside to eat.

He washed his hands in the kitchen sink as Marina placed a large salad and two bowls of minestrone soup on the table. She seemed to have forgotten all about their earlier disagreement. "So," she said, getting out the silverware, "how do these locks work?"

He sat down. "Simple. You push the bolt to lock the window, pull the bolt to open it."

"How come you're putting them on the outside?"

"The lock itself is on the underside of the window, even though you lock it from inside the house."

The phone rang, and they looked at each other. Ordinarily, when someone called during dinner they let the phone ring without answering it, but Gordon did not want to take any chances. "I'll get it," he said.

Marina nodded.

He came back into the kitchen a few minutes later, embarrassed. "Brad," he said. He scratched his head. "He wants me to help him finish up tonight."

"Tonight!" Marina looked at the clock. "It's after six already!"

Gordon shrugged. "He's let me off early the past few days to take care of this break-in—"

"So what's that mean? You owe him your life?"

"That's the reason he's fallen behind. All he wants

me to do is help him deliver a few cases to the markets in town. That's it. With both of us working it shouldn't take more than an hour. Hour and a half at the latest."

"What about the door locks? You're just going to leave me here alone by myself? It'll be dark in less than an hour."

"We only have two doors," he said. "I don't have to meet Brad until seven. I have plenty of time to put both locks on."

"Hurry up and eat then." Marina shivered, though it was far from cold. "I want them done before you go."

All of the lights in the house were on, but Marina was still frightened. She should have gone with Gordon, should have gone to the stores with him and read magazines while he unloaded Pepsis.

The house sighed somewhere, creaking, and she blamed the wind, though she knew the air outside was still. She focused her attention on the TV, trying to get herself involved in the show, but the picture came in poorly, the dialogue interrupted by loud crackles of static, and she realized that there was a storm somewhere between Randall and Flagstaff. The thought made her aware of how isolated she really was from everything. She considered calling Ginny, but then decided against it. She didn't really have anything to say; she would just be calling to assuage her fears, to feign companionship.

Wasn't that reason enough?

No. She forced herself to watch the snowy television. Besides, Gordon would be home soon.

There was a knock at the door. Marina jumped from her chair and ran to the front. She peeked through the curtains of the living room window and saw a strange man in a gray business suit standing on her doorstep.

She gave a short, sharp cry and the man's sharp eyes veered instantly to her window. She let the curtain fall, backing into the room. She banged against a chair and reached behind her, grabbing it for support.

There was another knock at the door. This one firmer, less hesitant, more insistent. *The man wanted in!*

"Go away!" Marina yelled.

"I have come to speak with you and your husband," the man called through the closed door. His voice was loud, carrying with it the controlled authority of a public speaker.

"My husband's not home! Come back later!"

"I will talk with you, then."

Marina licked her lips, but her tongue was dry as well. She could feel her arms trembling with fear. Slowly, she crept forward until she was again at the window. She thought for a moment, then moved to another vantage point—the window on the other side of the door. She pulled the curtain slowly back and peeked out. The man's gaze was still fixed on the other window. "I would like to speak with you," he said.

"I can hear you fine!" Marina yelled. "Tell me what you want to tell me, then leave! Or I'm going to call the sheriff!"

His gaze swung immediately to her, and she blanched at the intensity of his expression. She noticed for the first time that he carried with him a Bible, tucked under his right arm.

"Who are you?" she demanded.

"I am Brother Elias. I have come to save you from your peril and to deliver you from the brink of the pit upon which you stand."

"Go away!"

Brother Elias took out his Bible and opened it to a previously marked page. " 'Children, it is the last hour; and as you have heard that antichrist is coming, so now many antichrists have come; therefore we

know that it is the last hour. They went out from us, but they were not of us; for if they had been of us, they would have continued with us; but they went out, that it might be plain that they all are not of us.'"
He closed the Bible and looked at her, his eyes holding hers.

Is this how these people keep their followers? Is this how Jim Jones got his disciples? She could not look away. It was as if he had her hypnotized.

"So it is written in The First Letter of John, chapter two, verses eighteen and nineteen. The antichrist is not coming, the antichrists are here!" His voice took on the rolling oratorical delivery of a fundamentalist minister. "We must fight this evil where it dwells! We must bring it out into the open sunshine of the Lord's divine light where it can be dissipated according to the Holy Word of God!" He opened up the Bible again, looking away, and Marina quickly let the curtain drop, retreating back into the room.

She could hear his voice, above the television, as she made her way to the telephone.

"'And the great dragon was thrown down, that ancient serpent, who is called the devil and Satan, the deceiver of the whole world—he was thrown down to the earth, and his angels were thrown down with him.'"

Marina, her fingers fumbling, found the number of the sheriff written on the emergency pad next to the phone. She quickly dialed. The line was busy, and she dialed again.

"'And when the dragon saw that he had been thrown down to the earth, he pursued the woman who had borne the male child—'"

"Shut up!" Marina yelled. "Shut up!" She was gratified to hear the loud voice stop for a moment. She picked up the phone again. "I'm calling the sheriff!" she announced. "I'm going to have you arrested!"

"I am here to save you from the darkness that

threatens, from the evil within. I am here to put you on the path of righteousness and—"

"Get the fuck out of here!"

Marina was aware that her voice sounded panicked, that she was becoming hysterical, but she was terrified. She saw in her mind the bloody kitchen, gray and red portions of Vlad scattered over the tile floor and the Formica countertops. She dialed the sheriff's number again, and this time the phone rang. Someone on the other end picked it up. "This is Marina Lewis," she said breathlessly into the receiver. "There's someone at my house. He's outside my front door, trying to get in—"

"We'll have someone there immediately," the receptionist told her. "Don't let him in. Do you have any firearms in the house?"

"No."

"Then I'd suggest grabbing a baseball bat or a knife or any sort of weapon you do have. Just in case." There was a click, and the receptionist's voice became muffled as she put out the call. "Deputy Chmura and Deputy Weiss will be there in a moment," she said, reconnecting into the line. "Don't panic."

"I'm not." Marina looked up, putting the receiver down. The voice outside had stopped. She listened for a moment, then ran over and turned down the TV. Nothing. Gathering up her courage, she pulled open the curtains and looked outside.

Brother Elias was gone.

Marina returned to the phone. "He left," she said. "Thank you." She didn't wait for the receptionist's reply but hung up the phone. She again moved to the front of the room and looked out the window, trying to spot any sign of movement in the darkness, listening for the sound of a starting car.

A moment later, she heard the sound of a siren, growing louder, coming closer. The trees lining the narrow dirt road soon glowed with the blue and red of the sheriff's flashing lights. Behind the sheriff's car, thankfully, unbelievably, was the Jeep.

Marina opened the front door and ran outside. Only then did she realize that she was crying.

FIVE

Father Andrews milled around after the prayer meeting, shaking hands and talking with parishioners. The meeting had gone much better than he'd expected. He had never conducted a prayer meeting before, and though he knew theoretically what was required of him, he was sure that the actual practice would be quite different. He wasn't sure he'd be able to do it. But Father Selway's congregation had been kind to him on Sunday, and the parishioners at the prayer meeting had been just as nice. They'd guided him through the meeting, letting him know how Father Selway had done things, but letting him know that if he wanted to make changes that was fine, too.

He grabbed a Dixie cup filled with red punch. An elderly woman next to him, wearing a large hat and too much makeup, reached for a cookie. She smiled up at him. "My name's Betty Murphy," she said.

He shook the woman's offered hand. "I'm glad to meet you, Mrs. Murphy, and I'm glad that you could make it to our meeting."

She giggled. "Oh, I wouldn't miss it for the world. I come here every week. Been coming ever since Jim died." She straightened her flowered hat. "I wanted to ask you what you think of that new preacher who's been preaching around town."

"New preacher?"

"Yes. I'm not sure exactly who he is, but I've seen him twice already this week. The first time, he was preaching in the parking lot in front of the old bowling alley. The second time, he was on top of a car parked near the post office, yelling at the people who walked by. It was real hellfire and damnation stuff, how we are all going to burn if we don't repent." She wrinkled her nose distastefully. "I never did go in for that sort of preaching." She put her hand familiarly on his arm. "That's why I became an Episcopalian."

"I couldn't help overhearing you." A thin middle-aged man, wearing a gaudy new western shirt and a bolo tie, turned from the small group he was with to face the priest. He held out his hand. "Jeff Haught."

Father Andrews shook his hand. "I'm glad to meet you."

The man turned to Mrs. Murphy. "Were you talking about that street preacher been around town the past couple days?"

She nodded, her hat bobbing up and down in assent.

"Did you hear what he said?"

Mrs. Murphy sniffed. "I heard enough."

The man faced Father Andrews. "That preacher's crazy. I was just stopping by the Circle K yesterday to buy some ice, and I saw this crowd gathered around the side of the building. I went over to investigate, and there was this preacher, wearing a heavy gray suit, in the hottest part of the day, standing on one of those empty wooden spools they use for telephone line. I stood there listening for a while and," the man shook his head, "I never heard anything like it. He started off like Mrs. Murphy said, regular fire and brimstone fundamentalism, but then he started on this . . . weird stuff. He started saying how Satan and God were going to fight it out here on earth and how we'd better start gathering up our weapons to fight. He said some people were going to be fighting on God's side, but some were going to be on Satan's. Then he started pointing out specific people in the crowd!"

Father Andrews smiled. "That's not unusual. A lot of these evangelists use such techniques to fire up the crowd and get people to listen to them."

"He said God and Satan were going to fight here, in Randall. Next week."

Father Andrews' smile faded. Mrs. Murphy laughed out loud. She let go of the priest's arm and grabbed the other man's. "Oh Jeff. You don't mean to tell me you actually believe that nonsense?"

He shook his head, smiling. "Of course not. But a lot of other people seemed to." He looked at Father Andrews. "That's what I wanted to talk to you about, Father. Do you think maybe you could give some kind of warning during your sermon Sunday? Tell people not to listen to this jerk?"

The priest slowly shook his head. "No, I can't really do that. It is not my place to criticize other religions, particularly on the pulpit."

"I understand. I just thought that maybe as a kind of public service . . ."

Father Andrews smiled. "No."

Jeff nodded. "That's okay." He started to go, then turned back around. "You know something, though? When I was leaving, he was starting to make predictions."

Father Andrews frowned. "What kind of predictions?"

"The only one I really heard was the first one. He said the churches in town were going to be struck down, one by one, by the devil's fire. Then I went to get my ice. He was still talking, but I didn't hear what he said."

"That is a little more serious," Father Andrews said. He was silent for a moment, thinking, but conscious of the two pairs of eyes on him, he forced himself to smile. "Of course, he probably just heard about the vandalism and what happened to the Selways and was trying to make the most of it," he said.

Jeff nodded. "Probably." He shook the priest's hand again. "I really enjoyed the meeting, Father. I just wanted to tell you that. I hope you're going to be around here for a while."

"I hope so, too," Father Andrews said laughing. But he stopped laughing almost immediately, aware of how callous and flippant that sounded in the wake of what had happened to the Selways. Though he had never met his predecessor, everyone here had been on close terms with him, and they had all liked him a lot.

But neither Jeff nor Mrs. Murphy noticed his faux pas, and he did not dwell on it, turning his attention instead to the excited chattering of Mrs. Murphy, who was filling him in on the details of everyone in the room. He watched as Jeff and two of his friends left by the front door. A few moments later, several other elderly ladies came up to talk to him, to tell him how much they'd enjoyed the meeting. He kept the conversation on a light tone. There was something in the story of that preacher that bothered him, and he found himself coming back to it, thinking about it, and not concentrating on the conversation around him.

By ten o'clock, everyone had left, even Mrs. Murphy, and he put away the leftover carton of punch, storing it in the church refrigerator, and picked up the crumpled Dixie cups left on the tables around the room. He gave the room one last cursory glance, and turned off the lights, locking the door behind him as he stepped outside.

He felt a smothering cloak of dread settle about him the second he stepped out of the church. The air suddenly felt thick and heavy, hard to breathe. He thought instantly of the preacher.

From the center of town, he heard a siren, loud in the still evening. A firetruck, Father Andrews thought. One of the churches is on fire.

But he pushed the thought from his mind. He was overreacting, still hyped up from his talks with the sheriff. He was jumping at shadows. He could not allow his emotions to run away with him. If he was going to be any help at all to the sheriff, he would have to think things through logically, reason everything out.

He got into the car just as it started to drizzle. The light rain and the windshield wipers cleared the small flecks of soot and cinder from the glass.

SIX

Jim sat in Ernst's office, squirming in the uncomfortable plastic chair the fire chief had filched from the elementary school last year when the cafeteria had caught on fire. Ernst nodded slowly, not looking up from his desk. "It's arson," he said. "We haven't had time for an official investigation yet, of course. But after a while you can spot these things. It's arson. I'd bet money on it."

Jim stood up and started pacing around the room. "Damn it, I knew it would be." He hitched up his pants. "That's the last thing I need right now."

Natalie Ernst stuck her head in the open doorway. "You two want anything to drink? Coffee?"

The fire chief shook his head, waving her away. "Not now, Nat. Maybe later."

She smiled cheerfully at her father-in-law. "Okay."

Ernst picked up a short stubby pencil from the top of his desk, turning it over in his hands. "This is the fire season, you know. The rangers do most of the work, but we have a pretty full load ourselves."

Jim nodded. "I know."

"But the monsoons have come," Ernst continued. "And if you and your men need a little help, we'll be glad to help you out. I can spare a few men, as long as things don't get too crazy around here."

Jim shook his head. "Thanks, but—"

The staccato clanging of a loud firebell sounded throughout the small building. Ernst stood instantly up, punching the intercom button on his desk. "What is it?" he asked.

"Church," Natalie said. "First Southern Baptist. Over on east Main."

Ernst stared at Jim. "Want to come along?"

The sheriff nodded. He followed Ernst out to the garage, where four other men were already putting on fireproof uniforms. Ernst quickly got into his suit and hopped into the truck. Jim jumped into the passenger seat, and the other men found places on the back of the vehicle. The fire chief flipped on the siren and pulled out onto the street.

"It's a hot one," Ernst said as they pulled up to the church. Jim saw multicolored shards of stained glass littering the church parking lot. The windows had exploded outward, and thick white smoke was billowing from the open holes. Small orange flames were licking out of a hole in the roof.

Ernst stopped the truck and jumped out. "Anybody inside?" he yelled, approaching a young man standing in the parking lot watching. The young man shook his head. The other firemen were already hooking up the hoses. "How long ago did it start?" Ernst demanded.

The young man shrugged. "It was already goin' when I got here."

"Did you call it in?"

"No." He pointed toward a teenage girl standing nearby, holding her hands over her mouth. "She did."

The firemen had hooked up the hoses by this time, and two of them grabbed axes from the back of the firetruck. Ernst hurried across the asphalt to join them, and Jim approached the sobbing girl. "You're the one who reported the fire?" he asked gently.

She nodded, still holding her hands in front of her mouth.

"I'm Sheriff Weldon. Could you tell me exactly what you saw? Did you see how it started?"

The girl shook her head. "I was just walking by on the way to the store, and I saw smoke coming out from under the door." She looked up at him. "That's my church, you know." She wiped the tears from her eyes with the back of a hand. "I ran over and opened the door, and all this smoke just poured out. I called out, to see if anyone was in there, but no one answered. I ran around the building, looking for Pastor Williams' car, but it wasn't there so I assumed there was no one in the church, so I ran across the street and called the fire department." She stifled a sob. "We just got that new Sunday school addition put onto the church last year. Now we're going to have to start from scratch."

Jim turned to watch the firemen put out the blaze. "Maybe they'll be able to save it," he said. "Maybe there won't be that much damage."

"It's destroyed!" the girl sobbed.

An overweight man wearing faded jeans, a Charlie Daniels T-shirt, and a CAT hat moved next to the sheriff. He stared at the firemen, who were running into the side doors of the church with long hoses. "You know, Brother Elias said this was going to happen."

Jim turned to look at the man. "What?"

"I said, Brother Elias said this was going to happen."

Jim was instantly on the alert. Brother Elias. The man who had been harassing Gordon's wife. "Who is this Brother Elias?" he asked.

The man shook his head dismissively. "A preacher I saw out by the Circle K yesterday. Crazy as a fucking bedbug."

Bentley Little

"But he said this church was going to be set on fire?"

The man chuckled, a low sound that came from deep within his massive chest. "He didn't say this church was going to be set on fire, he said all the churches were going to be burned. Satan was going to burn them, he said."

"Why?"

The man shrugged. "How the fuck should I know?" He stared at the smoking building, but it was clear that the firemen already had the blaze under control. He started to move off.

"Wait," Jim said. "Do you know where I can find this Brother Elias?"

The man shook his head. "Search me. I saw him at the Circle K yesterday, but I heard someone today say he was at the sawmill. You might try there."

"Thanks." Jim watched the man lumber away. Next to him, the young woman was still sobbing. From the front door of the church a yellow-suited fireman, Ernst presumably, gave him the high sign. Jim waved back and turned to the girl. "It's out," he said. "It looks like they saved most of it."

She did not hear him, or, if she did, she did not care. She continued to cry into her hands. Jim stared at the church. A small plume of smoke was still swirling upward from a hole in the roof, like the benign smoke from a chimney. The brownish bricks of the building were covered with soot and water.

Brother Elias, Jim thought.

SEVEN

The preacher stood on the small wooden bench, holding his Bible high in the air and glaring out at the assembled crowd before him. There were at least fifteen or twenty people standing on the rough asphalt sidewalk in front of the rodeo grounds, staring up at him in rapt attention. They had all been walking by on their way to other places, they had all been thinking of other things, but they had all stopped to listen when they'd heard the sound of his voice.

"The evil one is amongst you NOW!" the preacher screamed, gesturing into the crowd with his Bible. He smiled slyly, crouching low on the bench. "No, don't pretend that you are surprised. Because you are not surprised. He is here now, and you know he is here! In fact, YOU have had dealings with him!" The preacher jumped up, pointing to a long-haired young man drinking a Coke.

"Fuck you," the young man said tiredly. He held up a middle finger as he walked away. Several people in the crowd giggled.

"Yes, you can laugh now," the preacher said. "But there will be no laughter when Satan claims the earth for his own and walks freely amongst his subjects! For,

yes, that is what he intends to do. He will conquer
this earth and all on it and turn it into his own private
playground, his own annex of hell!"

Someone in the crowd stifled a laugh.

The preacher looked heavenward, straining his neck
as he faced the skies. "Oh Lord, why dost thou give
them brains when they do not use them to think? Why
dost thou give them eyes when they do not use them
to see?" Suddenly, he jumped down from the bench,
waving the Bible in his hand at the crowd. The people
backed up a step, shocked. The preacher's black eyes
burned with a crazed, fiery intensity. "He has come
once before, the evil one. He came to this town and
was defeated!" He looked around at the faces before
him. "Do you have enough faith to defeat him this
time? Are you willing to fight on the side of the Lord,
or will you lay down and die and surrender your souls
to the clutches of Satan?"

A frightened woman in the front of the crowd took
a dollar bill from her purse.

"I don't want your money!" the preacher yelled,
slapping her hand and sending the bill fluttering to the
ground. "I want your word! God has given you his
word, will you give him yours? Will you stand by your
faith? Will you fight against the forces of evil?" He
stared at the woman who had offered him the money.
"You," he said. "Your son is fighting on the side of
Satan. He is lost."

The woman paled. "I . . . I have no son," she
stammered.

But the preacher was already moving through the
crowd, touching certain individuals. "Your wife died
in childbirth," he said to one old man. "She has as-
cended to the bosom of the Lord. Your daughter is
burning in the pits of hell." He looked at another
man. "You could go either way," he stated.

"How do you know all this?" one skeptical voice

piped up. "What makes you think we should listen to you?"

"It has been foretold in the Bible," the preacher said loudly. "It has all been foreseen by Almighty God." He glanced around him. "This has happened before," he repeated, "and if we are successful in our attempts to combat the adversary it will happen still again. And again. And again. Satan has been banished for all eternity from the presence and grace of the Lord, and he will never give up in his attempt to usurp the power of God. Satan is gathering to him an army, and he will use that army to fight against the forces of good." He moved back through the crowd and once again jumped on top of the wooden bench. "We have no time to argue or debate. Either you are with God or you are against him. The time for indecision is past. The evil one is here and ready to strike!"

The crowd was silent.

The preacher closed his eyes and began swaying. "And the lightning will turn red, signifying the coming of the adversary," he chanted. "There will be flies, there will be earthquakes." He stopped speaking, opening his eyes, and he stared silently down at the crowd. He jumped down from the bench and, without a word, picked up his suitcase from the ground behind him and strode purposefully through the throng of people. He continued down the street, not looking back.

On the bench, he had left a pile of pamphlets, religious tracts. One man moved hesitantly forward, picking one up. "Blessed are the brave," the title announced, "For They Are the Armies of God."

EIGHT

Pete King sat in the metal swivel chair in front of the switchboard, his feet propped up on the counter. He stared at the randomly flickering lights of the board, wondering why they lit up when no one was calling. He never would understand how these damn things worked.

Judson came in from the back, from the bathroom, buckling his belt. He nodded toward Pete. "Any of them donuts left?"

Pete tossed him a crumpled white sack. "Some."

Judson pulled out half a crumb donut and a small piece of maple bar. He dropped them back in the sack and threw the sack at Pete in disgust. "That's it? You ate all the rest?"

"I saved two for you."

"Two pieces you bit out of."

Pete laughed. "I didn't bite out of them. I tore pieces off with my fingers. What a pansy."

"Pansy hell. I just don't want to get your AIDS germs." Judson pulled the chair out from Rita's desk and sat down, pushing his feet against the wood and tipping the chair back on two legs. He nodded toward the switchboard. "Anything?"

Pete shook his head. "Slow night."

"So what'd that dickhead from Phoenix have to say?"

"McFarland? Nothing new. I think the staters are concentrating more on the Valley than here."

"That's bullshit. More's happened here than there."

Pete laughed. "What is this? A contest? Sure, more's happened here than there, but they figure Phoenix is bigger, he'd have more place to hide. Up here, we'd notice someone new immediately, the town's too small."

"He, huh? They've narrowed it down to a single person?"

"Don't play goddamn word games with me. You know what I'm talking about. They think the perpetrator or perpetrators is or are in the Phoenix area, all right? Is that clear enough for you? They're concentrating their efforts in the Valley. McFarland's staying here, but Ralphs will be operating both here and in Phoenix."

"That's bullshit. Did you tell him about the preacher? What's his name?"

"Elias something. Yeah, I told him. He said he'd talk to Wilson about it, but he himself couldn't make any decisions. He said he'd tell him about the fire this afternoon, too, but he thought that last fire was totally unconnected. He has a real bug up his ass about everything being centered in Phoenix."

"Shit."

Pete shrugged. "That's the way of the world."

Judson put his feet back down on the floor and pulled a stick of gum from his shirt pocket. He slowly unwrapped the gum. "Tell me the truth. Do you think it was a good idea bringing these guys in?"

Pete thought for a moment. "I don't know," he admitted. "I did at first, but they don't seem to be doing any better than we did on this. Worse, maybe. And they treat us like shit. They're supposed to be cooperating with us on an investigation, but they act like we're their goddamn servants or something."

"Ain't that the truth."

"They think that just because we work in a small town instead of a big city, we're Podunk know-nothings and can't be trusted to work on an investigation."

Judson laughed. "The old Barney Fife situation."

Pete shook his head. "I don't know." He turned around and stared at the lights of the switchboard, flicking on and off for no discernible reason. Behind him, he heard Judson scoot across the floor in his chair and grab the donut bag. He stared at the lights for a moment longer, thinking, then swiveled around again. Judson was eating the last of the crumb donut, licking the excess spices off his fingers. He wasn't quite sure how to bring up what he wanted to say, and he almost turned back around, but he gathered up his courage and cleared his throat. "Jud?" he said.

Judson looked up. "Yeah?"

"Have you noticed anything . . . strange about all this?"

"What do you mean, strange?"

"You know, strange."

"You mean like those strange little footprints in the blood over at the farmer's place?"

Pete nodded excitedly. "Exactly!"

"No, I haven't."

"Come on. Be serious. You know what I'm talking about. You know this isn't any ordinary investigation."

Judson nodded reluctantly. He put the donut bag down. "Yeah," he said slowly. "Yeah, I do. I don't want to, but I do." He sighed. "I've been seeing things, hearing things, thinking things, and I wish to Christ they'd go away."

"What'd you see?"

Judson was silent for a moment. "The footprints," he said, finally. He looked at Pete. "You saw the footprints, too?"

Pete nodded.

"We all saw the footprints. So how come we pretended we didn't? How come none of us said anything? How come we didn't tell Jim?" He shook his head. "Jesus. Last week, right after all this started, about this time of night, Jim came running out of his office with his gun drawn. He was scared shitless. I could see it in his face. I was coming back from the head, and he ran into me in the hall, knocking me down. He said he saw something, something strange, running down the hall. I told him he was tired." He laughed mirthlessly. "Jesus, tired."

"You think he really saw something?"

"Hell, I saw the fucking thing too! It was running fast and keeping to the shadows. You know how shitty the lights are back there at night. But I could see that it was about the size of a small dog. It was hairless and pinkish, and it ran on four legs, babbling to itself. I saw it right after the sheriff left. Right after! He turned around the corner, and it sped by at the other end of the hall. I should've called out to Jim, or at least said something to him the next day, but I didn't. I ignored it, tried to forget about it, pretended it didn't happen."

Pete nodded. "I know what you mean. I saw those footprints too. Weirdest damn things I ever saw. What do you think they were?"

Judson shook his head slowly. "I don't know, and I don't think I want to know."

"And what about those bodies? The farmers' *and* the preacher's family. I mean, we were all acting like it was nothing, like we did this all the time, like we were trained to handle shit like that, but I know damn well that I wasn't trained for anything like that. I've never seen anything like that in my life. And I never thought I would, outside of a movie."

"Me either," Judson said softly.

Pete stood up and began pacing. "People are talking, too, in town. I hear them. At the store, at the gas station, at the restaurants. They know this ain't no normal situation here. People have a good nose for this sort of thing, and they know there's something strange going on. A lot of them are talking about that preacher, that Elias. They say he's making predictions, warning them about what's going to happen." He stopped pacing and stared down the hallway toward the back of the building. The lights were off back there, and the hallway disappeared into blackness. He shivered. "Something is going on here, but I'll be damned if I know what it is."

"I don't know either. And I don't think I want to know." Judson picked up the donut bag and pulled out the last piece of maple bar.

"Aren't you even curious?"

"Sure I'm curious. But I'm not going to do anything about it." He gave Pete a halfhearted smile. "It's not my job."

Pete moved back to his seat and slumped down in the metal chair, his eyes focusing on the blinking lights of the switchboard. "Yeah," he said. He stared at the lights. "Yeah."

NINE

Dr. Waterston tore up the duplicate copies of the test analysis, wadded up the pieces and threw them across the room in disgust. The crumpled paper fell far short of its intended mark against the opposite wall and landed benignly on the middle of the carpet. Waterston picked up the flask of whiskey next to his right elbow and took a long, healthy, medicinal swig.

Nothing. The test results revealed that there was nothing in the Geronimo Wells water. If anything, the water was cleaner, purer, than average. No chemicals, particulates down to almost nothing, only a few traceable minerals.

So what the hell was it?

There had to be some common denominator, something that linked Julie Campbell, Joni Cooper, Susan Stratford and possibly even old Mrs. Perry. But what could it be? The water was out. Chances of it being some type of food were slim to none. Could they have been exposed to hazardous waste being transported through Randall? It was possible. Though it was a much longer route, many trucks preferred to pass through Randall when transporting goods from Phoenix to either Prescott or Flagstaff in order to avoid the weigh and inspection stations on Black Canyon Highway. And who knew what those trucks carried? Who knew what sort of substances they were transporting?

Waterston took another swig from his flask. He realized that he was grasping for straws. If there had been any unfamiliar chemicals in any of the women's bloodstreams they would have shown up on the blood tests. There didn't seem to be anything physiologically wrong with any of the women, with the possible exception of Mrs. Perry. But something obviously *was* wrong. Dreadfully wrong.

He had to admit it: he was baffled.

But at least something good had come out of all this—the chances that something would go wrong with Marina Lewis' pregnancy had been whittled down to almost nothing.

Waterston pulled open his desk drawer and drew out the photographs he had taken of the miscarried babies before the autopsies. On the top of the stack, the half-formed mucilaginous eyes of Julie Campbell's fetus stared blindly up at him. In the next picture, the premature infant's reptilian hands were clenched into permanent fists.

Waterston put the photos down and took another swig of whiskey. He needed courage. He would have to call each of the women and tell them what he had found. Or what he had not found.

He shuffled quickly through the photos, and his eye was caught by the horrible face of Joni Cooper's infant. The smooth bald forehead was wrinkled into a frown, and the toothless mouth was twisted into a hideous grimace. The eyes, pure white, with neither irises nor pupils, bored into his own and caused him to shudder. He dropped the stack of pictures on the desk. It was impossible, but the tiny infant looked angry, furious.

Waterston picked up the phone and started dialing.

*   *   *

Joni Cooper stared into the blackness of the living room, letting the phone ring without picking it up. From the bedroom, Stan called out angrily, "Are you going to get that or what?"

She did not answer him.

"Fuck it, then!"

The phone rang three more times, then stopped. Joni sat unmoving. The drapes in the room were all closed, and the lights were off. She could see nothing. But she stared into the blackness, listening, thinking. She could hear Stan thrashing around in the bedroom, taking his aggression out on whatever inanimate object was closest to hand. They had had another fight tonight, or, rather, another battle in their ongoing fight. She knew she should be upset, but for some reason she just didn't seem to care.

She sat, staring, thinking, and after a while Stan shut off the television. Soon she heard his even, regular breathing—the breathing of sleep—loud in the silent empty house.

A year. It had been almost an entire year since she had lost the baby.

Though she knew there was something wrong with her, she had never gotten over the loss of her baby. It was affecting her still. She thought about it constantly, brooded about it, lamented it. She realized that her preoccupation with the incident was taking its toll on her marriage, her job, her friendships, but there didn't seem to be anything she could do about it. She had no control over the situation. She was losing her grip on everything.

It was stupid, she knew. Women had abortions all the time. It wasn't the end of the world. And she could always have another child. There was nothing physically wrong with either her or Stan. Theoretically, they could have a whole bunch of kids.

But she couldn't let this child go. Stan Jr., she thought. They would have named him Stan Jr.

She even imagined sometimes, in the middle of the night, staring into the darkness, that she could hear the baby crying, crying.

From the bedroom came the sound of something heavy being knocked over. A lamp. She heard the shattering of glass, followed by a loud hard thump. What was Stan doing in there, tearing the place apart? She knew she should get up to investigate, but she couldn't bring herself to move. Instead, she sat still, staring into nothingness, listening.

There was a muffled yelp.

And a baby's cry.

Joni stood up, her heart racing. The sound came again, and she hurried down the hall toward the bedroom. The lamp had been knocked over. The room was dark. The only light was the diffused glow of the bathroom overhead. She peeked into the room. "Stan?" she called softly.

Something small and soft nuzzled against her leg, and she felt a thrill of excited anticipation rush through her. She bent down on one knee and reached forward with both hands. Her fingers touched skin that was cold and slightly slimy. In the half-light, she saw something pinkish press toward her. *Stan Jr.?* She reached for it and instinctively pulled it toward her, cuddling it blindly against her breast.

Searing pain lashed through her as tiny teeth bit down and tiny claws dug in. She tried to push the small creature away from her, but it held tightly onto her breast, ripping open the skin. She fell forward, screaming, feeling the blood spurting from the open wound. Another pair of jaws bit into the exposed skin of her calf.

Her last thought, before the pain obliterated everything, was disjointedly coherent: We're too far from town. No one will hear us die.

TEN

The truck turned from Main Street to Old Mesa Road, cases of Pepsi sliding slightly across the metal floor in the back and bumping gently against the side as Brad pulled the wheel hard, trying to lessen the impact of the curve. The truck straightened out and they headed past the park toward the markets at the north end of town. Suddenly Brad bent forward and stared through the dirty windshield, squinting against the morning sun. "What in fuck's name is that?"

He pulled the truck to a stop in front of the parking lot next to the Valley National Bank building. A crowd of people had gathered in the parking lot and were standing in a tight group, facing the building, those in back pressing close against those in front and craning their necks as though trying to see something. Gordon looked over at Brad. "Why'd you stop? You want to get out and see what it is?"

Brad took off his Pepsi hat, threw it down on the seat next to him and ran a hand through his hair in a rough effort to comb it down. "Don't see something like this every day," he said in answer. "Must be fifty, sixty people out there."

They hopped out of the truck and started walking

across the pavement toward the crowd. They could hear the clear tones of a public orator, loud even without amplification. The crowd pressed forward, listening, trying to catch a glimpse of the speaker.

"Satan preys upon the young because they are WEAK! They do not KNOW they are doing his bidding, they simply do not under-STAND! They are INNOCENT! And innocence is NEITHER good nor evil! It is the absence of BOTH! THIS is why innocence is so easily corruptible, why the innocent so often become the wicked! We must not be innocent OR ignorant if we expect to do battle with Satan! We must be ARMED! Armed with the ammunition of RIGHT! With the Holy Word of God!"

Brad stopped walking before they were even halfway across the parking lot. He listened for a moment to the voice, then laughed loudly. A few heads on the periphery of the crowd turned to look at him. "I thought this was something important," he said. "It's just some preacher trying to drum up business. He's probably planning to have a tent meeting tonight and tell everyone about the evils of sex and drugs and rock and roll." He spit on the asphalt then nodded back toward the truck. "Come on. Let's get going. I don't want to hear this crap, and we have a lot to do today."

Gordon held up his hand. "Wait," he said. He was already walking forward. "I want to see something first."

Though he had been tempted, Gordon had said nothing to Brad about Marina's experience with Brother Elias the other night. He could hear Brad shuffling uninterestedly behind him, the heels of his cowboy boots scraping against the loose gravel on the asphalt. "You've heard enough," Brad said. "Let's go."

Gordon ignored him and moved forward.

"Chaos is Satan's goal! He will stop at nothing less! He intends to unravel ALL of God's work, ALL of man's accomplishments and bring about his OWN world! A world of evil, of blackness, of perpetual night!"

He knew that voice. He had heard it only once, and it had been much quieter, much more subdued, but it had been filled with the same demonic intensity and had been delivered in the same rhythmic cadences. He pushed his way through the crowd, shouldering past old men and young women, stepping over small children in strollers. Until he stood before Brother Elias.

The preacher, wearing the same gray business suit he had worn that day in the hospital, his short hair neatly combed and glistening with some type of application, stood on the small bench in front of the bank, holding a Bible in his right hand as he spoke. Behind him, Gordon could see the faces of the tellers and other bank workers pressed against the tinted glass doors of the building. Brother Elias was pacing, walking back and forth along the rectangular seat of the wooden bench like an animal in its cage. Periodically, he would stop pacing and point his Bible melodramatically at someone in the crowd, his voice rising with fervor. Sunlight glinted off his gold crucifix tie clip.

Brother Elias suddenly crouched low, pointing at a young mother standing next to her infant daughter. He straightened up as he saw Gordon. He stopped speaking, and his black eyes bored into Gordon's. The expression on his face was so fanatic, his look so hard and determined, that Gordon felt the anger which had been building inside him drain away and metamorphose into something like fear.

The crowd was hushed, waiting for the preacher to speak, and Brother Elias' voice was barely above a whisper when he spoke. " 'Humble yourselves therefore under the mighty hand of God, that in due time he may exalt you. Cast all your anxieties on him, for he cares about you. Be sober, be watchful. Your adversary the devil prowls around like a roaring lion, seeking someone to devour. Resist him, firm in your faith, knowing that the same experience of suffering is required of your brotherhood throughout the world.' First Peter 5:6.''

Gordon looked away, avoiding the burning black eyes, not quite sure why his heart was pounding wildly in his chest. From far off, on the other side of town, he heard the familiar whine of a siren. Someone, he realized, someone in the bank, must have called the sheriff. He looked again at Brother Elias and saw that the preacher was staring fixedly at him. The preacher had not yet said another word, and vague questioning murmurs were beginning to ripple through the assembled crowd. Brother Elias slowly lifted his Bible and pointed it toward Gordon. "You and your wife are not without sin. You are sinners in the eyes of the Lord. Yet you have been chosen by the Lord our God."

The siren grew louder then abruptly shut off as the car pulled into the parking lot. Gordon turned to look, along with the rest of the crowd, but he could see nothing. Too many heads were in the way. There was the sound of a car door being slammed.

"Out of the way. Come on, Flo, move aside. I have to get through here." Gordon heard the tired, slightly nasal voice of Carl Chmura as the deputy pushed his way through the crowd. He pressed between an old man and woman and nodded curtly to Gordon as he passed by. Brother Elias remained unmoving on top of his bench, staring at Gordon.

The glass double doors of the bank opened and Delmer Rand, the small weasel-like bank manager, stepped officiously out, followed by three or four curious tellers. "This man has been trespassing, creating a public nuisance and obstructing my business," he told the deputy. "I want him arrested."

Chmura looked at him condescendingly. "Let us decide if there are going to be any charges filed here, all right Del?" He turned to look at the preacher, still standing on the bench, and his expression grew tense. His hand snaked to the butt of his nightstick. "All right, mister," he said. "What's your name?"

"Brother Elias."

At the sound of the name, Chmura stiffened. He looked quickly at Gordon then stepped forward. "I'm afraid you are under arrest, sir. You are going to have to come with me." His hand closed around the nightstick, ready to use it.

Brother Elias nodded agreeably, as if the proposition met with his complete approval, but his eyes lost nothing of their black burning intensity. He stepped down from the bench and held his hands out in front of him, offering the deputy his wrists. "Would you like to handcuff me, officer?"

Chmura shook his head. "That won't be necessary. Just come with me to the car."

The crowd parted to let the two through and immediately began to disperse. Some people followed the deputy and Brother Elias, listening to the deputy read the preacher his rights, but most scattered slowly outward, resuming whatever they had been doing before stopping to listen to the preacher. Gordon looked around for Brad and saw that he was already back in the truck. There was an impatient honk as he saw Gordon walking across the parking lot. He rolled down the window. "Get your ass in gear! We're already behind schedule!"

Gordon desperately wanted to be there when the sheriff questioned Brother Elias. He had some questions he wanted to ask himself. But he knew that he dare not ask Brad for the day off. The deliveries *were* running behind schedule, and though Brad hadn't said anything, Gordon knew he was mad about the time he had already taken off.

He ran the last few feet to the truck and hopped into the cab. Brad had already started the engine, and he put the truck immediately into gear, peeling out. Gordon was thrown back into the seat.

Brad grabbed his hat from the seat next to him and put it on. He looked at Gordon. "So what the hell was all that about?"

Gordon thought for a moment. "Nothing," he said.

ELEVEN

Jim pulled into the parking lot of the sheriff's office and sat in his car for a moment, staring out at the low gray building. The meeting with McFarland had been a waste of time. He had met the state policeman at the cafe for a late breakfast, hoping to get some idea of where the investigation was headed, what leads were being followed up. But McFarland had been closemouthed, saying only that Wilson believed they should concentrate their efforts in the Valley. Jim had tried to tell him about Brother Elias, who seemed to him to be intimately connected with at least the fires, but McFarland, very patronizing, had said that the weirdos came out of the woodwork for something like this.

Jim had left early, furious, intending to call Wilson and give him a piece of his mind. This was supposed to have been a joint investigation, an equal partnership, and these young punks were treating him as if he were some rube who didn't know his ass from his elbow.

He drove around town for a while, radio off, windows open, trying to calm down. When at last he no longer felt like doing physical violence to that state asshole, he headed back toward the office.

Now he sat in the car, staring out the dusty windshield. He resented wasting half his morning talking to McFarland. It was like talking to a brick wall. He wished he had never called in the state police, publicity or no publicity. He didn't see where the staters were helping out a whole hell of a lot anyway.

He got out of the car, pulled up his belt and walked across the parking lot to the office. He nodded at Rita as he walked in. "Where's the posse searching this morning?" he asked.

"They checked in about an hour ago, said they were still in the Aspen Lake–Milk Ranch Point area. There's a lot of ground to cover there."

Milk Ranch Point.

Jim remembered the dream he had had about Milk Ranch Point, Don Wilson taking him on a tour of the small white gravestones, and he shivered, feeling the coldness seep through him.

"I'll be back in my office," he told Rita.

She nodded, pressing a button on the switchboard to answer a call.

Jim started down the hallway, toward the back of the building, when he heard Carl's excited voice behind him. "Sheriff! I've found him!"

Jim turned around to see Carl leading a conservative-looking business-suited man through the front door. The man was moving along voluntarily, not struggling, but there was defiance in his posture, fight in the movement of his muscles. His eyes, unnaturally black, were staring hard into Jim's. Jim noticed a black-bound Bible under the man's arm.

"Brother Elias!" Carl said excitedly. "I got a call about a disturbance at Valley National, and I found him preaching out there!"

"Good," Jim said, keeping his voice calm. "Bring him back to the conference room. I want to talk to him." He led the way down the hall, forcing himself to remain stoically detached though the adrenaline of excitement was coursing through his veins. He used his key to open up the conference room door and flipped on the lights. The fluorescent bars in the ceiling flickered into existence.

Carl led Brother Elias into the room and sat him down on a hard metal folding chair. The preacher looked at the deputy and smiled slightly. His eyes were cold. "Get out of here," said Brother Elias quietly.

Carl looked toward the sheriff.

"He's my deputy. He stays."

"Then I cannot speak." Brother Elias folded his hands on the table in front of him and stared at the bare whiteness of the opposite wall.

Jim looked at the preacher. Brother Elias sat staring with an expression of endless patience on his face. The patience of a true believer. He had seen that expression before—too often before—and he knew there wasn't a damn thing he could do to wipe the infuriating complacency off the man's face. If Brother Elias said he wouldn't talk, he wouldn't talk. The sheriff sighed heavily and motioned for Carl to leave the room. "All right," he said. "We'll have to play it his way for a while. Stay outside. I'll call you."

The deputy glared with hatred at the preacher as he walked out of the room. The door closed behind him, and Jim turned to Brother Elias. "Well," he said. "You've been pretty busy the past week or so, haven't you?"

The preacher turned to look at him, examining his features. "There's a lot of family resemblance," he said finally.

"What?"

"You look an awful lot like your great-grandfather."

Jim stared at the preacher, unsure of how to react. Behind the man's cold black eyes, he could detect an inner insanity. He forced himself to smile benignly. He'd let the preacher determine the course of the conversation. "My great-grandfather?" he said.

"Ezra Weldon," the preacher replied.

Jim's polite smile faded. Ezra Weldon *had* been his great-grandfather's name. But how could Brother Elias know that? He stared into the preacher's unflinching black eyes and felt the first vague stirrings of fear inside him.

"He was a good man, and a good sheriff," the preacher said.

Jim stood in front of Brother Elias. "Who are you?" he demanded. "What the hell are you doing here?"

"I am Brother Elias," the preacher said calmly. "I have come to fight the fight of the good. I have come to repel the wicked and do battle with the forces of evil. For the evil one is here." He looked into the sheriff's eyes. " 'And the adversary also came among them.' Job 1:6."

"How do you know my great-grandfather's name? And how do you know he was a sheriff?"

Brother Elias smiled. "I knew him," he said. "He was with me the last time."

Jim began pacing around the room. The man was obviously crazy. He had gotten ahold of Ezra Weldon's name somehow, and now it happened to come in handy. There was no secret to it, nothing mysterious. Any one of the fifty-odd members of the county historical society could have given him detailed information about the Weldons, the Murphys, the Stones, the Smiths, or any of the other local families who had lived in Randall for several generations.

But why would any of them talk to Brother Elias about Ezra Weldon? Why would Brother Elias ask about Ezra Weldon?

Jim stared defiantly at the preacher. "What do you know about the First Southern Baptist Church?"

"It was consumed by fire."

"And the Catholic church, St. Mary's? And the Presbyterian church?"

"They, too, were burned by the unholy flames of hell."

Jim glared at him. "And didn't you predict that they would burn? Didn't you know they would be set on fire?"

Brother Elias nodded. "All is as it was foretold. I have seen this in a vision of the Lord. The Lord came unto me and told me that here the adversary would be. He told me that first there would be sacrilege, then fire, to the houses of God."

"And you don't know how these fires were started?"

"I know," the preacher said.

"How?" Jim demanded.

"The minions of Satan started these fires. They are preparing for the coming battle against the forces of the Lord."

The sheriff pressed a hand against his forehead. Jesus. How come he always ended up with this kind of crap?

"There will be fires," Brother Elias continued, his voice chanting in a monotonic cadence. "And the lightning will turn red, signifying the coming of the adversary. There will be flies. There will be earthquakes."

Jim opened the door in disgust and motioned for Carl, standing directly opposite the door on the other side of the hall. "Lock him up," he said.

Carl grinned, pleased. "What's the charge?"

"Suspected arson," he said. "Disturbing the peace, harrassment. Have Gordon Lewis' wife come in here later and sign a complaint."

"Will do."

Jim watched as Carl walked into the conference room and escorted the preacher down the hall to one of the holding cells. Part of him wanted to believe that

Brother Elias knew what was going on, but the police training in him was too strong. The man seemed to have really gone off the deep end. He heard Carl slam shut the iron door to one of the holding cells. He had no proof to back up the arson charge, but he refused to admit that McFarland was right, that Brother Elias was just a crazy who had crawled out of a hole and who really knew nothing of what was going on. He wanted to keep him in incarceration for a few days at least, to see if he could discover something. Anything.

He shook his head in frustration and walked down the hall to his office. He slammed the door behind him.

TWELVE

They finished delivering to the town stores an hour earlier than expected, despite the heavy afternoon rain, and Brad decided to call it quits for the day. Tomorrow they were delivering to the outlying areas and they'd be starting early. Gordon declined Brad's offer to stop off for a beer at the Colt and headed home instead. He was half-tempted to drop by the sheriff's office and talk to the sheriff about Brother Elias, but he knew he should drive home first and pick up Marina. She was the one who would have to identify the man and press charges anyway, if there were any charges to be pressed.

The Jeep sped past Char Clifton's 76 station, and Gordon was surprised to see that it was closed. As far as he knew, the station had never closed this early in the day before. Come to think of it, there had been quite a few places in town that had been unexpectedly closed today. He wondered idly if there was a flu going around. *Or something worse?*

He pushed the thought from his mind, concentrating instead on the narrow road curving through the trees. Ahead, through the ravine, he could see the flat-topped outline of the Rim and a curling wisp of smoke coming from somewhere on its top. Lightning from the storm must have hit up there and started a minor forest fire.

A few minutes later, he pulled off on the small dirt road that led to their house. Marina came out of the kitchen as the Jeep rolled to a stop. The air was still slightly chilly from the recent rain, and she walked toward him slowly, avoiding the puddles in the drive, her hands buried deep in her jeans pockets for warmth. She kissed him lightly on the mouth, and he put his arm around her as they walked toward the house. "The sheriff called," she said. "I tried calling the warehouse around lunchtime to let you know, but no one answered. I called Connie, and she said that you and Brad were in town somewhere."

"Did he say what it was about?"

"No. He just said to have you call him back as soon as possible."

Gordon was silent for a moment. "They caught Brother Elias this morning," he said. "I saw it. They found him preaching in front of Valley National."

Marina stopped walking. "Why didn't he tell me?"

Gordon shrugged. "I guess he didn't want to worry you or anything. I don't really know."

"But I'm the one who's going to have to sign the complaint."

"You're right." They walked into the kitchen and Gordon grabbed an apple from the wire fruit basket on the counter next to the sink. "Do you want to go down there?"

Marina shivered, remembering the strange black eyes that had held her spellbound. "I don't know. I don't think I want to see him."

"You don't have to see him to swear out a complaint." Gordon walked out into the living room and headed toward the back of the house. "I have to go to the bathroom. After I'm finished, we'll go."

Marina moved into the living room and stood in

front of the screen door, staring outside. The storm had died, but a new one was brewing on top of the Rim. There was a flash of lightning, and she blinked her eyes, not believing what she had seen.

Gordon put a hand on her shoulder, and she jumped. "Jesus! Don't scare me like that."

He grinned. "Sorry."

She pointed toward the top of the Rim. "Look up there," she said. "Watch that lightning."

Gordon followed her finger. "I don't see anything."

"Just keep watching."

He stood there for a moment, staring. "That's weird," he said finally. "It's red."

Gordon was right. Marina did not have to see Brother Elias to sign a complaint. She simply filled out the form the sheriff gave her and signed her name at the bottom. Jim looked over the form and nodded. "Fine," he said. He handed it to Rita for processing.

Although Marina had not mentioned the kitten, she was somewhat cold to the sheriff, and Gordon was happy when the complaint had been signed and it was time for them to leave. It had been a somewhat awkward situation. They were about to step out the door, when he heard the sheriff loudly clear his throat behind them. He turned around.

"Could I speak to you for a moment?" Jim asked. "In private?"

Gordon looked at Marina. "I'll wait in the car," she said flatly. She walked out the door without even glancing at the sheriff.

Jim smiled. "Still mad at me, huh?"

"Well, you know—"

"Happens all the time," the sheriff said, waving his hand dismissively. "Don't worry about it." He opened the small gate next to the front desk and motioned for Gordon to follow him back to his office.

"What is it?" Gordon asked when they were alone.

"It's Brother Elias. Tell me what you think of him."

Gordon shrugged. "I don't know. I only met him that one time. I thought he was crazy. Marina thinks he's crazy."

"He didn't . . . scare you?"

Gordon looked at the sheriff. "What are you getting at?"

Jim chewed on his upper lip for a moment, thinking. "Okay," he said. "I don't want you to breathe a word of this to anyone."

"You know I won't."

"He's been around town here for a couple days now, preaching." He paused. "Predicting. He predicted those church fires, and he said he didn't have anything to do with them starting, and I believe him."

Gordon remained silent.

"And he talked about my great-grandfather as if he knew him. I've been thinking about this all day, going over it in my head, and I don't see how he could know anything about my great-grandfather. Not realistically." He looked at Gordon. "To be honest, he scares the shit out of me. I've gone back there a couple of times today, to check on him, and each time I do he's always staring at me, waiting for me, as if he knows when I'm coming. It gives me the creeps. There's no logical connection other than the fires, but I think he's involved in all this. It's nothing that'll hold up in court, but . . ." He trailed off. "I think I'm going to ask Father Andrews to come here and look at him, see what he thinks."

"What other predictions has he made?" Gordon asked.

The sheriff shook his head. "I don't know. Something about flies, an earthquake, different colored lightning—"

"Red?" Gordon asked.

The sheriff nodded, looking at him. "Yes."

"Look outside," Gordon said. He found that his hands were trembling.

Jim moved over to the window, glancing out at the town. His eye was captured by the building storm on the Rim. He saw a flash of red lightning, and he paled. He turned back to Gordon. "How long has this been going on?"

"I don't know. We just noticed it about a half hour ago."

"Do you think it's some type of legitimate weather disturbance? I mean, do you think he could have known about it ahead of time?"

Gordon shook his head. "I don't know."

The two men stared at each other. "Do you want to see him?" the sheriff asked finally.

"Not now," Gordon said. "Right now I just want to take Marina home and forget about this whole damn thing."

Jim nodded, understanding. "But what if we have an earthquake in the middle of the night?" he said softly.

"Then I'll hold her even closer. And I'll wait for it to go away."

"But we can't just ignore it. We can't pretend there's nothing going on."

"What else can we do?"

"I'm going to call Father Andrews," Jim said. "He's dealt with this kind of stuff before. We'll see what he has to say about all this. Maybe he can make some sense out of what Brother Elias is saying."

"Are you still having nightmares?" Gordon asked.

The sheriff nodded. "Of course. You?"

"Yes. I had a hell of a one last night."

"What was it about?"

"I was at the dump, then I was at this place with little white crosses and there was a boy—"

"Jesus," Jim said. He sat down hard on his chair. "I had the same dream." He stared at Gordon. "You take your wife home," he said. "Then you get back here. I'll call Father Andrews. We're going to talk to Brother Elias."

Gordon nodded silently.

The sheriff looked at his watch. "It's four right now. Be back here at five-thirty. We're going to get to the bottom of this."

"Are you sure we want to?" Gordon asked.

"We have no choice."

Gordon left the sheriff in his office and walked back toward the front of the building. He nodded politely to Rita as he passed by, then moved through the double glass doors. As he walked across the parking lot toward the car, he couldn't help glancing at the storm on top of the Rim.

The red lightning was flashing much more often now. And was getting much stronger.

THIRTEEN

The day's storm hit earlier than usual, just after twelve, and Father Andrews found himself staring outside for most of the afternoon at the torrents that fell from the gray-black sky, trying to gauge the damage being done to his recently planted seedlings. He stared, almost hypnotized, as the rain fell in never-repeating patterns on the concrete floor of the open patio.

Another of God's small miracles.

He turned away from the window and was surprised by the darkness of the house. He walked across the kitchen and switched on the light. The light illuminated the kitchen but sent the rest of the house and the world outside into further darkness. He found himself, against his will, listening for noises from the back of the house, from Father Selway's study. But there was nothing.

He put on some water for tea and sat down at the kitchen table. He picked up the Episcopal Concordance where he had left it. Several of the pages were marked with small bits of paper. Next to the concordance, on the table, was a list he had written. A list of everything the sheriff and Gordon had told him, as well as what he had learned on his own. Most of the things he had written, he knew, would not be found in the Bible. But he hoped to somehow link together what elements he could, to discover some meaning in the emerging patterns.

He had begun by reading all relevant passages relating to Satan or the devil. Though he had studied all such passages thoroughly in the seminary and knew most of them by heart, he felt it important to double check. Just as he had thought, the passages concentrated on Satan's acts rather than on descriptions of the fallen angel. The only description he could find— and that one an analogy—had been in Revelation. Satan here was described as a dragon and a serpent. Not the traditional cloven-hoofed devil he had been searching for. He had underlined the passage anyway, marking it with a scrap of paper, and had moved on to accounts of dreams and visions, but dreams and visions were so prevalent in the Bible that he had barely begun to scratch the surface before he had had to quit for the evening.

Now, he picked up the concordance and leafed through it. He happened upon the description of Satan in Revelation and reread the blue underlined verse. His eye moved back to the beginning of the chapter: "And a great portent appeared in heaven, a woman clothed with the sun, with the moon under her feet, and on her head a crown of twelve stars; she was with child and she cried out in her pangs of birth, in anguish for delivery. And another portent appeared in heaven; behold, a great red dragon, with seven heads and ten horns, and seven diadems upon his heads. His tail swept down a third of the stars of heaven, and cast them to the earth. And the dragon stood before the woman who was about to bear a child, that he might devour her child when she brought it forth."

Father Andrews shivered and put down the book. He knew that the woman was Mary, her son Jesus

Christ and the dragon Satan, and he knew the traditional explanation of the symbols, but there was something about the passage that spoke to him, that somehow had a bearing on the disjointed thoughts whirling around in his head. He had no alternative interpretation of the passage, but he had a gut feeling—*premonition? insight?*—that it related to the situation in Randall.

The situation in Randall. It was amazing how quickly he had come to believe that there *was* a "situation" in Randall, that there was something going on which could not be explained away by logic or any of the other placebos of rationality. Something was happening that encompassed all of the recent bizarre occurrences. Something so big that the obvious crimes comprised only a small part of its totality. Something entirely unseen and possibly incomprehensible.

Father Andrews knew that such a line of thinking could not be supported by an objective look at the available facts. But what the mind could *deduce* and what the mind actually *thought* were often two different things. And he had always been one to trust his feelings and instincts rather than his rational mind. What he felt and what he sensed were always more important than what he thought. Although a similar leap of faith, a similar trust of feeling rather than fact, was required of anyone practicing a religion, he knew that the bishop would frown upon such a practice from one of his priests. Particularly in regard to an ostensibly secular matter. He smiled as he thought of Jim Weldon's description of the bishop. The sheriff had dismissed him with one short blunt word: "Prick." He wouldn't go quite so far, but he knew that he and Bishop Sinclair did not see eye to eye on many matters. Unfortunately. He needed someone to talk to on this matter, someone with more experience, someone he could trust.

The sheriff. The phone. These thoughts, neither

words nor images, forced themselves upon his consciousness, separate but connected. In the split second after his brain received and acknowledged the thoughts, the phone rang, and he knew immediately that it would be the sheriff. He picked up the receiver. "Hello?"

"Hello, Father? It's me, Jim."

The priest felt an icy finger of fear shiver down his back. "I know," he said. "I knew you were going to call before the phone rang."

The sheriff sounded surprised. "Really?"

"Just a routine psychic experience." He tried to make his tone light. "So why did you call, Sheriff? What can I help you with?"

"Actually, it's along those lines."

"What lines?"

"Psychic lines." The sheriff's voice lost its open, friendly tone. It was now very serious, and Father Andrews thought he could detect a slight note of fear in it. "We have someone here, in custody. He's a street-corner preacher. We found him preaching in front of the Valley National this morning. A few nights ago, he was out at Gordon's house, scaring the heebie-jeebies out of Gordon's wife."

"Brother Elias," the priest said.

The sheriff was silent for a moment. "You know him?" he said finally.

"No. But I know of him. I've heard a lot of things about him the past couple days."

"You're going to be hearing a lot more about him. I want you to come down to the station right now. I think you should hear what he has to say."

"What's this about?"

"I'd rather not tell you over the phone," the sheriff said hesitantly.

He's scared, Father Andrews thought. The sheriff is scared. "Okay," he said aloud. "I'll be right over." He told the sheriff good-bye and hung up the phone.

He sat unmoving for a few moments, staring at the black receiver, feeling the cold seep into his bones. He had a sudden premonition of death, of destruction.

Outside, the rain had abated somewhat, the torrential downpour of the early afternoon tapering off to a constant drizzle. The sound of thunder rolled down from the top of the Rim. Father Andrews ran across the yard to his car. He had not brought a raincoat with him to Randall because he had not anticipated the monsoons. It seldom rained in Phoenix during the summer. He hopped in the car and started it up, turning on the windshield wipers. The driver's wiper worked all right, but the passenger blade flopped around with each sweep across the windshield.

He pulled out of the driveway, driving slow, trying to see through the small curved rectangle of clearness created by the single wiper blade. The road curved next to the river, now brown and muddy because of the rain, and crossed the water on the east side of the sawmill. Through the windshield he.could see the billowing smoke of the smelter, fighting bravely against the rain. There was a sharp flash of red, and he braked to a stop.

What was that?

The flash came again, a crimson light that flashed over everything and turned even the trees a blood red.

Lightning. It was lightning, and Father Andrews stared out his windshield in wonder. He had never seen red lightning before. There was another flash. And another. And another.

He took his foot off the brake and started moving again. There was something strange about the colored lightning, something he didn't quite like, something that disturbed him. But he concentrated on the road, not letting his mind dwell on the extraordinarily loud thunder or the lightning flashes that were now almost constant.

He turned right on Main and headed for the sheriff's office. He parked the car as close as possible to the door and dashed through the open entryway. He stomped the water off his feet and wiped his shoes on the entrance mat, shaking the rain from his hair. He smiled at the pretty receptionist staring at him. "I hate this weather," he said.

The receptionist smiled back. "We like it around here. The monsoons make things a lot easier for us." She stood up and moved to the counter next to him. "May I help you?"

"I'm supposed to see Sheriff Weldon. My name's Donald Andrews."

"Father Andrews! The sheriff's been expecting you. Come with me." She pushed through the swinging gate that separated the back of the counter from the front and led the way down a wide corridor. "They're in the conference room." She stopped in front of a door and pushed it open, sticking her head in the room. "Father Andrews is here," she announced. She held the door open to let him in.

The sheriff stood up from a chair, offering his hand. "I'm glad you're here, Father."

Father Andrews shook his hand, but his attention was focused on the business-suited man sitting on the other side of the table in the center of the room. Brother Elias. He walked forward slowly, looking into the preacher's face. Brother Elias' eyes, the pupils glaringly black, stared back unflinchingly.

The sheriff worked his way around the table and sat next to the preacher. He motioned for Andrews to sit down as well. The priest pulled out a chair opposite the sheriff and sat. He pushed his chair closer to the table. From this vantage point, he could see that Brother Elias' tie clip was a small gold crucifix. His cufflinks were also in the shape of crosses.

The sheriff took off his hat and placed it on the table in front of him. He cleared his throat loudly and nodded toward Father Andrews. "You said you'd heard about Brother Elias," he said. "What exactly have you heard?"

Father Andrews looked at the preacher. He felt awkward talking about him in the third person, as if he weren't there. "Not much," he admitted. "Rumors."

"Like what?"

"Some of my congregation members have been talking about him. They said he's been preaching around town, making predictions—"

"The predictions," Jim said, nodding. "Have you heard those predictions?"

Father Andrews shook his head.

"He predicted that churches would be burned," the sheriff said, his voice low. "And they were burned. He predicted there would be red lightning. And there is red lightning." He paused. "And he predicted there would be an earthquake."

"And flies," Brother Elias added, smiling slightly.

"And flies," Jim agreed. He stared at Father Andrews. "What do you make of this?"

The priest shook his head. "I don't know yet. What should I make of it?"

"Talk to him," Jim said. "See if you can make any sense out of what he says."

The priest turned to Brother Elias. "Why are these predictions coming true?" he asked.

"The adversary is among us," the preacher said. "The evil one is here."

Father Andrews leaned forward. "What do you mean the adversary is among us? Do you mean that Satan is here? Actually, physically, here?"

"Satan is here," Brother Elias said. "And he is recruiting disciples to help him accomplish his work."

"But where is here? Do you mean here on earth? Or do you mean Randall specifically?"

Brother Elias' black eyes bored into those of the priest. "He is here," he said, hitting the table with his forefinger to punctuate his words. "Here in this town. He is recruiting disciples in preparation for the coming battle with the forces of the Lord. This is to be the battleground."

Jim stood up, running a tired hand through his hair. "What makes you think he's here?" he asked. "Churches in Phoenix have been desecrated, too. How do you know he's not down there?"

"He is here."

"Why?"

"Who knows why Satan does what he does, why he goes where he goes? It is enough to know that he is here among us, that he is gathering together his army in preparation for the final battle, the battle that was foretold—"

"Look," Jim said loudly. "I've had just about enough of this crap." He glanced toward Father Andrews. "I'm not sure I believe all this end-of-the-world shit he's spouting, but it seems pretty obvious to me that he's involved in all this. I don't know how. Maybe he's crazy, and maybe I'm crazy too, but I think he knows what's going on here. What do you think?"

The priest nodded.

"All right, then. Now what I want is specifics. What, where, and when. Don't give me this vague crap about visions and prophecies."

Brother Elias smiled. "You are just like Ezra," he said. "Just like your great-grandfather."

Jim looked exasperatedly at Father Andrews for help. "You try to talk to him, Father." He began pacing around the room. "Jesus fuck." He glanced quickly and shamefacedly at the priest. "Sorry."

Andrews smiled, shaking his head, signifying that no apology was necessary. He turned his attention back to the preacher, seated across the table from him. There is something wrong with this man, he thought, something basically and fundamentally wrong. Something inhuman. He stared into the preacher's calm face and felt the fear rise within him. He could sense, beneath the surface calm, an inner twistedness. Outwardly, Brother Elias' suit was neatly pressed, his hair combed to perfection, his. . . . Andrews bent forward, squinting, not believing what he was seeing.

On Brother Elias' earlobe was a small cross. It had been tattooed on. He looked closer. No, not tattooed. Carved. The cross had been carved into his flesh. Andrews looked at the preacher's other ear. The skin here, too, had been savagely marked with the carving of a crucifix.

The door to the conference room opened, and Rita let Gordon in. He stood by the doorway for a moment, taking everything in, unsure of what to do.

"Sit down," the sheriff told him. "We're just getting started."

Gordon nodded politely to Father Andrews, but his attention was focused on Brother Elias. The preacher, likewise, was staring at Gordon. "I was wondering when you would arrive," he said.

"Let's get back to the questions," the sheriff said. "What exactly is Satan doing here in Randall?"

Gordon looked up at the sheriff, but he knew enough not to interrupt or ask any questions. He would just follow along with the conversation and ask questions afterward, if he had to.

Brother Elias continued to stare at Gordon. "He is recruiting disciples for the coming battle—"

"How is he recruiting them?" the sheriff demanded. "Who is he recruiting? And where is he getting them? From the prisons? From the bars? From the people who don't go to church or don't believe in God?"

Brother Elias stared at him as though he had just said something profoundly stupid. "Where is he getting them? He is getting them from the womb. He is gathering to him the babies."

The babies.

Gordon looked at the suddenly pale faces of the

sheriff and Father Andrews, knowing that his face
must appear even more shocked and scared. He tried
to lick his dry lips, but the saliva had fled his mouth.

Brother Elias picked up a black-bound Bible from
the floor next to his chair and opened it to a marked
page. "Revelation 20:14," he said, and his voice was
filled with calm authority. " 'Then Death and Hades
were thrown into the lake of fire. This is the second
death, the lake of fire; and if any one's name was not
found written in the book of life, he was thrown into
the lake of fire." ' He looked up and repeated the last
portion of the verse in a softer voice. " 'And if any
one's name was not found written in the book of life,
he was thrown into the lake of fire.' "

There was silence after the preacher had finished
speaking.

Brother Elias closed the Bible and put it back on
the floor next to his chair. "The lake of fire is hell,"
he said. "And those who are not written into the book
of life, those who are not born, those who are aborted
or miscarried or stillborn, are cast into the lake of fire
to become the disciples of Satan. These unborn infants
are blank slates, neither good nor bad, but Satan cap-
tures them in his web, forcing them to do his evil
work, converting them to his evil purpose."

Father Andrews shook his head. "You're wrong,"
he said. "You don't know what you're talking about.
The lake of fire is not hell, and the book of life is not
life. Any seminary student could tell you—"

"Go not by the interpretations of the past," Brother
Elias said. "For they are incorrect."

"You have no idea what—"

"The Lord," Brother Elias said calmly, "has spoken
to me in a divine vision. He has shown me what must
be done." He looked from Gordon to Andrews to the
sheriff. "And you are to help me."

"Why do you need us at all?" Andrews asked.

"You obviously know what needs to be done and how to do it, why don't you just do it on your own?"

"The adversary is crafty. He is a liar and the father of lies, and he can call forth his minions to aid him. He will do everything in his power to stop me from doing my duty."

Jim sat down heavily in the chair next to Brother Elias. He thought for a moment, then sighed. "I don't know what to believe," he admitted. He looked at the preacher. "I believe you know what's going on here, but I'm not sure you're telling us the truth. Or all of the truth. I need more proof. I need proof before I can act on any of this. I can't just take your word for it all."

Brother Elias fingered the gold cross of his tie clip. His black eyes were bright and alive. "By tomorrow, you will have your proof," he said. "If you wait any longer than that, it will be too late."

FOURTEEN

Tim McDowell, armed only with a flashlight and a kid's walkie-talkie, walked for the thirteenth time that day across the water-cut path that dissected the ravine at the north end of Aspen Lake. A low drizzle had started several hours ago, burgeoning into a full-fledged storm, and most of the searchers had since gone home for the day. A few others were waiting out the monsoon in their cars, parked along the dirt road next to the lake, staring out their windshields at the flashes of alternately red and blue lightning, perplexed. Only he and Mac Buxton and Ralph Daniels were still trudging around and actively looking. He knew that the odds were against finding anything, particularly in this ravine, which had been covered more than any area save the campground itself, but he was determined not to give up the search until he found out about Matt. One way or the other.

Several of the other searchers had tried to hint gently that it was possible the boys were dead, and he knew, intellectually, that they were probably right, but emotionally he felt otherwise. He had a feeling, a gut feeling, that Matt was alive, only lost or hurt.

"Matt!" he called. "Matt!"

No answer.

His voice was getting hoarse, and his arms and legs were aching, but he didn't care. He pulled a wad of chaw from his Skoal can and put it between his cheek and gum. The tobacco tasted good. He spit, wiping the excess off his beard. He took off his CAT hat and squeezed some of the water out of it before putting it back on.

The walkie-talkie crackled, and he held it up immediately next to his ear, but it was only another false alarm. He put the walkie-talkie down and looked back toward the lake. Through the natural green of the ponderosas he could see the red and blue metal of pickup cabs. Ron Harrison and Joe Fisk were in one of those trucks. Drunk, probably. He spit in disgust. How could they sit there when their kids were still missing? What kind of fathers were they?

"Shitty," he answered himself. He looked around, walking forward, trying to spot a shirt, a shoe, something. "Matt!" he called.

The walkie-talkie crackled. He held it up to his ear.

"Tim. I've found something."

His heart stopped. His lips were dry in spite of the rain. He held down the "talk" button with his finger and took a big gulp of air. "Is it . . . Matt?"

"You . . . have to come here." Ralph's voice sounded strange.

"What's wrong?" He was scared. "What is it?"

"You have to come here. You too, Mac."

"Where are you?" Mac's voice sounded faint, far away.

"I'm behind the hill on the west side, probably straight across from the campsite."

Tim was already running. His feet sank in the mud and he tripped over an occasional rock or branch, but he was moving too fast for it to slow down his momentum. He found a deer trail leading up the side of the ravine, and he sprinted up the path. Branches whipped

against his face. He was breathing heavily, both because of the exertion and the panic, but he forced
himself to keep moving, despite the pain in his chest.

He topped the hill and saw, down below, the red
flash of Ralph's jacket through the trees. From somewhere off to the side of him, Mac was yelling loudly
for the rest of the search party to follow him. Tim
listened, as he ran, for the telltale sound of slamming
truck doors, but he heard nothing. The other searchers, sitting in their vehicles, probably with the windows
up, could not hear Mac over the rain. The walkie-
talkie crackled, and Mac's harried voice came through
clearly. "I'm going to get everyone else. Hold on, we'll
be right there."

Tim slipped in the mud and slid down the last
twenty or thirty feet of the hill. He scrambled to his
feet and ran over to where Ralph stood looking into
the darkly clouded sky and breathing deeply. "What
is it?" he demanded, grabbing Ralph's shoulder.
"What did you find?"

Ralph looked at him, the rain dripping down his
face looking almost like tears. He said nothing but
pointed off to the right. Tim's gaze followed his finger,
but he could see nothing at first. There was only a
dead half-rotted log, a copse of small saplings, some
ferns, and . . .

Tim walked slowly forward, his heart thudding pro-
pulsively in his chest, feeling as though it would pound
a hole through both his ribcage and his skin. On some
of the light green ferns he could see trails of watery
pink. He moved closer. Now there was a definite form
lying in the midst of the ferns. A form wearing a T-
shirt and jeans.

Matt?

"Ohmygod ohmygod ohmygod . . ." He realized he
was babbling, but he did nothing to stop himself. He
didn't care. This close, he could see that the pink trails
on the ferns had been formed by splattered blood wa-

tered down with rain. Darker blood had seeped into the mulchlike groundcover, and other, lower, sheltered plants were speckled with various hues of red. He bent next to the body, falling to one knee, praying, pleading wildly in his mind, *Don't let it be Matt, please don't let it be Matt,* as he tentatively touched the form.

The T-shirt gave under the pressure of his prodding finger and collapsed inwardly. There was nothing there. There was no back to the figure. He pushed his finger forward again and felt squishiness. Squishiness and bone. The dirty whiteness of the T-shirt began to disappear under a creeping soaking red.

The hair was blond, he noticed suddenly. Matt had black hair.

He dared not turn the body over, so he shifted his position, moving in front of it.

He closed his eyes immediately.

The figure's face had been eaten away. Ragged clumps of bitten, gnawed flesh hung in tattered patterns from an almost visible skull. An eye lolled limply on a torn optic nerve. Red-stained teeth grinned in a dead idiot's smile.

He stood up, opening his eyes only when he was once again on his feet. He stared into the sky, trying to blot the horrible image from his mind, trying to cleanse his senses of the sight. Even in the rain, he could smell the thick, heavy, disgusting odor of blood. Taking a deep breath, he looked down again, checking out the rest of the body. Hands and feet were all gone. Although the backs of the jeans and T-shirt had been untouched, the fronts were ripped to shreds. All that was left of the body was a bare outline, a hollow shell.

He stepped back over the body and stopped before Ralph. He swallowed audibly. "Where are the rest of them?" he asked.

Ralph looked at him, his face pale. "I don't know. I didn't want to look."

There was the sound of voices and cracking twigs

and branches as Mac led the rest of the searchers over the hill. Tim looked up, watching the others make their descent. Half of him wanted to search immediately for Matt's body, but the other half wanted to wait until other men could help him search, afraid of what he might find. He was sure Matt was dead after seeing that other body, but he dreaded the confirmation and wanted to put it off as long as possible.

One of the men on the hill stumbled and went down, slipping in the wet mud. Tim heard a disgusted "Jesus Christ!" and then, seconds later, a panicked "No! Please, God, no!"

"Ja-a-a-ack!" Ron Harrison's cry of animal torment cut through the whispered hissing of the rain and the mumbles of the other men like a knife through Jell-O. Jack. They had found the body of Jack Harrison. Tim glanced instinctively back at the body couched in the ferns. That must be Wayne, then. Wayne Fisk.

But where was Matt?

He looked at Ralph and their eyes met. They did not have to climb up the hill to know what the other searchers had found. Neither of them said anything, but both moved in opposite directions, their eyes on the ground, searching for the last body. Matt's body.

Tim's muscles hurt, not from exhaustion but from tension. The muscles in his arms and legs were knotted with fear and anxiety, and he could feel his neck cords straining. His teeth were clenched against whatever he might find. He stared at the ground, moving slowly, looking behind every fern, every shrub, every fallen tree for any sign of blood or clothing. His shoe hit against a rock, almost tripping him, and he stopped to catch his balance, looking up.

Ahead, lying against a tree trunk, almost hidden by underbrush, he could see the bloody, pulpy remains of what had once been a body. The body of his son.

He ran forward, screaming as he did so, hearing his cries echoed by Ralph and taken up by the men on the hill. He reached the tree and stopped, looking down, his arms dangling uselessly at his sides. He didn't know what to do. Some part of him, some primal fathering part of him, felt the need to cry and grieve and hug his son's dead body. But there was no body to hug. What remained of Matt was a broken and twisted lump of bloody, almost gelatinous, flesh. There was no sign of head or hands or feet or anything recognizable. It looked as though his body had been torn apart, then turned inside out, then completely restructured. Only a tiny scrap of cloth remained of his clothing, and it was glued by blood to the tree trunk.

Tim looked away, staring down at his feet instead. He wanted to cry, but he could not. He was too horrified. For some reason, he could not conjure up Matt's image in his brain. When he tried to picture his son, only the bloody lump of flesh came to mind. He tried to force his brain to concentrate on Matt's good points, to remember the times they had had together, to somehow recover those moments that had been lost and would open the floodgates to his grief, but his senses were too shocked, his mind too numb.

From far off, behind him, he heard someone gagging, then retching.

His eye caught on a small footprint next to his foot. He stared at it. What the hell could it be? It looked almost like a baby's footprint. He looked closer, and saw that there were many such footprints in the open mud around the tree. Quite a few of the footprints had been either obscured or obliterated by the constant rainfall, but the deeper ones had remained and stood out sharply.

Ralph walked up behind him and clapped a sympathetic hand on his shoulder. "Sorry," he said. His voice was filled with genuine hurt, genuine understanding. He glanced toward Matt's body and looked instantly away.

Tim touched his arm and pointed at the footprints. "Look at that," he said.

There was a rustling movement in the ferns off to the right. Both men watched as something small scurried away from them, pushing ferns and grasses aside as it moved. Around them, other rustling noises sounded.

Tim felt an instinctual fear supersede his pain and disgust. The rain became suddenly heavier, its loudness drowning out the rustling noises in the underbrush. He turned to Ralph. "What do you think it is?" he asked.

Something grabbed his legs from behind and jerked, sending him sprawling. In the split second before his eyes were clawed out, he saw Ralph fall as well. Small creatures, creatures brown with mud, were hanging onto Ralph's legs and pulling him down. Others were darting out from under the ferns, babbling and cackling in some high-pitched alien tongue.

Then his eyes were gone and he was fighting blindly against his unseen attackers. His hands found flesh, soft flesh, and punched, grabbed, squeezed. Others were upon him now, small claws ripping and tearing, small mouths biting. He screamed in agony as he felt his legs being torn apart, the pain shooting up through his spinal cord and bolting through his brain in one shock-inducing instant.

Where were the other searchers? Couldn't they see what was happening?

The last thing he heard, before he lost consciousness for the last time, was the sound of other men screaming.

FIFTEEN

The rain had abated and the lightning had stopped while Gordon had been in the sheriff's office, but there was still a light mist in the air and the sky was darkly overcast. He pulled out of the parking lot and onto Main. Ahead of him, above the road, across a telephone line, two raincoated workers were stringing a large banner. He slowed down. Through the wet windshield he could read the purple words written on the white cloth: "Thirtieth Annual Randall Rodeo Sept. 1, 2, 3."

The rodeo. He had forgotten that it was coming up. He and Marina had been planning to go this year. Gordon stared at the two men wrestling with the banner, both standing on the top rungs of twin tall ladders, as he passed between them. He wondered how many other people had forgotten about the rodeo this year.

The whole town's on edge, the sheriff had told him before he'd left.

Gordon passed the Valley National Bank building, now closed, and sped up as he passed the Circle K. By the time he hit the ravine on the other side of Gray's Meadow, he was doing well over sixty. He

knew for a fact that the sheriff wasn't hiding behind
bushes trying to catch speeders, and he had a feeling
that handing out tickets wasn't high on his deputies'
list of priorities right now either. Rounding a curve,
he swerved to miss a small boulder that had fallen
from the adjacent cliff onto the road during the storm.

"Shit," he said, turning the wheel sharply. He
slowed down. He didn't want to kill himself.

By the time he pulled off on the small dirt road
that led to their house, it was almost dark. He could
see the warm comforting yellow lights of home
through the irregularly spaced black shadows of the
trees. He pulled to a stop and Marina, peeking out of
the living room window, unlocked the front door. She
met him on the porch. "So what happened?" she
asked.

He looked down at her big brown eyes and put a
hand protectively over her stomach. He wasn't sure
he should tell her. Well, he *should* tell her, but he
wasn't sure he wanted to. He didn't want to worry her
unnecessarily. Though he didn't know if he believed
everything Brother Elias had said, both the preacher
and his theory scared the living hell out of him.

"Nothing," he said.

She looked up at him, forcing him to meet her eyes.
"You're lying. I can tell. What happened?"

"Nothing," he said.

"Bullshit."

Gordon smiled. "I never could fool you, could I?"
He kissed her, but she pushed him away.

"Don't try to change the subject," she said.

Gordon assumed a look of unhappy resignation.
"The sheriff doesn't think we have much of a case
against Brother Elias," he lied. "He might do thirty
days at the most, then walk." He met her eyes, feeling
like a prick for not leveling with her, for not even
being honest about his real reason for meeting with
the sheriff.

Marina was outraged. "The man's crazy!" she exclaimed. "What does he have to do, kill me before he can be put away?" She shook her head in disbelief. "Jesus, I used to think the conservatives were idiots when they said our judicial system's gone to hell."

"I know," Gordon said sympathetically.

"That Weldon's an incompetent jerk. God, I hate that man."

Gordon said nothing. He held her close, kneading the muscles in her shoulders until he felt some of the tension drain out of them.

Marina pulled away from him. "Come on," she said. "Let's eat. Dinner's been ready for a while now. I thought you'd be home sooner." She led the way into the house. "You'd better enjoy these home-cooked meals while you can, you know. School's starting in a few weeks, and you're going to have to start helping around here again."

He followed her into the kitchen and sat down at the table while she pulled a casserole from the oven. She turned the oven off and used a spatula to dish out two equal portions of the casserole. "I don't know how that man ever rose past patrolman," she said, grabbing two wine glasses from the cupboard. "He doesn't know what the hell he's doing."

"Oh, he's all right," Gordon said halfheartedly.

She sat down at the table next to him. "How did you two get to be such bosom buddies? Our cat gets torn apart in our own kitchen, and he sits on his butt all day and does nothing."

"He caught Brother Elias," Gordon pointed out.

"And now he's going to let him go." She looked at Gordon. "You know, they say that reporters who cover the police beat become more like cops than reporters if they stay there too long."

He made a face at her. "Very funny."

"Oh. I almost forgot." She stood up and opened

the refrigerator, bringing out a tray of sliced carrots and cucumbers.

Gordon looked down at the tray and grinned. "Phallic vegetables," he said. "Are you trying to tell me something?"

She picked up a carrot stick and slipped it suggestively between her lips, letting her tongue flick lightly across the tip. "After dinner," she promised.

They ate quickly and washed the dishes together. Gordon turned off the lights in the kitchen, and they headed back toward the bedroom, hand in hand. Marina pulled down the bedspread and slipped off her T-shirt. She was wearing no bra. She pulled down her pants.

Gordon had taken off his shoes and was unbuckling his pants when he stopped for a moment, listening. He looked over at Marina, who was already naked and under the covers. "What's that?" he said.

"What?"

He held up a hand. "Listen."

Marina remained unmoving, her head cocked, listening. From far off, she thought she heard a low buzzing. "That?" she said. "That buzzing noise?"

Gordon nodded. "It sounds like it's coming from outside."

"It's probably just electricity in the wires. Or bugs or something."

Flies.

He stood up, buttoning his pants. "Stay here," he said. "I'm just going out to check for a moment." He walked slowly toward the front of the house, switching on lights as he did so. Nothing. There was nothing there. He stopped in the middle of the living room, listening. The buzzing was louder now, and it was definitely coming from outside.

Slowly, afraid of what he might find but knowing he had to look, he pulled aside the front drape and pressed his face against the glass.

Flies were all over the Jeep. A swath of blackness ran up from the vehicle's gray hood to the windshield. Even from this far away, he could see that the flies were not still. They were moving, swarming over one another, and in the dim light shining from the windows of the house, the Jeep looked almost alive.

Gordon dropped the drapes, terrified and repulsed, and he closed his eyes, trying to blot out the vision. But he could still see the flies in his mind, and he could still hear their maddening drone.

He walked back to the bedroom, forcing himself to appear calm though his heart felt ready to burst through his chest. He tried to smile at Marina, hoping his face gave nothing away. She was sitting up in bed, leaning back against the headboard, the blanket folded over her lap, her breasts exposed. For one horrifying second, he imagined her covered with flies.

"What is it?" she asked, frowning. "You look pale. Do you feel all right?"

"I'm fine," he said, crawling into bed. "Fine." He hugged her tightly and closed his eyes, hoping that none of them would get into the house.

SIXTEEN

After taking Brother Elias back to the holding cell and saying goodbye to Gordon and Father Andrews, Jim returned to his office. He sat for a moment, staring down at the pile of papers on his desk, then opened the bottom desk drawer and drew out the telephone directory. He found the number of the county historical society and dialed.

Millie Thomas answered the phone. "Hello?"

"Hello, Millie? This is Jim Weldon."

The old lady's voice instantly brightened. "Jim! How are you? I haven't heard from you in a while."

He smiled at her enthusiasm. "I'm fine, Millie. How are things going with you?"

"Great," she said. "Great. As you know, we've been trying to put together this book on the history of Randall for the past year, and we're supposed to get it to the printer next week. That's why I'm here so late. I'm rechecking everything to make sure we haven't forgotten something."

Jim saw his opening. "Is there anything in there about Milk Ranch Point?" he asked casually.

"Why do you ask?"

"Oh, I was just thinking of those stories we used to tell when we were kids."

Millie laughed. "Those ghost stories? Those were old when your mother and father and I were children. And I suppose the kids today are still telling them."

Jim tried to keep his tone light. "Did you mention any of those stories in your book?"

"Actually, we did." Millie's voice grew excited, the voice of a historian in love with her subject. "Like most stories that are passed from generation to generation, this one too has a grain of truth in it. You've been to Milk Ranch Point, I assume? You've seen the crosses, the graves?"

"Yes," Jim said. "Only I didn't go there until I was a teenager, long after I'd heard the stories."

"Well, that really is where people from this area used to bury their dead babies."

"But why did they do it so far out of town?"

"Because," Millie said, pausing for dramatic effect, "not all of the babies were dead. Most were stillborn, but sometimes, if a baby was born sick or deformed, the parents would take it there and leave it to die."

"Jesus," Jim breathed.

"That's where the stories started."

"I can't believe anyone would do that," Jim said.

"Don't judge them too harshly," Millie said. "Three out of four babies died anyway in those days. The people were just doing what they thought practical. They were weeding out the weak and the infirm before they had anything invested in them. Times were hard. Most families could not afford more than one child, and they wanted to make sure that one child was strong and healthy enough to pull his own weight. And birth control was unknown."

"I can't believe it," Jim said. "I'd always thought those stories were made up. And I didn't think those crosses marked real graves. I thought they were . . . I don't know what I thought they were. But I didn't think they were real graves."

"Oh, they're real all right. And that's not all. Before that, before the white man settled here, the Indians, the Anasazis, used to do the same thing. In the same spot. I wouldn't be surprised if that's where our ancestors got the idea."

Jim felt his heart pounding in his chest, the blood thumping in his temples. His stomach was knotted with fear. "I seem to recall a story about a preacher," he lied. "A preacher who was connected somehow to Milk Ranch Point."

"Why, yes," Millie said, "there was such a preacher. Only it's not a story. In our research, we've turned up documentation, corroboration from several diaries and journals, that confirms the man's existence."

He closed his eyes, holding the receiver tight to his ear so he wouldn't drop it. "Really?" he said.

"Yes. It was about a hundred and fifty years ago. An itinerant minister, wandering through the area, found out somehow about Milk Ranch Point. He preached about the evil of such practices on any soapbox he could find. He scared the heck out of everyone in town. He'd been here for a week or so when he started trying to get people to go up there with him. But no one wanted to take him. Finally, a few of the men accompanied him up the Rim. In fact—" She paused for a moment. "Wait a minute. Yes. Your great-grandfather was sheriff at that time. I think he went up there with them."

"What did this preacher look like?" Jim asked. "Do you know?"

"There was only one physical description, and it seemed to dwell on his eyes. His eyes, apparently, were black, unnaturally black."

Jim licked his lips, which were suddenly very dry. "What happened then?"

"We don't really know. An entry in one of the diaries made it sound as though there was some type of exorcism or something, but we're not sure. We don't even know what they were supposed to be exorcising. It's fascinating though, isn't it?"

"Yeah," Jim said mechanically.

"Now you see how rumors and ghost stories get started. Of course, we did get most of this from personal remembrances, and you know those records aren't reliable. Still, it's food for thought."

"Yeah," Jim repeated. He cleared his throat. "Whatever happened to the preacher?"

"That we don't know," Millie admitted. "But we turn up something new all the time. I expect we'll find out eventually." She laughed. "I guess you'll have to buy the sequel for that."

"Yeah. Well, thanks Millie. You've been a lot of help."

"May I ask why you wanted to know all this?"

"Oh, nothing. Curiosity."

"Okay," she said. "I'll let you go. You are going to buy one of our books when it comes out, aren't you?"

He smiled. "Of course."

"I'll let you go then. Bye-bye."

"Bye." He hung up, feeling numb. He glanced involuntarily toward the hallway. At the end of the hall, he knew, Brother Elias was sitting calmly in his holding cell.

He had the sudden feeling that, within that cell, Brother Elias was looking toward him and smiling.

Jim stood up. He had to get away from here. He knew he should talk to Brother Elias, confront him, but he did not want to see the man right now. Not until he had had time to sort things out. He picked up his hat and walked out to the front desk. Rita had just left, and Pete and Judson were signing in, coming on duty. He waved tiredly, perfunctorily, at them and walked across the silent parking lot to his car.

He drove home on instinct, his mind still on Milk

Ranch Point. He thought of the stories he and his
friends had told each other when they were kids. The
ghosts of abandoned babies, perpetually crying in the
forest for mothers who would never come. Infants left
at the point to fend for themselves who had grown
into wild, animalistic killers. Goose bumps arose on
his arms, though the air tonight was warm.

He parked the car on the street in front of his house
and walked across the unmown lawn to the front door.
His mind was preoccupied. He did not see the pools
of unfamiliar shadow next to the garage. He did not
see the shadows move. He did not see the shadows
buzz.

SEVENTEEN

Father Andrews drove to the church after leaving the sheriff's office. He had a Bible study group to meet with at seven, and though he didn't really feel like going through with it, he couldn't cancel out now. He parked the car and walked across the gravel toward the front door of the church. Looking down, he could see minuscule bits of multicolored glass in the gravel. His eyes moved up to the twin stained-glass windows in the front of the building. Good as new. No one could ever tell that anything had happened here, save for the slightly lighter tone of the new paint on the bricks.

He took out his key and opened the door, turning on the lights as he walked in. He poked his head in the chapel, to make sure everything was all right. The setting sun, its rays converted to red and blue and yellow and orange as it streamed through the chapel windows, fell on the altar. Everything was as it should be.

Father Andrews walked down the short hall to the large Sunday school classroom that was used for the Bible study group. He wondered idly why this church hadn't been burned. He thought of Brother Elias and

felt a cold finger tickle his spine. He was suddenly
aware of the fact that he was all alone in the church.
He hurried into the classroom and pulled the small
portable radio out of the storage closet, turning it on,
grateful for the sound of another voice.

He busied himself preparing for the meeting, trying
to keep his mind off of what had happened at the
sheriff's office.

Billy Ford and Glen Dunaway were the first to arrive, driven by Glen's mother. Both were giggling as
they came into the classroom. Father Andrews smiled.
"What's so funny?" he asked.

Billy shook his head. "Nothing." Both boys giggled
again, whispering to each other.

Susie Powell stepped through the doorway a moment later. She was running her hands through her
hair, as though she were trying to comb something
out. She looked up at Father Andrews. "What are all
those flies doing out there?" she asked.

"You know what they're attracted to," Glen said,
and both he and Billy laughed loudly.

Flies? Father Andrews felt the fear well up again,
and he strode out of the classroom toward the front of
the church. He stood for a moment in the open doorway. Two pairs of headlights pulled into the parking lot.
It was dark, and he could see nothing.

But he could hear, even above the engines of the
cars, a droning buzzing.

Flies.

Brother Elias had predicted there would be flies.

His mind went over all of the Biblical plagues. Was
that what was happening here? He felt like calling the
bishop. He was not equipped to deal with something
like this. He did not have the experience. But he knew
the bishop would not understand, would think he was
crazy, would dismiss him from his position.

Maybe he should be dismissed from his position.
And get as far away from Randall as possible.

But, no, he couldn't do that. He had responsibilities. And he owed it to the sheriff to stay. He was involved with this, whether he liked it or not.

He stood by the front door and watched two more groups of children run to the church, swatting the flies away as they ran. More headlights pulled into the parking lot.

An earthquake was supposed to come after the flies, Father Andrews thought, and he suddenly felt sick to his stomach. What if it happened while they were at their Bible study? The church might cave in, killing all those kids.

But it was too late to call it off now. Most of the parents had already driven off and wouldn't be back for an hour.

They would practice civil defense tonight, he decided, duck-and-cover.

Ann Simon, the last member of the study group, came running through the doorway, and Father Andrews closed the heavy wooden door behind her. "To keep the flies out," he explained.

"We have a whole bunch at our house, too," Ann said as they walked toward the classroom. "I don't know where they all came from."

Father Andrews told the children the story of Joseph and his brothers, they practiced civil defense and talked for a moment about earthquakes, they had refreshments.

Nothing happened.

After the children had left, Father Andrews locked the door behind them and went into the chapel. He spent the night there, on his knees, praying.

He prayed for guidance but none came.

EIGHTEEN

The earthquake hit at precisely ten after midnight.

Gordon and Marina had been making love, and they stopped in midmovement, hardly daring to breathe, as the ground beneath them jolted in harsh irregular waves. There was the sound of shattering glass from the kitchen, the sound of something crashing in the bathroom. The hanging lamp above their bed was swinging wildly. "What is it?" Marina screamed, clutching his back.

"An earthquake," Gordon said, feigning a calm he did not feel.

"Oh God," Marina said, closing her eyes. "Oh my God."

They held each other tight.

Jim had lain awake all night, waiting for this moment, knowing it would happen, preparing himself, but he still felt a helpless primal feeling of panic as he felt the earth shift beneath the bed. He jumped up, shaking Annette awake and rushing down the hall to the kids' rooms. He took Suzonne in his arms and jerked Justin out of bed, running back to his own bedroom.

He and Annette and the kids stood under the doorway, waiting, until the quake was over.

Father Andrews, kneeling before the altar of the church, closed his eyes tighter, prayed more fervently, and hoped that the shaking would stop.

On the "Today" show the next morning, John Palmer said it was the first recorded earthquake in Arizona in over a hundred years. He said the quake measured 4.5 on the Richter scale and was centered just above the small town of Randall on the Mogollon Rim.

NINETEEN

Jim sat in his office, the door locked, the phone off the hook, waiting for Gordon and Father Andrews to show up. He pulled a small piece off the glazed donut on his desk in front of him and swallowed it down with a sip of lukewarm coffee. The damage from the quake hadn't been that bad. He'd compared notes with Ernst at the fire department, and both of them had agreed that the damage was much less than either of them had expected. Of course the actual monetary amount of damages hadn't been assessed yet and probably wouldn't be for another week or so, but none of the buildings in town had collapsed and no one had been seriously injured.

That hadn't stopped people from calling, however. He had tried getting ahold of Pete right after the quake had stopped, and it had taken him a full fifteen minutes to get through. The office phones had been ringing nonstop ever since, which was why he had taken his own phone off the hook. He didn't feel like listening to petty complaints about broken china or smashed teacups. He'd let Rita and Tom handle that.

He had much more important things to think about.

He took another bite of the donut and another sip

of coffee. He knew he should go back and talk to Brother Elias, but he did not want to go back there. He was afraid. He would wait until Gordon and Father Andrews got here.

There was a knock at the door.

"Who is it?" he called.

"Andrews."

Jim stood up and walked across the room to open the door. The priest, he noticed immediately, was wearing the same clothes he had worn yesterday. He had not shaved. His skin, normally pale, now looked even paler. The sheriff looked at him with concern. "Are you okay?"

Andrews shrugged. "I didn't get much sleep last night."

"Who did?" Jim said. He glanced back toward his desk. "Listen, do you want to wait here until Gordon comes, or would you rather go back and see Brother Elias right now?"

The priest licked his lips. "Let's see him now."

Jim closed the door behind him and led the way down the hall, past the conference room, past the supply room to the thick iron door that led to the trio of holding cells in the back. Even through the door, they could hear Brother Elias loudly singing hymns to himself. They looked at each other. "Are you sure?" Jim said.

Father Andrews nodded.

The sheriff unlocked the door, and they walked over to the first holding cell. Brother Elias stared at Jim and smiled. "You have your proof," he said.

The sheriff nodded. "Yeah. I have my proof." He unlocked the cell door. "What do we do now? I assume you have some sort of plan."

Brother Elias rose slowly to his feet. He was clutching his Bible under his right arm. "We must wait until we are all here," he said. He moved forward. "We will wait in your office."

"Okay," Jim agreed. "Come on."

They returned to his office to wait.

Ten minutes later, Gordon rapped softly on the door then pushed the door open. He stepped into the room and saw the sheriff seated at his desk, his fingers fiddling with a bent paper clip. Father Andrews was sitting on the couch opposite the sheriff's desk, holding his hands between his knees, staring at the carpet. He looked up as Gordon entered the room and smiled, but his smile seemed wan and forced.

In front of the window, silhouetted, staring out at the town, was the unmoving form of Brother Elias.

Brother Elias turned away from the window, stepping into the center of the room, metamorphosing from a silhouetted shadow to an almost normal looking man. He smiled at Gordon, though his black eyes remained unreadable. "We have been waiting for you," he said.

Gordon nodded slowly, unsure of what to say. He felt intimidated, though he was not quite sure why. He was aware that the balance of power in the room had shifted since the meeting yesterday. On the previous day, the authority had rested with the sheriff. Today, Brother Elias was in charge.

The sheriff stood up. "All right," he said. "We're all here now. Why don't you tell us what's going on?"

Brother Elias looked from Gordon, to the sheriff, to Father Andrews. "You have all been chosen by the Lord our God to combat the evil of the adversary. Satan has been banished for all eternity from the comforting presence of the Lord, and in his impotent rage he has vowed revenge on the Heavenly Father. He has been gathering to him an army to thwart the Lord's will, and if he is not stopped in time his efforts will be successful." He looked at Gordon, then the sheriff. "You have had nightmares, have you not?"

Both men nodded.

"The Lord has chosen to speak with you through

visions," Brother Elias said. He fingered his tie clasp. "He has seen fit to warn you of the coming evil through your dreams, as he did of old, as he did with Joseph and many of the prophets."

Jim cleared his throat. "So what's that mean? Whatever we saw in our dreams is going to come true?"

"The Lord works in mysterious ways," the preacher said. He looked at Father Andrews. "As the good father can tell you, God often speaks in parables or allegories."

Father Andrews found himself nodding.

"Maybe that was true at first," Jim said, "but I've been having some damn specific dreams lately. A kid I knew was in those dreams." He looked hard at the preacher. "I dreamed about Milk Ranch Point."

"Me, too," Gordon added.

Brother Elias smiled. "As the time draws nigh, as the powers on both sides approach their peak, the visions become less vague. My visions, too, are clearer."

"I've had no nightmares," Father Andrews said softly.

"You were chosen nonetheless." The preacher looked at Jim. "Your friend, the boy. He was chosen by the Lord our God. Now he is guiding your visions, doing the Lord's work on the other side. You," he turned back to Father Andrews, "have been chosen to fill his role."

"Why have I been chosen?" the priest asked. "Why have we all been chosen?"

"You are psychic," Brother Elias said simply. "The Lord has blessed you with powers beyond those of ordinary men. Now he wants you to use those powers. You must speak with the adversary, you must communicate with the evil one."

Father Andrews paled.

"Your family," he said to Jim, "has always aided in

the Lord's work. Your ancestors fought bravely against the adversary. Now it is your turn."

"This has happened before," Jim said.

Brother Elias nodded.

"At Milk Ranch Point."

"Yes."

"How far back does it go?" Jim asked. "How long has my family been involved?"

"You would not believe me if I told you."

"Tell me anyway." He paused. "My great-grandfather went up there, didn't he?"

"Ezra Weldon," the preacher said. "And Ten-Hano-Kachia before him. And Nan-Timocha before him. And Ware-Kay-Non . . ."

"And you were there, weren't you? All the way back then?"

Brother Elias only smiled.

Jim looked at the business-suited preacher and shivered. How had he appeared to his great-grandfather? he wondered. As one of those frontier ministers with the dusty black suit and stovepipe hat? And how before that? As a wandering Indian? How about originally? A caveman? He wondered how his very first ancestor, way back when, had gotten involved in all this. Someone, sometime, had to have made a conscious decision to go along with all this.

But he was making a conscious decision, wasn't he? This was his own choice.

Not really. It had already been decided for him.

"Why was I chosen?" Gordon asked.

Brother Elias shook his head. "That I cannot yet tell you," he said. "You are not ready for it. I will tell you when the time comes."

"Tell me now," Gordon said.

"I will tell you when the time comes," Brother Elias repeated. His black eyes bored into Gordon's, and Gordon felt his will crumble beneath the gaze. The preacher moved over to the sheriff's desk and picked up a pencil and pad of paper. "We have little time," he said. "The hour of action is drawing nigh. We must prepare if we are to be successful."

"And what if we are successful?" Jim asked. "Will that be it? Will that be the end of it?"

Brother Elias shook his head. "We were successful in the past," he said. "If we had not been, the four of us would not be here today. Satan has been beaten and humiliated by Almighty God, and he will never give up in his attempt to usurp the power of the Lord. He is immortal. And though we may beat him in these small battles, he can afford to wait. He will try again and again, gathering to him new armies, until he is successful."

"What if we lose?" Gordon asked.

"Satan will walk the earth. The earth will be his, and all in it his subjects. He will twist lives to his own purposes and mock the creations of God. He will laugh in the face of the Lord."

"Why doesn't God do something about it himself?" Father Andrews asked quietly. "Why must he work through our imperfect vessels?"

"Do not dare to question the decisions of the Lord," Brother Elias said angrily. "Do not presume to know the mind of God."

Jim stepped between the two. "How much time do you think we have?" he asked Brother Elias.

"I do not know," the preacher admitted. "The evil has already started, and it will intensify as more are converted. I would estimate that it will be twenty-four hours before Satan and his minions have the strength to take what they are after. We must strike before then. If we don't, we are lost."

They were silent, looking at each other, each of them feeling numb.

Brother Elias began writing on the pad of paper. He tore off the top sheet and handed it to the sheriff. Jim looked over the penciled list. He handed it to

Father Andrews, who read it and handed it to Gordon.

Gordon glanced at the paper. "Items we need," it said in a thick bold hand. He scanned the list. Thick rope, an unspecified amount. Pickup trucks. Four copies of the Revised Standard Version of the Bible. Plastic tarp. Four crucifixes. Four pitchforks.

Pitchforks?

Four high-powered rifles. Four hand-held axes. Matches. A gallon of human blood.

Gordon looked up from the paper at Brother Elias. "What are we going to be doing?" he whispered.

Brother Elias ignored him. Jim took the paper back from Gordon, looking it over. "Most of this should be fairly easy to get," he said. "The blood might be a little difficult, but I think I can requisition it from the hospital."

"I want you to get your families out of town," Brother Elias said. "Take them to a safe place, away from here." He looked at the sheriff. "Have your wife and children stay with relatives for a few days, until this is over."

Jim nodded.

The preacher looked at Gordon. "Make sure your wife is far away from this area," he said. "This is very important. She must not be here come tomorrow."

"Why?" Gordon asked.

"I cannot yet tell you. The time is not right. But you must get her away from here."

Gordon felt his mouth go dry. He imagined Marina killed, torn apart like the Selways, like Vlad. He licked his lips, looking up at the preacher. "I don't know if she'll go. I don't know if she'll even believe all this when I tell her."

"It does not matter what you tell her as long as you get her away from here."

"It's her decision," Gordon said firmly. "I can't force her to do something she doesn't want to do."

"Take her from this town," Brother Elias said. " 'For the husband is the head of the wife as Christ is the head of the church . . . As the church is subject to Christ, so let wives also be subject in everything to their husbands.' Ephesians 5:23." The preacher pulled out the Bible he had been clasping unobtrusively beneath his arm and began flipping through pages. He pulled a recently taken photograph from between two pages of the Bible, handing it to Gordon.

Gordon stared at the color photo. It had been taken near a beach somewhere. In the background, he could see the ocean. In the foreground were several dead and bloody bodies.

A tiny infant, with grinning bloody teeth, was pushing its way out of a pregnant woman's abdomen.

The implication was obvious.

Gordon handed the photo back, sickened. His rational mind wanted to protest, to label the photograph a fake, to attribute the horrible scene to darkroom trickery, but he knew the picture was genuine.

The preacher turned to Jim. "We need a camera as well," he said.

Jim reached over and grabbed a pencil. "Camera," he wrote at the end of the list. "Film."

"What exactly are we going to be doing?" Gordon asked.

But Brother Elias had moved back in front of the window and was staring out, unmoving, at the black shape of the Rim far above the town.

TWENTY

Ted McFarland pulled his white government-issue Pontiac into the closed and abandoned Texaco gas station next to the Colt Saloon. Shutting off the engine and the headlights, he sat in the darkness for a few moments, staring out the windshield, thinking. He felt lonely, depressed. He knew he wasn't doing a damn bit of good on this investigation, and he could feel the resentment of the local authorities every time he tried to make a conjecture or offer an opinion. He sighed. He didn't know why Wilson had assigned anyone to this case at all. State police shouldn't have the responsibility of bailing out locals when they screwed up.

A pickup truck pulled in behind him, the bright headlights reflecting back off the rearview mirror and almost blinding him. He tilted the mirror up to keep the light out of his eyes. A minute or so later he heard the sound of the truck's doors being slammed and the sound of boots on gravel as its occupants made their way toward the bar.

He knew he should call Denise. She was probably waiting by the phone for him to call. But listening to her talk, hearing her voice, would probably only accentuate his loneliness and make him more depressed. He stared out the windshield of the car at the lighted doorway of the saloon. He could hear, from inside the building, the raucous sounds of people having a good time, the music of Charlie Daniels. He knew that, in the state he was in, if he *didn't* call Denise he would be likely to do something stupid, something he would later regret.

A young buxom woman wearing tight jeans and a skimpy halter top came stumbling out of the bar, her arms around a tough-looking man in a cowboy hat.

McFarland looked at her, thought for a second of Denise, then rolled up the window of the car door and got out, locking it. He walked over cracked slabs of asphalt and hopped the low, crumbling brick wall that separated the gas station from the Colt. The parking lot of the saloon was filled with pickups. A few were high-riding customized jobs; a few were small foreign gas savers. But the vast majority of them were good, healthy, American stock trucks. Fords primarily. Nearly all had the obligatory trailer hitch on the rear bumper and the gun rack in the back window.

He walked into the bar. It was smoky and humid, the smell of cigarettes and beer and human body odor almost overpowering. The music was loud, too loud, and conversation appeared to be difficult if not impossible. He scanned the room for a familiar face and, seeing none, made his way toward the bar. He motioned for the bartender. One song ended, and before the next began he shouted: "Coors!"

There was a hard clap on his shoulder. McFarland jerked around. Carl Chmura, Weldon's right hand man, was standing behind him, grinning. "Hey," he said. "How's it goin'?"

McFarland nodded as the bartender brought his beer. "All right." He stared at the deputy. Carl Chmura had been one of those who had resented his presence the most, and he had made it clear that he did not want and would not accept the help of the state police, though he would comply technically with all of the sheriff's orders. Now the young deputy was smiling at him, apparently friendly, all hostility gone. Apparently, he was one of those people who could successfully separate all aspects of his job from the rest of his life—something McFarland had never been able to do.

He tried to smile at the deputy, but the smile felt strained and he was aware of the fact that it probably looked false. "So," he said, "what are you doing here?" The question was stupid, and he knew it was stupid, but he could think of nothing else to say.

Chmura took a swig from the bottle he held in his hand. "I have the night off, I just broke up with my girlfriend, I thought I'd celebrate. Want to join me?" He looked around the bar. A group of cowboys and their dates were two-stepping to the Marshall Tucker Band. Several unattached women stood around the fringes of the dance floor, looking around for partners. "I bet we could pick up on one of those bimbos there."

McFarland shook his head. "Not tonight. I don't really feel up to it."

Chmura grabbed his arm, and McFarland realized that the deputy was already drunk. "Come on."

He shook his head more firmly and peeled the deputy's hand off his arm. "I can't. I'm married."

Chmura laughed. "That don't mean shit. I was married once, too. Who cares?"

McFarland looked at the younger man. Married and divorced? He couldn't have been any older than mid-twenties. McFarland shook his head and pretended to look at his watch. "Sorry. It's almost time for me to call my wife. I've got to get going." He downed his beer and stood up. He'd head back to the hotel and see what was on TV. Maybe he *would* call Denise. Who could tell? It might cheer him up. It certainly couldn't be worse than this. He clapped an arm on

Chmura's back in an expression of camaraderie he didn't feel. "I'll see you later."

"Wait," the deputy said, and there was a tinge of desperation in his eyes. "You sure you wouldn't like to just stay here and talk or something?"

McFarland shook his head. "Sorry, but I have to go. Maybe some other time."

There was a sudden jumble of loud voices in the back of the bar, near the jukebox, and both men turned to look at the disturbance. Something slammed hard against the jukebox and the obnoxious sound of a needle being scratched over a record surface blared through the Colt's PA system. Chmura put his bottle down on the bar, hitched up his belt and grinned. "It's times like these that it's fun to be a deputy." He started toward the rear of the bar and noticed suddenly that the crowd which had been gathered there was slowly backing up toward him. One older woman abruptly turned and ran for the front door. A new song had started playing on the jukebox, a Waylon Jennings song, and Waylon's already low voice became even lower as the power plug to the jukebox was pulled out and the record slowed to a stop.

McFarland watched Chmura hesitate for a moment, patting his waist for a gun-and holster that weren't there, then start slowly forward, against the tide of people. He swore to himself, wishing that he, too, had brought along some type of weapon, and reached for the deputy's bottle. He smashed it against the bar and held the jagged edge out in front of him, moving forward to help Chmura. You could never tell what would happen in these redneck bars. You could never be too careful.

The bar was silent now, all conversation stopped, and the dancers and drinkers in the front of the building were looking curiously toward the rear, trying to figure out what was going on. Some of the other patrons were still backing up, and some were standing

their ground, staring toward the door next to the jukebox, but the vast majority of them were making a
hurried beeline for the front exit.

McFarland followed Chmura through the crowd of
people and stopped.

A small infant, legless, its arms mere underdevel-
oped stumps, was flopping along the wooden floor of
the saloon through the doorway, laughing and cackling
to itself. The sound was low and barely audible, but
McFarland could hear it clearly through the silence of
shuffling feet and it sent a cold chill down his spine.
He moved a step closer and stared at the baby. It was
small, undersized, and appeared to be newly born. Its
pink skin was still wet with blood, and behind it on
the floor stretched a red trail, like that of a snail. Its
eyes blinked rhythmically at even intervals as it
flopped forward, staring at nothing. Its mouth continued its hideous cackling.

McFarland looked around at the faces of fear and
disgust on the staring patrons. He would have expected, under the circumstances, that some woman in
the crowd, some compassionate mother-type, would
have picked up the baby, feeling sorry for it, and tried
to help it. But there was something so decidedly wrong
about the infant, something so evil, that he could well
understand why most of the people were backing away
from the creature, why some were running away. He,
too, felt a primal sort of fear at the sight, and he had
an instinctive desire to rush over and stomp on the
thing, crushing it beneath the heel of his boot as he
would a particularly large and repulsive bug.

There was a loud female scream off to the right, and
McFarland looked toward the sound. Another infant,
equally small and equally deformed, also laughing, was
crawling through the open window at the side of the
saloon. Its tiny body was halfway over the windowsill,
crooked arms flailing wildly in the air. The window,
he knew, overlooked a drainage ditch that ran along

the side of the building to the field out back. It was a good twenty feet to the bottom.

How had the baby gotten up that high?

McFarland glanced toward Chmura. The deputy was staring at the window, his face a blank expression of disbelief. Shock had apparently nullified the effects of alcohol. He turned to look at McFarland. "What's happening?" he said.

The state policeman shook his head. He had no idea. He saw another baby crawling through the door next to the jukebox, following the red blood trail of the first. This one had a huge oversized head. In the front of the bar, near the entrance, several people screamed.

They were coming in from all sides.

McFarland looked around. The bartender had taken a sawed-off shotgun from beneath the bar and was holding it in both hands, ready to use it if something happened. He was staring at the fragmenting groups of panicked people in the saloon, confused. McFarland nodded quickly at Chmura, catching his eye, and ran over to the bar, pulling his badge from his front pocket. "State police," he said. He reached for the shotgun.

"Hold it right there, motherfucker." The bartender lowered the weapon and snaked a finger over the trigger.

"I'm a policeman," McFarland said in a louder, more authoritarian voice. "Please let me see your weapon. Mine is out in the car."

The bartender's eyes darted quickly around the saloon and he saw, through a hole in the parting crowd, the first blood-wet infant flopping along the hardwood dance floor. His hold loosened on the shotgun, the weapon drooping, and McFarland wrenched it from his hands. The bartender looked up at McFarland. "What is it?" he asked. His voice was quiet, subdued, filled with either terror or awe.

"I don't know," the policeman said. Holding the shotgun tightly, he started back across the floor toward Chmura. Before he had reached the deputy, however, the saloon was rocked by a harsh shock wave. There was a loud metallic crash from the front of the building, and the crowd, as one, stepped slowly, silently, backward. There were no screams this time, no grunts or groans or mutterings of any kind. No one spoke. No one made a sound. There was only the quiet ragged breathing of the terrified patrons and the sickening wet slapping sounds of the strange infants as they flopped forward on the floor.

Then McFarland saw it.

A charred and blackened figure, wearing what looked like the tattered remnants of a priest's collar and uniform, stood at the front of the saloon, gazing at the crowd with unnaturally white eyes. The skin on its face was burnt horribly, peeling off in large flakes. Its hands and fingers were twisted almost into claws. Behind the figure, a large hole had been torn through the wall next to the door.

McFarland sidled up to the deputy, swallowing hard. "What is it?" he whispered.

Chmura shook his head.

"Sinners," the black figure said, then chuckled. Its voice was grating, inhuman.

Chmura gasped. "Selway," he said. "Father Selway."

McFarland could hear the whisper traveling through the crowd as others recognized the figure.

"Ask and you shall receive," the thing said, its voice mocking. It smiled, revealing crooked blackened teeth. "I have come to set you free." Its grating voice chanted something in an alien tongue, and it pointed into the crowd with one charred finger. Through the hole in the wall, more infants came, fifteen or twenty of them moving slowly forward en masse. There was the sound of workmanlike scratching from atop the roof.

Chmura looked around crazily. "It's not human," he said. He grabbed the shotgun from McFarland's hands and pointed it toward the figure's head. He pulled the trigger. There was a deafening roar and then . . . nothing.

The slug neither tore the figure apart nor passed cleanly through it. Instead, the blackened head seemed to accept the slug and *absorb* it. The head did not even move backward from the impact.

Chmura fired again. Nothing happened. And again. Nothing. The figure smiled.

McFarland grabbed the shotgun from the deputy.

"You've been *bad,* Carl," the thing said. "You have been straying from the path." It moved forward, the crowd parting in front of it as people scurried out of its way. McFarland found himself inching away from the deputy. The figure stopped directly before Chmura. "Bad Carl."

The deputy did not even try to move away. He remained rooted to the spot, apparently in shock, and he did not flinch as the creature reached out and grabbed his arm, ripping it from its socket. It held the arm high, blood dripping onto the floor, and grinned.

Still Chmura did not move. He remained standing, blood flowing freely from the open socket, and stared up at his severed limb.

The noises on the roof grew louder.

McFarland could take no more of this. He raised the shotgun high and shoved it hard into the figure's blackened face, pulling the trigger. The end of the shotgun sank easily and deeply into the burned head, but the creature did not seem to notice. No slug emerged from the back of the skull.

The thing turned to appraise McFarland, jerking the weapon from his hands and tossing it aside. It smiled at him.

There was the sound of splitting wood, and McFarland saw out of the corner of his eye tiny malformed infants dropping from the roof onto bare heads and cowboy hats. These were not slow and plodding like their brethren flopping along the ground. They moved quickly, surely, with purpose. One landed on a burly man nearby and started digging in, small arms and small mouth working in tandem as it ripped apart the flesh on the man's head, the man trying in vain to pull it off him.

The Colt was filled with wild screaming as more fell from the roof and began attacking.

"I hope you said your prayers before going to sleep last night," the burnt figure said in its grating voice. It laughed.

McFarland struggled as a strong hand gripped his neck. He could smell the fried flesh.

Denise! he thought. *I should have called Denise!*

And then Father Selway pulled his head from his body.

TWENTY-ONE

Brother Elias sat alone in the well-lit conference room of the sheriff's office, thinking back upon the time when he was not known as Brother Elias. He had had darker hair in those days. And shabbier clothes, in keeping with the times. Then, he had called himself Father Josiah. Before that, it had been Iktap-Wa. And, before that, Wikiup-Asazi.

Names changed, but people remained the same.

Evil remained the same.

He stared down at the black-bound Bible on the table in front of him and smiled slightly. He liked Christianity. It was a simple religion, with few standardized ceremonies, and it was easier to incorporate into the ritual than most. And, unlike some of the more holistic Eastern religions, Christianity understood that there was a clear dichotomy between good and evil.

Even if it didn't understand the true nature of evil.

Brother Elias maintained the placid smile on his face and stared benignly at the wall, aware that he was being observed through the small window of safety glass embedded in the steel door. One of the sheriff's deputies came to check on him every few hours, keeping tabs on what he was doing. As always, the man stared through the window for a moment then quickly disappeared.

Brother Elias knew what was happening in the town. He knew that attacks were being made at various weak points. He knew that the evil was growing quickly now, that it was making firm inroads. He had seen it all before. In other towns, other times.

In Randall.

Brother Elias touched the small gold crucifix that served as his tie clip. He could not afford a debacle like the last Randall excursion. That time, four of the six men involved had been killed. The evil had been contained, its power effectively drained for the next century and a half, but they had come perilously close to failure. Only he and Ezra Weldon had come down from the Rim alive.

He was afraid the same thing would happen this time.

Or something worse.

It might be too late already, he knew. He should have gotten to Randall much earlier. Things were getting out of hand. But neither he nor Andrews nor the sheriff nor Gordon would have been ready. He was not sure they were ready now. The chance that they would succeed in their mission was slim.

But he could not voice his fears. He could not show his lack of faith. He had to be strong for all of them. He had to provide the courage they did not possess themselves.

If the ritual was done correctly, if everything went according to plan, there would be no mishaps, there would be no sacrifices. But nothing ever went perfectly. There were always variables. There were always changes to be made according to circumstances.

There were always deaths.

TWENTY-TWO

The narrow dirt road wound through the forest, tall pines lining the rutted trail like silent sentinels, black and forbidding against the moonless sky. Gordon walked forward, his eyes trained ahead, tripping periodically in shallow shadowed holes he could not see, stubbing his bare toes on rocks he could not quite make out. Before him, the trees seemed to be growing closer to the road, edging deliberately in on the dirt path, and it appeared as though eventually the road would dwindle away entirely.

Gordon continued walking. He did not know what lay ahead of him, but he felt an increasing sense of menace, a growing paranoia, the deeper he penetrated into the woods. He wanted to turn back, but something inside him made him press on. On the sides of the road, between the trees, he could hear sinister whispering noises and what sounded like low chuckling. He increased his pace.

Ahead, something large and black lurched out from behind a tree and stood directly in the middle of the road, blocking his way. The night was dark, but the figure was darker, and it loomed before him, standing completely still, not moving. Its very lack of move-

ment seemed threatening, and Gordon forced himself
to stop. He nervously coughed. "Who are you?" he
asked.

The figure did not speak.

"*What* are you?"

Gordon was aware that the figure moved, but he
could see no movement and it scared the hell out of
him. He turned to run away, and . . . he was standing
in the middle of Old Mesa Road, staring around him
at the wreckage of Randall. In front of him, the Valley
National Bank building was demolished, large chunks
of concrete and metal protruding from a pile of
charred ash. Two people, dressed in torn rags and
leaning on one another for support, were staggering
away from the smoldering hulk of what had once been
the Circle K store. Further up the road, people were
running as fast as they could away from him, away
from the center of town. Above everything, high on
the Rim, an enormous black storm cloud grew ominously, slowly shaping itself into the form of a gigantic
clawed hand.

Something bumped against his leg, and Gordon
looked down. Something that looked like a large rat—
a rat as big as a small dog—was crouched on the asphalt in front of him, grinning up in malevolent glee.
Before he could react, before he could kick out at the
animal or even scream, the creature had leapt up and
attached itself to his face, clawing wildly, its carnivo-
rous teeth biting with relish into the soft flesh of his
cheeks. He could feel the blood gush warmly out of
his face as the skin was ripped apart. Trying to pull
the creature from his face, he fell backwards and . . .
landed with a soft thud on a pile of wet garbage.
Stunned, it took him a moment to get his bearings.
When he realized where he was, he sat up and looked
around. It was morning, and the sunlight glinted
brightly off strips of chrome and shards of steel in the
pile of metal next to him. On the other side of him,

the pile of wood and combustibles was burning, and
the air around the fire shimmered in liquid waves of
heat. Gordon stared at the burning pile, transfixed.
Though he did not want to, he could see within the
fire strange shifting shapes. Figures. Faces. The figures
were almost but not quite human, and the faces were
known to him but not immediately recognizable.
Though he tried to concentrate on one face at a time,
he could not. They changed too rapidly for him to get
a fix on them.

Out of the bottom of the burning pile crawled a
charred, smoldering baby. The infant was blackened
almost beyond recognition, but Gordon could see that
even if it had not been burned, the baby would have
been horribly deformed. Its bones were heavy and
oddly formed, and as it crawled out from under the
fire, pulling itself over stray pieces of garbage, it
smiled, revealing unnaturally long and crooked teeth
that stood out in white relief against its scorched skin.

The baby looked up at Gordon. "Daddy," it said.

Without thinking, Gordon jumped to his feet and
grabbed a long broken stick from the pile on which
he was standing. He shoved the pointed end of the
stick with all his might into the center of the infant's
back. He could feel the point piercing the tiny body.
The baby emitted one long loud shriek of sudden pain,
jerked once and was still.

Gordon looked up and saw in the fire the wavering
figure of Marina. Her face was unclear and indistinct,
but it seemed to him that she was crying.

He glanced around and saw, to his surprise, a ring
of people surrounding the fire. Some of them were
holding long sticks similar to his own. Many were not.
He recognized among the faces Father Andrews and
the sheriff. Standing next to the sheriff, looking up at
him with something like admiration, was a young teenage boy with dirty clothes and greasy unkempt hair.

The boy from his previous dream.

He stared at the youngster and the boy smiled at him, nodding in recognition.

Gordon walked across the gravel toward the boy and the sheriff and grabbed both of their hands. Across from him, he could see the face of Char Clifton, and, next to Clifton, Elsie Cavanaugh from the drugstore.

Something large rose up from the fire . . . and Gordon was standing before the black metal smelter of the sawmill. He was alone. Around him, the wind whistled and howled, driving the dried leaves on the ground into a frenzy. The door to the smelter slowly opened.

And out rushed the massive head of a raging demon, babbling incoherently in the tongue of the damned.

Gordon sat bolt upright in bed, a scream caught in his throat.

Marina held tight to his shoulders, hugging him close. "It's okay," she murmured reassuringly. "It's all right. It's just a dream."

He clasped her hard and said nothing.

She let her hands wander up and down his back then lightly caress his sleep-disheveled hair. "Are you okay?"

She felt him nod against her shoulder, but still he said nothing.

"Do you want to talk about it?"

He pulled back from her and looked her full in the face. His eyes were worried, scared. "You have to leave," he said. "You have to get out of here."

She held him and said nothing.

"You have to get out of here," he repeated. "Before morning."

"I'm not leaving," she told him.

"I'm serious."

"I'm serious, too," she said. She sighed and kissed

him lightly. "Look, let's get some sleep, okay? We'll talk about it in the morning."

Gordon started to protest, but she pulled him to her, holding his head tightly against her breast. In a few moments he was fast asleep, and she carefully laid his head upon the pillow. She stood up slowly, so as not to disturb him, and moved in front of the window, not exactly sure why she suddenly felt so frightened and alone.

Something large rose up from the fire, and Jim was standing before the black metal smelter of the sawmill. He was alone. Around him, the wind whistled and howled, driving the dried leaves on the ground into a frenzy. The door to the smelter slowly opened.

And out rushed the massive head of a raging demon, babbling incoherently in the tongue of the damned.

Jim awoke gasping into his pillow, his hands clutching the pillow's fluffy edges, his mouth opened against the cotton material of the pillowcase. He was drenched with sweat. Beside him, Annette still slept, though she tossed fitfully. He was tempted to wake her but decided against it. She would be leaving early in the morning and needed all the sleep she could get.

They had argued long and hard over her leaving, and finally she had said, "I'm not setting a foot out of this house until you tell me what this is all about. Are you in danger? I don't want you pulling any *High Noon* crap on me."

"I just want you to leave town for a few days," he'd told her.

She'd just stared at him. "Why can't you at least have enough respect for me to level with me, to tell me the truth instead of treating me like I'm one of the kids?"

That had gotten to him. He'd apologized and meant it, then had lied to her and told her that they were closing in on the murderers, a cult, and that as the family of the sheriff, she and the kids might be prime targets. She'd seemed to buy the story, or at least had realized that the children probably were in real danger, and she'd agreed to visit her sister for a few days.

She'd made him promise that he would be careful, that he would let someone else play hero, and he had lied again and said okay.

He pushed a wisp of hair from her face. He felt isolated, alone, in the quiet darkened house. But he was isolated neither by the quiet nor the dark. He was isolated by his knowledge.

He closed his eyes, trying to will himself back into slumber.

Across town, Father Andrews slept peacefully and without dreams.

Brother Elias stared at the bare wall of the lighted conference room, wide awake.

PART THREE

ONE

Gordon awoke well before the alarm went off at four. Next to him, Marina had kicked off the covers and lay unmoving, her face half-buried in the pillow, her arms resting at her sides. He watched her back move slowly up and down as she breathed. He should have made her leave. He should have forced her to go.

But she did not want to go. And trying to force her would have made her all the more stubborn.

He had to convince her to get out of town, to at least go down to Phoenix for the day and shop. What he and the sheriff and Father Andrews and Brother Elias were going to do was dangerous. There was a strong possibility that one, or more, of them might be injured. *Or killed.*

Gordon thrust the thought from his mind. He didn't want to think about that possibility. He wasn't one to believe in self-fulfilling prophesies, but on some superstitious level he didn't feel comfortable dwelling on such thoughts. Perhaps if he didn't think about it, it might not happen.

He looked down at Marina. She seemed to be sleeping so innocently, so peacefully. His hand touched her back, and she jerked awake.

"Sorry," he said. "I didn't mean to startle you."

She opened her eyes, rubbing them. She stared blearily at him. "What time is it?"

"Almost four."

She sat up on one elbow, looking at him. "I'm sorry about last night." Her eyes were serious, her mouth grave. "I've been thinking about what you said, and I think you're right. It is dangerous here for me and the baby."

"You mean you'll—"

"And for you, too. I think all of us should get out of here."

He stared at her stupidly, thrown off by her unexpected change of mind. He had been planning to fight an uphill battle in order to get her to leave, and now she not only wanted to get out of Randall, she wanted him to come with her. He was not quite sure how to react.

"I want us to go to Phoenix or Flagstaff until everything blows over."

He shook his head slowly. "No," he said. "I can't do that." His voice was regretful and apologetic, but there was no hesitation in it, no openness to debate.

Marina's mouth tightened. "I'm not going alone."

"I have to stay here. I have to—"

"Help the sheriff? Help Brother Elias? Come on, you don't owe any of these people anything. Your duty is to me and to your daughter." She pressed a hand against her abdomen. "Your family."

"It's dangerous here," Gordon said. "You know that. After you drop me off at the sheriff's office, I want you to—"

"I'm not taking orders from you." She glared at him. "Stop talking to me as if you were my father."

He took a deep breath. "Look, I just want you to be safe. And I want to make sure nothing happens to the baby. Please, promise me you'll take the car and go down to Phoenix for the day."

"I'm not leaving here without you. If you stay, I stay."

He shook his head. "Now you're just being stupid."

"Maybe I am," she said. "Maybe I am being stupid. But so are you. I don't know what's happened, but lately you've been a real macho asshole." She threw the covers off angrily and slipped into her jeans, which were lying on the floor next to the bed. She pulled on a T-shirt and ran a hand through her hair. She picked up her keys from the dresser.

"What are you doing now?"

"I'm going to take you down to the damn sheriff's office, then I'm going to get the hell out of here."

He reached across the edge of the bed, and the tips of his fingers touched her back. "I only want you to be safe," he said. "I worry about you. I care about you."

Marina pulled away, facing the wall. She said nothing.

He got out of bed and pulled on his own jeans. He stared at the back of her head. "You are going to Phoenix, aren't you?" She said nothing, and he walked around the bed to where she stood. Hesitantly, he put a hand on her shoulder.

She pulled away. "Fuck you."

"Marina—"

"I'm only doing this for the baby. If it wasn't for her, you'd never get me out of here unless you came with me."

Gordon looked relieved. "You take first shower. I'll make us some coffee. Then you can drop me off and head back around to the highway."

"I'll take a shower after I drop you off. I just want you to get the hell out of here right now."

"Okay," he said. "Okay." He grabbed a shirt from the closet and took a pair of underwear from the dresser. "I'll take a quick shower, and then we'll go." He started out the door, then turned around to look at her unmoving form. "You are going to Phoenix, right?"

She did not look at him. "Just take your goddamn shower."

He went into the bathroom.

TWO

Father Andrews awoke to the sound of static from the blank hissing television. He had left the TV on, he remembered. And the lights. He felt, for a second, embarrassed, but that passed immediately. He remembered what they were to do today, and a black cloud settled over him. He did not feel right about this. No, that was not true. He did not feel good about this, though it felt right.

He felt scared.

That was it exactly. He was scared. Like Jim and Gordon, he had only a vague outline of Brother Elias' plan. But that outline was enough to terrify him.

He got out of bed and turned off the television. He was half-tempted to call the bishop and tell him what they were planning. It was not yet four, and the bishop had probably not yet awakened, but he knew his superior would want to know about this.

And he knew the bishop would disapprove and would forbid him to go along with it.

That was the real reason, wasn't it? That was why he wanted to tell the bishop. Not because he respected the other man's opinion, not because he was worried about the moral and ethical implications of what they were going to do, but because he was scared and wanted to find an easy way out of it. He wanted to remove the responsibility for his actions from his own shoulders and place it on someone else. He wanted to pass the buck. He wanted to fall back on the oldest, safest excuse in the book: "I can't. I'm not allowed to."

Father Andrews bowed his head in embarrassment, though no one was there to see him. He looked up, toward the window . . . *and Brother Elias was standing alone in the middle of a grassy meadow. His face was covered with a light stubble, and his dirty hat and clothes were typical of the type worn by many western-ers of the mid-nineteenth century. At the meadow's periphery stood a small group of similarly dressed men, one of whom bore an uncanny resemblance to Jim Weldon. As the men looked on, Brother Elias raised his hands and cast his eyes toward the sky. The bushes surrounding the meadow began to rustle ominously, and the preacher reached down to grab a pitchfork.*

Father Andrews looked away from the window and closed his eyes, his head reeling from the strength of the vision. He sat down on the bed, waiting for the dizziness to go away. He had never experienced a psychic flash of such length and magnitude before. He had never been the recipient of such a clear and literal vision.

He opened his eyes, and his gaze fell on the four Bibles he had promised the sheriff he would provide. The Bibles were bound in white and were unused, completely new.

Trying to think of nothing, concentrating only on the tasks immediately at hand, Father Andrews dressed in nondescript street clothes and put the Bibles in a bag. Before he left the house, he bent down next to the bed, his hands folded before him on the mattress like a child. He began to pray.

THREE

Pete King was sitting in front of the switchboard, waiting for the phone to ring, when Jim walked into the office. He jumped at the sound of the sheriff's boots on the tile and swiveled immediately around. "Thank God you're here!"

Jim stared at the deputy, shocked by the deep circles under the young man's eyes, by the look of haggard frustration on the normally implacable face. Even Pete's hair, ordinarily combed to perfection, looked unkempt and in disarray. "What's up?" the sheriff asked.

Pete shook his head and picked up a huge pile of scratch paper from the table in front of him. "I don't know where to begin," he said. "The members of the posse out looking for those kids on the Rim never came back. There was some type of huge fight at the Colt, I really don't know how many people were killed or exactly what happened. The whole place is in shambles. The Department of Public Safety's been calling in every hour or so with reports of giant accidents on the highway. Eight people from three different neighborhoods called in saying they heard screams and gunshots from their neighbors' houses—"

"Okay, Pete. I get the picture."

"I don't think you do. Judson hasn't called in since he went out to the Episcopal church. Tom said Carl was—"

The sheriff stopped him. "I understand. Where's the preacher?"

"He's still in the conference room."

Jim nodded and was about to walk down the hall when he stopped. "You can go home, Pete," he said.

"Who's taking over the shift?"

"No one. We're closing down the office for a while."

Pete shook his head. "That's okay. I'll stay."

"You need some rest. You look like hell. Now get home. That's an order."

"No." Pete met the sheriff's eyes for a moment then glanced away. "We have to have someone here. We can't just close down the office. What if something happened? What if someone was in real trouble? Who would they call?"

"I'll call Elise and have her transfer all our calls to the DPS. I'll explain the situation to Nelson. He and his men can handle things for a day."

"I'm sorry. I don't think so, sir."

Jim sighed heavily, running a hand through his hair. "All right. Stay here then." He started down the hall.

"Sheriff?"

Jim turned around. "Yes?"

"What's going on here?"

"I'll be damned if I know."

"Me and Judson were talking about it the other night, and we decided that there's a lot of weird stuff's been going on."

Jim smiled tightly. "You got that right."

"No, I mean really weird stuff. We never told you, but we found little footprints out at the farmer's house. Strange little footprints. And I've been seeing a lot of strange things lately. A lot of people have. I've heard 'em talking."

"I know."

"The other night? When you thought you saw something in the back of the building? Judson said he saw it too, only he never told you."

Jim looked at his deputy sympathetically. The young man had been through a hell of a lot lately. "It's okay," he said reassuringly. "We have it all under control. Hopefully, we'll have all this cleared up by the end of today. You just keep manning the phones there. I'll keep you apprised of all developments."

"Sheriff? If you need any help, you let me know. I don't know exactly what it is you're doing, but whatever it is, I'd be willing to help out."

"I know you would. And if I need your help, I'll tell you. Okay?"

Pete nodded. "Okay."

Jim smiled at the deputy. "Thanks, Pete. For everything." He paused, thinking. "You know Gordon Lewis?"

"The Pepsi guy?"

"Yeah. How about Father Andrews?"

Pete shook his head.

"Well, he's the priest that came to take over for Father Selway. If either of them come looking for me, send them to the back. I'll be in the conference room. And hold all calls." The deputy nodded acquiescence, and Jim walked down the hall toward the conference room. Behind him, he heard the telephone ring and Pete answer.

Brother Elias was seated in a stiff-backed chair, wide awake, staring at the blank wall opposite him. He did not move as the sheriff entered the room. His eyes did not waver from their fixed point on the wall. Jim stared at the back of the preacher's head. Technically, Brother Elias was still in custody, and Jim wanted to retain some measure of control over the preacher. Jim knew that he would not be calling the shots today, but he did not feel entirely comfortable subordinating himself completely to Brother Elias. He walked farther into the room and cleared his throat loudly, unsure of what to say, hoping the preacher would speak first.

Brother Elias remained silent.

"I got everything we need," Jim said, trying to make the statement sound as casual as possible under the circumstances. "The hospital gave me several different blood types. They said they couldn't spare a gallon of a single type. They don't have enough on reserve, and in case of an emergency, blood would have to be flown in from Phoenix. I wasn't sure what type we needed, anyway."

"It does not matter," Brother Elias said.

Jim pulled out a chair across the table from the preacher and sat down. "Where are we going to start looking?" he asked. "How are we going to begin this thing?"

Brother Elias smiled slightly, but his eyes were cold. Jim recalled the nightmare he had had during the night, and as he looked into Brother Elias' eyes, he realized that he was a little afraid of the preacher.

"The others will be here soon," Brother Elias said. "We will talk then."

Jim sat back in his chair, glancing around the conference room. Though he had spent a lot of time in here interrogating suspects, he had never noticed how dingy the walls looked, how much in need of a paint job the room was. He would have to look into that, see if he couldn't get some funds to repaint the entire office. Perhaps make it a more cheerful color, get rid of that ugly grayish green the county had forced on him the last time.

If everything worked out today. If they survived.

"Most people believe that God has a penis," Brother Elias said.

Jim looked up sharply, shocked. "What?"

"Most people believe that God created man in his own image. Man has a penis. Therefore, most people believe that God has a penis."

Jim smiled. "It must be an awfully big one."

Brother Elias did not smile.

The sheriff coughed, embarrassed. "You don't believe God has a penis, I take it?"

The preacher shook his head. "God does not have specialized organs as does man. He does not have a penis, he does not have a stomach, he does not have a spleen."

Jim said nothing. He looked away from the preacher. He assumed that this bizarre conversation was Brother Elias' equivalent of small talk. He said nothing more, hoping to drop the subject.

There was a knock on the outside of the conference room door.

"Come in!" Jim called.

Gordon stepped into the room, looking pale and a little scared. He was wearing a pair of ripped and faded jeans and an old checkered shirt. Over his shoulder was slung an expensive 35-millimeter camera. He nodded silently to Brother Elias and to the sheriff.

"Grab a seat," the sheriff said.

Gordon sat down to wait. A few moments later, Father Andrews entered the room. The sheriff stood up and motioned for him to take a chair. He turned to face Brother Elias. "Well," he said, "we're all here."

The preacher nodded slowly. He looked at Gordon, his black eyes clear and unreadable. "I assume you would like to know why you are with us."

"Yes, I would," Gordon admitted.

Brother Elias stood up. "We all have our parts to play," he said. "We must all take the roles for which we were meant." He nodded toward the sheriff. "He is a protector, like his great-grandfather before him, and his great-grandfather before him. The adversary is strong, and there is an element of physical danger in our endeavor. We need his protection." His gaze shifted to Father Andrews. "He is a man of God, blessed with extrasensory ability. We need his ability to communicate with the adversary."

"Why do you need me?" Father Andrews asked. "Why can't you communicate?"

"I cannot," the preacher said simply.

"But you're a man of God as well."

Brother Elias smiled but said nothing. He turned to Gordon. "You, too, are to be a protector."

"But why me? I can't even—"

"Your wife is pregnant. The evil one wants your unborn infant. We need the added insurance provided by your personal involvement."

Gordon tried to swallow but his mouth had suddenly gone dry. He felt as though he was going to faint. He stood up and clumsily knocked over his chair. His legs felt weak. *Marina!* "I have to go," he said hurriedly. "I have to get her."

The preacher's eyes held him, forcing him to remain still. "You cannot leave."

Gordon willed himself to look away, he rushed to the door. "I have to get her!"

"If you do not come with us now, the adversary will surely get your unborn daughter."

Gordon's hand let go of the doorknob. He turned around.

"We need your strength. Your daughter needs your strength."

"Why?" Gordon asked.

"The Lord," said Brother Elias, "has always chosen special people to carry out his work, be it artistic, intellectual, or spiritual. The Bachs and Beethovens, the Thomas Edisons and Albert Einsteins, the Ghandis and Martin Luther Kings. He places these special individuals in different parts of the world, in different countries. Not all of them survive. In his jealousy and rage, Satan attempts to gather these individuals to him before they are born, to convert them to his own evil purposes, to spite and mock the Lord our God." He looked at Gordon. "Your daughter is just such a person. That is why the adversary is after her."

"You mean," Jim said, unbelieving, "that all of this, all this chaos, happened when Bach was born, when Thomas Edison was born, when all those other people were born?"

Brother Elias shook his head. "The adversary is lucky that the unborn infant is here at this place at this time." He shrugged. "Perhaps he planned it that way. I cannot say."

"I have to call Marina and warn her," Gordon said.

The sheriff nodded and gestured toward the door. "Call her. Tell Pete to let you use the phone."

Gordon pulled open the door. He turned suddenly around. "What will my daughter be when she grows up?" he asked.

Brother Elias only smiled.

Gordon ran out into the hall.

Jim stood and looked at the preacher, a mixture of fear and bewilderment visible on his features. "This is the first time this has happened?"

"I did not say that."

"Were any of these . . . special people ever born in Randall?"

"No," the preacher said. "We were not in time. The boy was never born."

Gordon ran into the front office, got the phone from Pete, dialed the number of his house and let the phone ring. Six, seven, eight times. He waited until the twelfth ring and hung up. Marina had had plenty of time to return home since she'd dropped him off. He was worried, but he knew Brother Elias would not let him drive back home to check on her. Maybe he could convince the others to stop by the house for a few minutes on the way to wherever they were going. He knew they would be heading in the direction of the Rim.

The other three men walked into the front office.

"We must go," Brother Elias said. "It is getting late. Time is short."

Angry as she had been with him, Marina was scared, Gordon knew. She might not have believed everything he'd told her, but she instinctively felt the danger. She had probably already left for Phoenix. She was probably well out of Randall by now.

Yes, he decided, adjusting the camera over his shoulder as he followed the other men out of the office. She was probably long gone by now.

He hoped to God she was.

Marina, taking a hot shower, did not hear the telephone ring.

FOUR

A line of light orange was just beginning to infiltrate the fading purple of the eastern sky as the two pickups pulled off the paved highway onto the control road. Brother Elias had originally said that he wanted enough pickup trucks for each of them, plus a few extra vehicles just in case. But the sheriff had been able to scrape together only three county trucks and one private vehicle—Carl's. As it turned out, they only needed two of the trucks. Father Andrews could not drive a stick shift and so was forced to ride with Gordon. And Jim did not want Brother Elias driving by himself. Not with a county truck.

The preacher had said nothing to Jim during the twenty-minute ride to the control road but had instead stared silently out the window at the passing trees. Jim had tried to talk to the preacher, had tried to ask questions, had tried to get some type of conversation going, but Brother Elias had refused to speak, and soon he had given up. He turned on the radio for a brief while, but the only station that came in was an obnoxious rock station out of San Francisco, and he ended up turning the radio off. "You get the strangest stations in the early morning," he said to Brother

Elias, but the preacher ignored him and they drove in silence the rest of the way.

Gordon and Father Andrews drove in silence as well, each thinking private thoughts. Gordon had looked at the priest as the truck before them had sped past the turnoff to his house, and Father Andrews, as if reading his thoughts, had smiled reassuringly. "Don't worry," he said. "She'll be fine." They had driven the rest of the way in silence.

Ahead, the right taillight of the sheriff's truck began blinking slowly on and off, and the truck turned onto the control road. Gordon slowed down as he followed the sheriff's lead. What little light they had had from the not-quite-rising sun was cut off instantly as they entered the low darkness of the forest. Here it was still night. They descended the dirt road down from the highway and wound through a small ravine. Around them, the trees grew high and tall and close to the road. Even the high beams of the truck did not penetrate far into the blackness. To their left, past the trees, unseen but felt, rose the huge majestic form of the Mogollon Rim.

The sheriff's truck moved carefully over the one-lane road, taking the sharp turns slowly. The road straightened out, and the truck's red taillights increased in brilliance as the sheriff braked to a stop. Gordon pulled to a stop as well. Jim came jogging back. He motioned for Gordon to roll down the window. Instead, Gordon opened the door and stepped out. "What is it?" he asked.

"Come here," the sheriff said. He walked briskly forward, past his own truck and stood in the middle of the road. "Look familiar?"

Gordon nodded, feeling the coldness creep over him, the goose bumps rising on his arms. This was where he had been walking in his dream. He recognized the shapes of specific trees, the convergence of certain silhouettes. Beneath his feet, even the dirt of the road felt familiar. "This was where part of my dream took place."

"Mine too."

He turned toward the sheriff. "What does this mean?"

Jim shook his head. "I don't know." He nodded toward the truck. "Our friend there's not talking."

"We are wasting valuable time," Brother Elias said from inside the pickup. "We must start moving. There is much to do." His voice sounded stronger in the forest darkness, even more authoritarian than usual, and there seemed to be a hint of urgency in it.

Brother Elias, his skin the dark brown of a full-blooded Anasazi, wearing only a loincloth, clutching a spear, standing before a ceremonial bonfire as around him warriors stood hushed.

Father Andrews shut his eyes against the vision, forcing the unwanted picture out of his mind through a sheer effort of will.

"Go back to your truck," Jim told Gordon. "Let's get going." He climbed into his own cab, slammed the door shut and put the engine into gear. Behind him, he heard Gordon's truck start up.

They moved forward. The narrow dirt road was now straight, moving toward the landfill in a direct line through the trees. A doe hopped onto the road, froze for a second in the glare of the oncoming headlights, then bounded off. They saw no other animals. Finally, they came to the open chain link gate of the landfill and stopped. Before them, blocking the entrance, parked sideways across the dirt road, was a truck.

Brad Nicholson's Pepsi truck.

Gordon got out of the pickup, his heart pounding. The cab was empty, he saw, its door open. The canvas strap used to close the back gate of the truck was swinging gently in the open air.

"Stay back!" the sheriff ordered. He had gotten out of his truck and was advancing toward the gate, gun drawn. Gordon remembered the rifles sitting in the bed of his pickup and he was tempted to grab one, but he remained rooted to the spot, watching as the sheriff moved cautiously forward.

Jim put one foot slowly in front of the other, trying desperately not to make any noise. He glanced from side to side, listening for the sound of movement, prepared to defend himself against whatever might jump out at him. He reached the open door of the cab and cautiously peeked in. Empty. He moved around the front of the truck, still preparing himself for an unexpected attack. From here, he could see the rest of the dump. A reddish orange glow emerged from the smoldering embers of the cumbustible pile in the middle of the cleared area, and he shivered. He scanned the space immediately around him. Nothing moved. He continued walking around the truck. The canvas strap of the rear door had stopped swinging, and the sheriff realized that there was no breeze. Something must have hit the strap to make it move. His grip tightened on his gun, and he peeked into the back of the truck.

Nothing.

He relaxed. Puzzled, he looked again into the interior of the truck then toward the bright headlights of the two pickups. He shook his head in an exaggerated motion. "Nothing!" he called.

Gordon moved forward and Father Andrews got out of the truck. Both of them approached the gate. "That's Brad's truck," Gordon said. "How did it get here?"

"I don't know," Jim said.

Brother Elias emerged from the cab of the first pickup, clutching his black-bound Bible in his hand. The preacher walked through the open gate of the landfill and moved around to the back of the truck where the others were standing. " 'Just as the weeds are gathered and burned with fire, so will it be at the close of the age. The Son of man will send his angels, and they will gather out of his kingdom all causes of sin and all evildoers, and throw them into the furnace of fire.' Matthew—"

"—13:40," Father Andrews finished for him. He looked into the preacher's black eyes, and the preacher smiled.

The sheriff glanced around the dump. The sky was becoming progressively lighter. Although the sky to the west was still a dark purple, to the east it was an orangish blue, almost daylight. The tall ponderosas were no longer black silhouettes but were now identifiable as trees.

Brother Elias focused his cold gaze on the sheriff. "Get the pitchforks from the trucks," he ordered. "Get the rope."

"What about the rifles?" Jim asked.

"We do not yet need them."

Jim started for the pickups and Gordon moved to follow him, but Brother Elias clapped a strong hand on his shoulder. "He will get the weapons," the preacher said. "You move the truck. We must have the way clear."

Jim returned with four pitchforks and the coils of rope. Gordon, to his surprise, found the keys still in Brad's ignition, and he moved the vehicle away from the gate. Glancing down at the seat next to him, he saw an empty can of Pepsi, a few wet drops of the beverage visible on the vinyl upholstery, and he thought of his boss. He shut off the engine and hopped out of the truck. He saw the sheriff run back to his pickup and pull the smaller vehicle through the gate into the dump. Brother Elias waved for him to park in the center of the landfill, near the smoldering woodpile. Jim stopped the truck, turned off the lights and came running over.

Brother Elias picked up the pitchforks and handed one to each of them. Gordon accepted the implement and hefted it in his hands. It felt heavy, lethal. The shiny steel of the pronged points captured the first rays of the rising sun and reflected them back at him. He wasn't sure exactly what Brother Elias had in mind, but he knew that as a weapon a pitchfork was good for only one thing—stabbing.

The thought did not comfort him.

Jim and Father Andrews accepted their weapons from the preacher.

" 'Take care, brethren,' " Brother Elias said softly, " 'lest there be in any of you an evil, unbelieving heart, leading you to fall away from the living God.' Hebrews 3:12." The preacher stared hard at each of them, then picked up his pitchfork. "Let us go forth," he said.

FIVE

After taking her shower, Marina dried off, slipped on a robe and went back into the bedroom. She sat on the unmade bed and stared at herself in the full-length mirror on the front of the closet door. The house was silent, she thought, too silent. And she wished, not for the first time, that they lived a little closer to town. Outside, it was still dark. The moon had long since set, and the sun was not yet peeking its face above the eastern horizon. The forest outside the window looked ominous and vaguely threatening.

That was nonsense, Marina told herself. It was the same forest that was out there in the daytime, the same trees she walked amongst in the light. She was just spooked because of what Gordon had told her.

She stood up and moved over to the dresser for some underwear. She would get dressed and drive to Phoenix, spend the day shopping in the bright clear heat of the Valley, surrounded by miles of steel and concrete and people and civilization.

She slipped on her panties and stood still for a moment, listening. Was that a scratching noise she heard coming from the kitchen?

No, she told herself. But she did not move, dared not breathe. She listened carefully.

Yes.

Something was out in the front of the house. Something small. She pulled her robe closed, then rushed over and slammed shut the bedroom door. Moving quickly, she pushed a chair against it. She put her ear to the door.

All was silent.

Marina moved over to the window. It was dark and she could not see very well, but she thought she detected movement in the underbrush. Scared now, she inched her way across the room to the phone, still watching the window. She dialed the emergency number. The phone rang five times before someone answered. "Sheriff's office." The voice was tired, harried.

"Hello," Marina whispered into the phone. "My name is Marina Lewis. Is my husband Gordon there?"

"Gordon Lewis? He went someplace with the sheriff. May I take a message?"

"I think there's a prowler in my house," Marina whispered. "I'm in the bedroom, and I barricaded the door. I heard noises out in the kitchen."

"Stay calm, ma'am. We'll have someone out there as soon as possible. We're a little understaffed right now, so it may be a while before we can get to you. I suggest you call a neighbor and try to find some type of weapon—"

"I need help!"

"I understand that, ma'am." The voice was clearly under stress.

"I'm pregnant!" Marina screamed. She dropped the phone, willing herself not to cry. The house was still silent, but she knew someone—something—was out there. She could feel it. She moved next to the door and crouched down, pressing her ear against the wood. Never before had she been so conscious of the child inside her, never before had her unborn baby seemed so alive, so in need of protection. She felt an unfamiliar predatory instinct flare up inside her—the instinct of a mother prepared to protect her young against all odds.

Something just outside the door gave a small yelp, and Marina jumped. She pressed against the door with her shoulder, pushing all her weight against it so nothing could get in. With one hand, she held the chair in place. There was the sound of rough gnawing on the wood outside the door.

"Get out of here!" she screamed.

Tiny voices in the hallway laughed, and there was the sound of little feet running away. Marina began sobbing, still pressing her shoulder to the door.

A rock flew through the window, glass shattering on the floor, and she screamed. She threw open the bedroom door, kicking the chair aside, and looked out into the hall.

Nothing.

She ran across the hall into the bathroom and shut the door, locking it. The shutters Gordon had put over the window were securely in place. Whatever was out there was playing with her, she realized. If it had wanted to kill her, it could have done so easily. She sat down on the toilet and bent over, her hands over her head, her head between her knees.

SIX

The four men walked slowly across the gravel of the
dump in the early morning half-light, toward the spot
where the Selways' bodies had been found, Brother
Elias in the lead, Jim bringing up the rear. The harsh
white light of the rising sun shone in barlike beams
through the branches of the trees. At the far end of
the landfill, the side mirror of a large parked bulldozer
reflected back the sunlight in a single concentrated
flash.

Brother Elias moved toward the large pile of garbage at the edge of the cliff. He stopped, cocking his
head, listening. He began walking forward more
slowly now, staring at the ground, his pitchfork held
out before him.

The other three followed silently.

Suddenly Brother Elias made a harsh stab into the
pile of garbage in front of him. There was an ear-
piercing squeal, and the preacher lifted his pitchfork.

Stuck to the points, still squirming, was a fetus.

Gordon turned away, feeling nauseous. Even the
sheriff flinched. Father Andrews stood with his eyes
closed, leaning heavily on his pitchfork for support,
his lips moving in silent prayer. Though all of them

had known, deep down, why they had been carrying the pitchforks, though all of them had known what Brother Elias expected of them, none of them had visualized the experience, had realized just how repellent the actual act would be.

What if Brother Elias was wrong? Gordon thought, sickened. What if he had just stabbed a real baby? But what real baby would be crawling through the dump, through the garbage, at six o'clock in the morning?

The preacher turned toward them. "This is what we are up against," he said. He held his pitchfork forward for them to examine the fetus. The thing was still alive, still squirming, though it did not seem to be in agony. Indeed, it appeared to feel no pain at all. Instead, it struggled furiously to free itself, as though the long steel points protruding from its body were nothing more than a harmless restraining belt. Its face was hideously malformed and was twisted into a malevolent grimace of hate. Thick fur grew on the unnaturally short arms. It stared up at them and spat angrily. There were tiny pointed teeth within its too-red mouth.

Brother Elias nodded toward the sheriff. "Get the blood," he said.

Jim ran off toward the truck.

Father Andrews moved forward gingerly. He was tempted to touch the fetus to make sure it was real. "What is it?" he asked. "I mean, is it alive? I thought these were infants who had died before birth. Shouldn't they be rotted? Or decomposed?"

"I thought they'd be like ghosts," Gordon admitted. "Not real babies."

"They have corporeal form," Brother Elias said. "But they are not real babies."

The sheriff returned, lugging a box filled with the four quart jars of blood. He set the box down in front of the preacher.

Brother Elias nodded to the sheriff. He lifted the pitchfork, the fetus still struggling on the points, and ran it hard into the ground. The hideous creature screamed, wiggling crazily. The preacher looked at Gordon. "Get the camera," he ordered.

Gordon ran to his truck and returned a moment later with the camera. He snapped a picture of Brother Elias standing next to the impaled fetus.

The preacher picked up two jars of blood, muttered a short incomprehensible prayer, and walked across the gravel to the smoldering woodpile. Chanting something in a strangely guttural foreign tongue, the words rising and falling in ritualistic cadences, he began walking in a circle around the pile, sprinkling the blood on the ground as he did so.

"What's he saying?" Jim asked.

Father Andrews shook his head. "It sounds like he's repeating some type of liturgy, but I'm not familiar with the language. It's not Latin, I know. And it doesn't sound either European or Oriental." He listened, cocking his head, and his face turned suddenly pale. "I . . . I don't think it's human," he said.

Brother Elias continued chanting until he had completed his circle around the smoldering woodpile. He knelt on the ground and dribbled the last of the blood on the dirt in a peculiar spiral pattern. He waved his hands over the ground, said something in the alien tongue and looked up into the sky. His fingers traced in the air a cross, a spiral, and an unnaturally angular geometric shape.

The circle of blood erupted immediately into flame. Within the circle, the ashes of the woodpile began to burn again until the flames had become a full-fledged conflagration.

The fetus on the pitchfork was now struggling harder and screaming wildly. From other parts of the landfill, other tiny bodies, other babies, other fetuses, pushed their way up through the wet slimy garbage, crawled out from between sheets of metal, and moved toward them. They moved slowly but surely, like large retarded slugs.

"Jesus," Gordon breathed. "How many of them do you think there are?"

"Hundreds," the sheriff said, and Gordon realized for the first time the enormity of what they were fighting against. He felt weaker, smaller, more impotent than he had ever felt in his life. What were they? A ragtag group of four stupid pitiful men fighting an evil so powerful, so organized, so all-encompassing, that it could animate these hundreds of bodies and will the bodies to do its bidding. There was no way they could hope to battle anything this large. He stared at the small wiggling forms moving toward them across the dirt. This was all part of a long-range plan, a plan that was coming finally to fruition. Something that could do this, that could capture these babies over a period of years, perhaps decades, and save them, hoard them, until needed, could not be fought. Not by them.

Brother Elias grasped the handle of the pitchfork and matter-of-factly pulled both it and the impaled fetus from the ground. He shoved the end of the pitchfork into the fire, and the fetus disintegrated in a flash of blood red light. The preacher turned toward them. "Now you know what you must do," he said.

Gordon stared at him. "It'll take us all day to get them all."

Brother Elias' tight lips curled into a smile, and for the first time his eyes joined in. He looked almost happy. "We are not going to get them all," he said. "We are using them for bait." He walked toward another small fetus flopping along the dirt and speared it through with his pitchfork. He shoved the pitchfork into the fire, and the creature disappeared in a squealing flash of red. "Get to work," he said, and his voice was filled with a powerful authority. "We have no time to waste."

Gordon found himself walking toward the large pile of scrap metal to his right. He had seen pink movement against the dull gray and silver of the discarded metal. He stopped in front of the pile. Before him, moving awkwardly toward him, was a hunchbacked creature much smaller than an ordinary baby, about the size of his fist. This, he realized, was one of the fetuses that had been aborted or miscarried early in the pregnancy, not one that had been stillborn. The creature had bent misshapen arms and a thick tuft of coarse black hair atop its pink elongated head. Gordon raised his pitchfork above the fetus, ready to bring it down, but he could not do it. He could not bring himself to stab the creature. Slowly, he lowered the pitchfork. He had never been able to kill. He did not hunt. Hell, he had a hard time getting rid of bugs; he usually took them outside and threw them into the bushes rather than kill them. He realized that these creatures were not exactly alive, but stabbing them felt the same inside as it would stabbing a normal baby.

He looked around. The sheriff, grimacing, was carrying a squealing, squirming infant to the fire, which was still burning as strongly as ever. Even Father Andrews was gingerly holding a tiny creature he had impaled on his pitchfork. Brother Elias was vigorously and enthusiastically spearing infants left and right.

Thou shalt not kill, Gordon thought.

He felt a sharp flash of pain in his foot, and he looked down. The fetus's twisted little hands had clawed a hole through the canvas material of his tennis shoe and were digging into his flesh. He stepped backward, and the fetus crawled toward him. Slowly, grimacing distastefully, Gordon scooped up the fetus, using his pitchfork like a shovel. He held the pitchfork way out in front of him, balancing the still moving creature carefully on the prongs, but before he could reach the fire it fell to the ground. The fetus looked up at him and laughed nastily.

He carefully picked it up again the same way, using the pitchfork as a shovel, but as he approached the fire the creature threw itself off the prongs onto the ground. He was about to pick it up yet again when another pitchfork speared the fetus through its mid-section. Gordon turned to see Brother Elias standing next to him. The fetus gave a tremendous screech of rage and agony, way out of proportion to its small size, and the preacher shoved it into the fire where it disintegrated.

"You're too slow," Brother Elias said.

It was a criticism, but Gordon did not care. He could not bring himself to stab anything in cold blood, no matter what it was. He looked up. The sun had risen by this time, and the morning sky was clear and cloudless. The trees on the side of the Rim stood out in green relief against the brown rock cliffs, and over-head a lone hawk circled lazily. Gordon started to walk toward the far side of the dump. He stumbled and looked down . . . and saw, protruding from be-neath a leaking shopping bag filled with garbage, a hand. An adult hand.

He pushed the bag aside with his foot, cleared away some rancid food and old newspapers, kicking them off, and found himself staring down at the lifeless form of Brad Nicholson.

Brad.

He was too shocked to even call out. There was a huge ugly gash in Brad's neck, and from the gash pro-truded a twisted bloody windpipe. The garbage be-neath his neck was soaked red with blood. Brad's eyes were open, staring, and his mouth was contorted in a silent scream. There was something else in his face as well, some other expression, and though Gordon did not know quite what it was, he did not like it.

He thought suddenly of Brad's son Bobby. Some-body would have to tell him that his dad had died. Had been killed. Had had his throat ripped out, bloody tubes yanked out of his body through a hole torn in his neck. The boy would grow up without a father. He might not even remember his father by the time he turned twenty. Not very well at least. And Connie. Someone would have to tell Connie. She and Brad may not have had the closest marriage in the world, but . . .

By the time Father Andrews and the sheriff had run up next to him, Gordon realized he was screaming.

"Jesus fuck," the sheriff breathed, staring down at Brad's body. Next to Brad's head, he saw a large brown rat, curled into a sleeping position. The animal awoke suddenly and stared into Jim's eyes. The sheriff watched in horror as the rat crawled into Brad's open mouth.

Gordon gasped and turned away. Father Andrews prayed silently.

Brother Elias came up behind them and glanced down at the body. Without speaking, he pulled a lighter from his pocket and touched it to the tattered remnants of Brad's shirt. The blood-soaked clothing started to burn, and the air was filled with a sickeningly acrid stench.

"What the hell are you doing?" Gordon said, shocked. He grabbed the preacher's arm. Brother Elias pulled away from his grip. "Let us hope we are not too late," he said.

Gordon stared down at the body of his boss, his friend, and watched the flames lick at the ragged edges of the gash in Brad's neck. The drying blood smoked and turned black, and the skin began to char and peel off. A tongue of fire leaped from Brad's blazing shirt to his beard, and his beard began to burn. Flames entered his mouth, blackening his teeth.

"We are too late," Brother Elias announced.

Gordon looked up and saw, coming toward them across the gravel, two adult figures.

One of them was Brad.

"Get the Bibles!" Brother Elias ordered. He rushed over to where the coils of rope were lying on the ground. The sheriff ran immediately toward the parked pickup. Suddenly remembering the camera around his neck, Gordon began snapping pictures. He could see the approaching figures even more clearly through the slightly magnifying lens of the camera. He did not know where they had come from or why they had not been noticed sooner. The figure next to Brad was jet black, its features unidentifiable. Brad appeared to be limping and was carrying his. . . . But Brad's body was burning on the ground next to him.

The sheriff hurried back, carrying the four white Bibles Father Andrews had brought along. "Give them to me!" Brother Elias demanded. Jim handed him the books. "Now pick up the end of that rope!" The preacher looked at Gordon and Father Andrews. "You two walk forward, holding your pitchforks in front of you! You're going to have to use them!"

Brad and the other figure had stopped.

"It's Father Selway," Jim said softly, picking up his end of the rope. "The other one's Father Selway."

He was right, Gordon saw immediately. The black figure was Father Selway. He saw the burnt face smile, teeth a lighter black against the jet skin, and he felt a wave of cold terror wash over him. He looked at Father Andrews, standing next to him, and wondered what the priest was thinking.

Father Andrews was trying not to think at all. Unwanted feelings, outside thoughts, alien impressions were pushing themselves into his mind. He saw the scene before him with unnatural clarity, his brain absorbing every detail, but it was intercut with other scenes, other events. *A group of settlers shoveling deformed infants onto a bonfire. Naked men and women dancing ritualistically before the unmoving form of Brother Elias in another guise. The blackened figure of an Anasazi woman standing amidst a sea of fetuses.*

The priest's head was pounding with the pain. He looked at Gordon, grasped his pitchfork tightly and forced himself to move forward, his face a mask of grim determination.

Brother Elias walked forward next to Father Andrews, three Bibles clutched under his arm, one held in his outstretched left hand. In his other hand, he grasped the end of the rope he and the sheriff carried between them.

Jim walked abreast of the preacher, keeping his eyes on the figures in front of him. He felt woefully unprepared, and he wished Brother Elias had told him what they planned to do. He felt extremely vulnerable walking toward these two . . . things . . . carrying nothing but a rope, and he cursed himself for leaving his gun in the pickup. He thought of the four high-powered rifles in the bed of Gordon's vehicle and wished that he had one of them with him. His jaw hurt from gritting his teeth, and his legs ached with nervous tension. This close, he could see the two figures quite clearly. And he did not like what he saw. Brad Nicholson's face was an inhuman blank, devoid of all thought and feeling. Only the eyes seemed alive. They burned with a piercing intensity not unlike that of Brother Elias'. The body appeared solid, real, though the stench of Brad's burning body singed his nostrils and the air was beginning to fill with the smoke of burning flesh. He could see the figure's skin darkening as Brad's real body burned, and he knew that when the body had been consumed completely by fire the form would be as black as the figure of Father Selway next to it.

Father Selway stood smiling, unmoving. His skin was charred by fire, and his features bore an expression of triumphant evil. The sheriff was unable to look into the hellish face for more than a few seconds.

Brother Elias stopped. They were only ten feet away from the unmoving figures. The other three men came to an abrupt halt. Around them, the wiggling and flopping infants were coalescing into a coherent group, coming from all parts of the dump toward them. Many of the tiny creatures were gurgling or mewing, making tiny sounds of pleasure.

Brother Elias placed the four white Bibles on the ground in front of him, along a straight line.

The figure of Father Selway raised a blackened hand into the air. "Do you really think your pagan rituals can accomplish anything?" The voice was grating, inhuman, filled with a disgusted contempt.

Brother Elias said nothing but passed his hands over each of the Bibles, muttering something in his strange unearthly tongue.

"Gordon," the figure said, turning toward him. "And how is your pretty little wife?" The black smile became wider, crueler. "And your daughter? Your daughter wants to be one of us, you know. She wants to claw her way out of your wife's thin little body and escape. Right now, your wife is coughing blood as her insides are being ripped apart. Blood is streaming from that pathetic little hole between her legs."

Gordon felt his muscles clench against this verbal assault. Hot anger rushed to his face. His grip tightened on the pitchfork. He felt like shoving it straight through Father Selway's head.

Brother Elias looked at him. "Satan is a liar and the father of lies," he said. "Ignore him. He is trying to provoke a reaction."

Father Selway turned toward the sheriff. "You have strayed from the path, Jim. You have forsaken the path of righteousness. You must be punished." The figure glanced around the dump. Its voice lowered. "The boy is here, Jim. Don Wilson. His body is burning. He is going to burn in hell for all eternity."

The sheriff smiled coldly. "Fuck you."

"And you, my successor." The figure turned to look at Father Andrews. "Is this what you were taught by the church? Is the bishop aware that you are taking part in these blasphemous rituals?" The creature laughed harshly. "You are a poor excuse for a priest."

Father Andrews looked away, saying nothing.

The figure of Father Selway lowered its head and, as if on cue, a look of joyous hatred passed suddenly over Brad's blank features. Behind the two, hundreds of infants appeared from nowhere. They were much larger and much more coordinated than the others. They moved forward in ranks, propelling themselves with precision.

Brother Elias stood up calmly. He looked at Gordon and Father Andrews, pointing toward the still-darkening figure of Brad. "He is weak," the preacher said. "Stab him when he comes forward and hold him down, pin him to the ground. The sheriff and I will take care of the other one." He moved next to Jim, took a deep breath and lowered his head in a position of prayer. "We ask thee for protection, O Lord. We seek only to do your bidding. Do not let us walk alone. In the name of the Father, the Son, and the Holy Ghost, amen."

Jim glanced over at the figure of Father Selway, still smiling, still unmoving, as hundreds of tiny infants and fetuses massed together behind it.

"Hold tight to the rope," Brother Elias said. "We are going to tie him up."

The figure of Father Selway said something harsh, guttural, and incoherent. A command. Brad rushed forward. The fetuses and infants swarmed suddenly over the dump in a liquid wave.

Gordon held tightly to his pitchfork as Brad ran toward him, and he pushed the weapon deep into the running figure's dark flesh. Brad let out a cry of rage and frustration, but there was no pain in the sound. The metal spikes sank easily and deeply into the soft body, coming out the other side. Gordon's weapon went through the stomach and Father Andrews' hit higher in the chest. Both used their weight to force the struggling body to the ground. Brad's arms were flailing wildly, trying to grab the handles of the pitchforks and pull them out, but it was no use. They had the creature pinned.

Jim and Brother Elias moved forward slowly, gripping the rope tightly. They waded through a sea of tiny bodies, all snapping and clawing at their legs and feet, but the creatures seemed to have no effect on them. The sheriff looked down. He could not see the gravel for the bodies. Hundreds, perhaps thousands, of the tiny infants were swarming on top of each other. He could see little hands grasping at air, little mouths snapping at nothing. His feet stepped on the bodies as he moved forward. They felt soft, squishy. He could feel small bones snapping as his legs sank deep into the sea of flesh.

Before them, the figure of Father Selway was slowly backing up. It was no longer smiling. A look of hatred—fear?—crossed its features.

"In the name of Jesus Christ, our Lord and Savior, we command you to recognize the power of the Word," Brother Elias chanted. "In the name of Jesus Christ, our Lord and Savior, we command you to bow down before the power of God."

The figure was not moving but was now standing stock-still. It appeared trapped, though Jim was not sure why. They had done nothing.

Was it the prayers?

They walked on either side of the figure and circled twice, pulling the rope tight. The rope sank deep into the black flesh—so deeply that it was no longer visible—but held nonetheless. The figure said nothing, made no sound, and Jim had the feeling that whatever power had been animating the body, whatever had inhabited the burnt form, had left, leaving only a lifeless husk.

Instantly, the form became animate. A hand lashed out and struck Brother Elias full in the face. The

preacher fell, letting go of the rope, blood streaming
from his nose. The black face grinned, the features
filled with an evil intelligence.

"Grab the rope!" Jim screamed, whipping his head
around. But both Gordon and the priest were struggling with the now jet figure of Brad, and he knew
neither of them could pick up the slack without letting
Brad escape.

Brother Elias struggled to his feet, shaking his head
as if to clear it. He reached down and grabbed the
rope with both hands. Blood was pouring from his
nose, which had been crushed. One eye was starting
to swell.

"I am very impressed with the power of the Lord,"
the figure said in its grating voice. A black arm swung
out again, but Brother Elias ducked successfully.

"Pull!" the preacher yelled. He leaned backward,
using all of his weight to drag the bound figure toward
him. Jim pulled as well, putting his strength into it.
The black form was heavy, much heavier than its size
would indicate.

"Pull!" the preacher yelled again. His eye was now
swollen shut. "Pull hard!"

With one quick yank, they pulled the figure over
the line of white Bibles. The body stiffened noticeably,
and Jim felt all of the power drain out of it. A look
of agonized rage cemented itself onto the burnt features. The Bibles on the ground blackened and burst
into flame. A terrible scream of primal pain erupted
simultaneously from the thousands of tiny mouths surrounding them. The sound was deafening.

"Drag it to the fire!" Brother Elias yelled. "It can't
hurt us now!" He looked toward Gordon and the
priest. "Bring him to the fire, too!"

Behind Jim, Gordon was struggling alone to keep
Brad pinned to the ground. Father Andrews' pitchfork
was sunk deep in Brad's chest, but the priest himself
was rolling on the ground in agony, holding tightly

onto his arm. Blood was pouring out from between his fingers. Dozens of little fetuses were swarming around the priest, but they seemed not to notice him. They were squirming blindly, panicked, and the sheriff realized that they were now lost, leaderless. They did not know what to do. A few of them bit into the skin of Father Andrews' arm, causing him to scream in pain, but it was the random biting of dumb mindlessness and not the concentrated frenzy of a few moments before.

"Get him up!" the sheriff called to Gordon. He was running out of breath as he tugged the inert form of Father Selway toward the fire. "You . . . have to bring . . . Brad to . . . the fire!"

"He's hurt!" Gordon said.

"Then you bring him by yourself!"

Gordon looked at the crazed hellish figure struggling beneath him. "I can't! I'm not strong enough!"

"We'll get it," Brother Elias said. His voice was slurred. He spat blood. He pulled hard on the rigid form of Father Selway. They were almost to the fire now. The flames were still burning bright.

Three more pulls on the rope and they were there. Brother Elias stopped. "We'll have to push!" he said. He dropped his end of the rope and moved next to the sheriff. He grabbed Jim's arm, leading him behind the unmoving form. This close, Jim could smell a faint sulfurous odor underneath the powerful scent of burned flesh.

"Push!" the preacher said.

The body was soft, like raw dough. Jim felt his hands sink deep into the black form. The squishy flesh pressing against his skin was cold. It felt as though his hands and arms were being absorbed by the body. He pushed as hard as he could without meeting anything solid, anything substantial, but the push must have been enough. The black figure toppled forward into the fire.

"Stand back!" Brother Elias ordered.

The charred blackness melted off the figure, and inside Jim saw something white and shiny and vaguely translucent. The body disappeared in a long, sustained flash of red, and the entire fire suddenly turned the color of blood. A shock wave of foul-smelling heat rolled outward from the blaze.

Fifteen feet away, Brad's struggling body suddenly went limp. Gordon held the pitchfork in place for a moment, but when the figure did not move again he let up. Jim came running over, and both of them picked up the body, carrying it to the fire and throwing it in. There was another flash of light, this one not as long, and the body was gone.

Blood was still streaming down Brother Elias' face from his crushed nose and eye, dripping down onto his suit. The preacher was standing before the blaze, hands outstretched, speaking loudly in his alien tongue. The red flames lent an unearthly tint to his features, highlighting the liquid redness of the blood on his face. The flames flared suddenly then died down to nothing. The fire devolved to its original smoking embers, and the burning ring of blood surrounding it went out completely. A thick wave of oppressive black smoke poured out from the now dormant woodpile.

Gordon looked down at the camera around his neck and saw that it had been broken. The lens was smashed, and light was leaking into the camera through a crack in the body, ruining the film. None of his pictures would come out.

The smoke was spreading upward, carried by an unfelt wind, blocking out the rays of the morning sun, covering the sky. Though the fire had died and there was nothing left to burn, the smoke continued to pour forth in great gusts. Gordon looked up and saw that the tip of the smoke cloud had formed a clawed hand.

Brother Elias picked up the box with the remaining jars of blood. "There's more to do," he said. "It's not over yet." He carried the box to the car. "Come on. We must go."

"To Milk Ranch Point," the sheriff said.

"To Milk Ranch Point," Brother Elias agreed.

Gordon moved toward them, supporting a weakened Father Andrews on his arm. "One of them jumped up and attacked him," Gordon explained.

Brother Elias grabbed the priest's arm and squeezed it tightly. Father Andrews screamed, but when the preacher removed his hand the bleeding had stopped. "You must be strong," Brother Elias said. "God needs you now."

The four of them walked back to the trucks.

"We'll all go in the same truck," Jim said. "It'll be a little tight, but we can't afford any accidents."

Brother Elias nodded. As the other three piled into the cab of Gordon's truck, the preacher picked a stray piece of paper off the ground, took out his lighter, and set the paper on fire. He dropped it on the ground. It spread to another piece of paper and then to a dried tree branch. He got into the truck and Jim started the engine.

"Are you just going to let that burn?" Gordon asked.

The preacher nodded. "Rangers will spot the fire when it has done its work. They will put it out."

The fire reached the body of a mindlessly squirming infant and engulfed it.

The truck backed out, tires squishing bodies beneath them, small bones breaking. None of them even winced at the terrible sounds or at the bumpy feel of the truck as it drove over the tiny bodies on the way out of the landfill.

Before they reached the highway, they heard a massive explosion as the flames reached Brad Nicholson's Pepsi truck.

SEVEN

Marina searched frantically through the bathroom, looking for a weapon. She opened the medicine chest and quickly pawed through its contents, throwing the discarded and rejected items onto the floor. She held the can of Right Guard deodorant for a moment. She had seen a character in a movie once use an aerosol spray can as a flame thrower, holding a lighted match in front of the spray. But she had no match, no flame whatsoever. She threw the can onto the floor. A small pair of scissors was lying in the top drawer under the sink, amidst various makeup containers and old curlers. She picked up the scissors, but rejected the idea immediately. Too small.

There was nothing she could do.

She sat down on the toilet once again. She had panicked at first, crying uncontrollably and screaming at whatever was outside the door. Then she had forced herself to adjust to the situation, forced herself to calm down and think rationally. The creatures outside the door had taunted her. Something large had been thrown against the door. Small rocks had been thrown against the shuttered window from the outside.

Marina stared at her face in the bathroom mirror.

Her hair was disheveled; mascara ran down her cheeks in twin rivulets. Her lips were dry and cracked. She buried her face in her hands.

Outside the door, something small chuckled evilly to itself. Other voices joined in.

"Get the hell out of here!" Marina screamed.

The bathroom doorknob rattled as something tried to turn it. Marina held her stomach protectively, acutely aware of the defenseless baby within her. She knew that whatever was out there was only toying with her, playing games with her. They would tire of her soon, and then she would find out what was really in store.

Several small voices, in and around the house, outside, on the roof, babbled crazily in unison, and were suddenly silent. She held her breath.

Five minutes passed. Ten. Fifteen.

Marina stood up, pressing her ear to the door, listening.

Nothing.

She moved over to the shuttered window.

Nothing.

Slowly, cautiously, she opened the wooden shutter. Several shards of broken glass fell into the bathroom. She peeked outside, but there was nothing, no one, no sign of life. She walked back across the bathroom and carefully opened the door. The hallway was littered with broken glass and china. Two chairs had been dragged out from the kitchen and were over-turned next to the bedroom door. An antique porcelain lamp, given to her by her grandmother, had been smashed against the wall.

But there was no sign of life.

Marina opened the door wider. She saw nothing and moved slowly out into the hall. The china cracked under her feet. She stepped over an overturned chair. She moved toward the kitchen and stepped through the kitchen door.

Something pink, moving at lightning speed, dashed out from under the table and knocked her backward to the floor. Her head hit hard against a smashed plate. Small fingers grabbed her arms and legs and spread them wide.

Marina screamed as the point of an icepick was driven through her right hand. Her head whipped around and she saw two small malformed infants pressing the pick through her hand into the tile floor. She screamed again as steak knives impaled her other hand and her feet, but though she felt dizzy and weak she did not pass out.

Scores of tiny infants, all hideously deformed, were moving around the floor of the kitchen, cackling to themselves.

She closed her eyes in pain and disbelief. She opened her eyes to see a large evil-looking baby clutching in its hand her good carving knife. The creature smiled. Morning sunlight glinted off the polished metal of the knife, and Marina realized that the knife was going to be used to cut her open and kill her unborn daughter.

Screaming, she blacked out.

EIGHT

The truck moved slowly up the winding highway that switch-backed up the face of the Rim. From this vantage point, they could see the forest below them. Jim saw that the clouds of billowing black smoke were still spreading upward from the landfill, now augmented by the more natural gray smoke of a forest fire. Farther south, the morning sunlight glinted off the buildings of Randall, a small whitish patch in the sea of green trees.

Jim wondered what was happening back in town. He should have given Pete more explicit instructions. He should have brought along some type of two-way radio so he could communicate with the office and find out what was happening. He shook his head. There were a lot of things he should have done.

At least Annette and the kids had gotten out safely.

He looked at Gordon and felt immediately guilty. He should have allowed Gordon to check on his wife. It would have only taken an extra ten minutes or so. She was the one who was really in danger, anyway. He should have overridden Brother Elias and allowed Gordon to drive by his house. It was very stupid of him not to. What if something happened to her? Gordon met his gaze, and Jim glanced guiltily away, concentrating his attention on the road.

"We need to go faster," Brother Elias said, "or we will be too late. The adversary knows now that we are here. He knows we are coming for him and he will be prepared."

"I have to use low gears here," Jim explained. "We'll be able to go a lot faster once we get to the top."

Brother Elias said nothing, staring silently out the front windshield.

Gordon turned to look at Father Andrews, leaning against the door. The priest was forced into an uncomfortably tight position, but his eyes were closed and he was sleeping. He was exhausted.

The pickup finally reached the top of the Rim, and Jim shifted the truck into third, flooring the gas pedal. The vehicle shot forward.

The road wound through the forest, following the lay of the land. The two-lane blacktop skirted especially thick stands of tall trees and wound through gullies, finding the easiest route through the rough terrain.

Ahead, Jim saw the small brown Forest Service sign that marked the turnoff to Aspen Lake and he slowed down. He rolled up the truck's window and turned onto the dirt road. Once again, he sped up, and soon the pickup was flying over the innumerable bumps in the road, sailing past the close-growing trees.

Fifteen minutes later, the pines began to be replaced by aspens, and he could see the blue of the lake through the trees. "We're almost there," he announced.

He slowed down as they reached the lake, searching for the old dirt path that led to Milk Ranch Point.

"There it is," Brother Elias said, pointing.

Jim followed the preacher's finger. Several newly cut aspens were piled across the path, barring the truck access.

"Something doesn't want us back there," Gordon said.

Brother Elias nodded. "We'll have to walk."

The truck braked to a stop, and Father Andrews blinked open his eyes. "Are we there?" he asked.

"Yeah," Jim said. He opened the door and got out, stretching his tired muscles. Above, the sky was darkening, gray rain clouds from the north intermingling with the heavy black smoke still streaming up from the landfill below the Rim. A warm wind had sprung up from somewhere, and it brought to his nostrils the odor of burning flesh.

Brother Elias stepped out of the cab, carrying the box with the last two jars of blood. He moved to the back of the truck and put the box down on the ground at his feet. He drew from the rear of the pickup a small canvas bag containing the four crosses he had requested, and he dropped the bag into the box.

He pulled out one of the rifles and a box of ammunition.

"Does everyone know how to use one of these?" the preacher asked.

Gordon looked at Father Andrews, and both men shook their heads.

"You won't need one," Brother Elias said to the priest. He looked at Gordon. "You will." He handed Gordon the rifle and threw another one to the sheriff. "Show him how to use it," he said.

Father Andrews watched as Gordon and Jim walked to the front of the truck, grasping their rifles. He turned his attention to Brother Elias, who was staring at him with that black unflinching gaze. "Come," the preacher said. He put a strong arm around Father Andrews' shoulders and led him to the makeshift barrier that was blocking the trail to Milk Ranch Point. This close, the priest could see that the felled aspens had not been chopped down. They had been gnawed on. By tiny teeth.

He felt suddenly cold.

"How strong are your ties to your church?" Brother Elias asked.

The priest stared at him. "Why?"

"What I will ask you to do goes against everything you have ever been taught. It runs contrary to the very tenets of your faith."

Father Andrews smiled slightly. "So what else is new?"

"This you will not be able to rationalize. What I will ask you to do is specifically prohibited in the Bible. It is considered blasphemous before the eyes of God." He paused for a moment, his gaze focusing upward on the gray clouds and black smoke creeping across the sky above them. The air was hot, humid, uncomfortable. "Good and evil are not abstract concepts," he said finally. "They exist and they have always existed."

The priest frowned. "I have always thought so."

"They exist outside and independent of any religion. Religions, all religions, are merely crude attempts to explain their existence. Religions are created to label and categorize powers they do not understand."

Father Andrews looked at the preacher. He could feel the evil of this place. It suffused the trees, the bushes, the very ground they stood upon. Corruption thickened the air they breathed, and he felt almost overwhelmed by nausea as the evil pressed in upon his senses. He felt his arm, now healed, and that too seemed wrong somehow. His eyes met those of Brother Elias, and he looked away, frightened.

The preacher pointed up the trail before them. "This is an evil spot," he said. "It has always been an evil spot. The power that is here has always been here and always will be here." He paused, and his voice lowered as if he were afraid of being overheard. "In the countless centuries before man, animals brought their young here to die. Deer that were born crippled were dragged here and left by their mothers. Bears that were undersized and would obviously not survive their first winter were brought here and abandoned. The evil was fed, and its power grew."

Father Andrews paled. He knew where the conversation was headed.

"The first men also left their unfit young here instinctively. But as cultures evolved, reasons were needed for continuing these practices. Elaborate rationalizations were concocted by men. Sacrifices were incorporated into emerging religions. This was considered the home of the dark gods, and sacrifices of infants, healthy or unhealthy, were supposed to appease the deities and keep their anger at bay." He looked at the priest. "Always, the evil of this place was recognized."

Father Andrews licked his lips, which were suddenly dry. "So what happened?"

"The evil fed on the bodies, on the blank innocent energy of the infants. But rather than appease the evil, the sacrifices added to its power until it began to expand, until it had grown far beyond its traditional confines." He smiled, but there was no joy in it. "This is the lake of fire."

Father Andrews nodded dumbly.

"Religions, as they changed, abandoned the sacrifices and no longer condoned them, but the sacrifices were still practiced surreptitiously by the people of this area. Stillborn infants were brought here and abandoned. Unhealthy babies were dropped off to die. The people forgot the reasons why they brought the infants here, but the reasons had not mattered to begin with. They were only rationalizations." He looked again at the darkening sky, then down at Father Andrews. "Infants are still brought here to die," he said.

"It's not possible. Not in this day and age."

"Aborted fetuses are brought here by doctors. Dead babies are stolen from their rightful graves and deposited here. The people often do not know what they do or why, but the evil is strong and it demands to be fed. It stretches outward as it grows, exerting more influence as its power increases." There was the sound of one gunshot, then another, as behind them Jim and Gordon practiced shooting. The sound echoed like thunder in the wilderness. "There is nothing we can do to stop any of this. The evil exists and it will always exist. We can only keep it contained, diffuse it when its power begins to grow. This is why we perform the ritual."

"Why are you telling this only to me?" Father Andrews asked. "Why aren't you telling the others too?"

The preacher once again put a firm hand around the priest's shoulder. "Because you need to know. They do not. We all have our roles to play."

"And what exactly is my role?"

"You must communicate with it. You must allow it to speak through you and to hear with your ears while I recite the words of the ritual."

A wave of terror passed through Father Andrews as the import of the preacher's words struck him. Panic flared within him, and he pulled away from Brother Elias. "You want me to let it possess me? I'm supposed to willingly let myself be possessed by some . . ." He could not find the word to finish his sentence.

"It's not dangerous," Brother Elias said. "If we do everything right, there will be no danger to you whatsoever."

Father Andrews felt the lie of the preacher's words. "I don't believe you!" he shouted. He glared at Brother Elias, his eyes wide with fright, his head pounding. "You're lying!"

Brother Elias stood unmoving as a warm wind blew

around him. He looked at the priest but said nothing. His eyes were unreadable.

As Brother Elias talked in low tones to Father Andrews, Jim gave Gordon a crash course in firearm use. After showing him how to unlatch the safety, how to aim and fire the rifle, he shot a pinecone lying on the ground. The pinecone was blown into tiny fragments. He then coached Gordon through a shot of his own. Gordon aimed at a blue logger's marking on a tree, but the bullet whistled harmlessly through the nearby branches, missing the tree completely.

"That's okay," Jim said. He then showed Gordon what he had done wrong, demonstrating how to hold the rifle properly and how to sight by tilting his head and not the gun. After several more tries, Gordon was finally able to hit one of the wider trees. He shot the rifle twice on his own, with no help from Jim, and he hit the tree both times.

"That's good enough," Brother Elias said, walking over to them. "You don't need to be any more precise than that. Your target will be big."

"How big?" Jim asked.

Brother Elias did not answer.

Behind the preacher, Father Andrews came shuffling forward. His face was ashen, his walk slow and stilted. He looked from Jim to Gordon, but his eyes were blank. His hands were clenched into trembling fists.

"We must start walking," Brother Elias said, stepping to the back of the pickup. He picked up a box and put it down at his feet, drawing something hidden in a greasy rag from the rear of the truck and dropping it into the box. "I hope we are not already too late."

The four men climbed over the hastily made barrier of downed aspens, Jim and Gordon shouldering rifles, Brother Elias carrying his box. Father Andrews followed close behind the preacher, carrying nothing, lost in silence.

The warm wind that had been blowing around them grew stronger as they walked. It whipped around them in strange and unnatural currents, sending strings of round aspen leaves fluttering in tiny whirlwinds, blowing against their faces from first one direction then another. Above them, the clouds and smoke were slowly encroaching on the sun. Ahead of them, the trail was already shadowed.

Brother Elias walked fast. He was obviously used to walking, and even wearing a suit and dress shoes he strode quickly and purposefully over rocks and ruts, pushing his way past manzanitas and mimosas. There was a trace of urgency in his movements, a hint of desperation in his long-legged stride. The trail they followed wound gradually upward, climbing a graded slope, but the preacher did not seem to notice. He did not slow down as he climbed but maintained a consistently even pace.

Ahead, the trail widened into a dirt semicircle. It was here that the off-road vehicles able to navigate the rough trail parked. Beyond this point there was only a small narrow footpath. Brother Elias did not even slow down as he came to the trail's end. He stepped purposefully over the low border of intentionally placed boulders and continued walking.

The climb was much steeper now. They were walking almost straight uphill, and both Gordon and Father Andrews were soon gasping for breath. Even Jim was having a difficult time. In addition to the rigorousness of the climb, the altitude was quite high and there was a noticeable lack of oxygen.

But Brother Elias seemed not to notice any of this. If anything, his gait became quicker, surer. He continued forward at a rapid pace, undaunted by either the steep climb or the thin air. He did not even bother to look back to make sure the others were following him.

Finally, all four of them reached the top of the hill. Here the path ended. Around them, the top of the rise was flat, the trees spaced widely apart. To their left, down through the forest of aspens, they could see the shimmering blue of the lake.

Brother Elias strode along the hilltop, never glancing to the side, never looking back, sure of his destination. The other three followed, trying to keep up. The wind was blowing wildly. Although very few trees or bushes were moving, the four of them were being buffeted by extremely strong gales. It was as if the wind was sentient, alive, and wanted only to harass them. Gordon looked up. The sky was now almost completely overcast, the sun effectively blotted out.

Suddenly Brother Elias stopped. He pointed in front of him. Protruding from the tall weeds and grasses were scores of small white crosses. Gordon shivered, feeling his knees grow weak.

Brother Elias put down his box and turned toward them. His face was set in an expression of grim determination. "We are here," he said.

NINE

Marina slowly came to her senses. The first thing she felt, before she even opened her eyes, was the sharp agonizing pain that burned through both the palms of her hands and the soles of her feet.

"Marina," Dr. Waterston said softly. "Marina."

She tried to stretch, but she could not move, and the pain ripped through her hands and feet like razor blades, flaring up through her body. She screamed in agony, opening her eyes wide.

Before her, standing in the middle of the kitchen, staring down at her, was the charred and blackened form of Dr. Waterston. He was burned horribly, and he smiled, his teeth unnaturally white. "We have been waiting for you to awaken," he said.

Marina noticed that her robe was wide open. Her panties had been ripped off.

"We wanted to make sure you could see and enjoy what we are about to do," Dr. Waterston said.

The evil-looking fetus with the large carving knife moved between Marina's legs.

"NO!" she screamed.

TEN

Brother Elias motioned for the rest of them to file past him into the unholy graveyard. The wind was howling wildly now; the sky was black. The preacher clapped a hand on Jim's shoulder as the sheriff moved past him. "You are a good man," he said. "I know you will protect us well, as your family always has." There seemed to be a note of regret in his voice, a hint of apology. His hand clasped Gordon's shoulder as Gordon walked into the field of crosses. "You, too, will be strong," he said. "For us as well as for your wife and daughter."

His black eyes met those of Father Andrews as the priest filed past. "Are you ready, Father?"

Andrews nodded silently.

He looks scared, Gordon thought.

Brother Elias drew from the box he had placed on the ground before him the two jars of blood. He opened the jars and passed his hands over the mouths of both, chanting quietly to himself. He took a small sip from each. Standing straight, his short hair blowing in the hard wind, he began walking slowly around the unseen perimeter of the makeshift graveyard, dribbling the blood on the ground as he did so. The wind was strong, but it was not strong enough to scatter the blood, and the heavy red liquid fell straight to the earth and weeds below.

Gordon did not think the supply of blood would hold out, but Brother Elias finished the entire circle and returned to them. From the box, he drew something small wrapped in a greasy rag.

He pulled open the sides of the rag to reveal the dried body of a long-dead fetus.

Gordon looked at the sheriff, who returned his troubled gaze. Both men watched silently as Brother Elias took the four small crosses from the canvas bag. He embedded three of the crosses in the ground at his feet, and immediately the wind doubled in strength. A tree branch cracked, falling to the ground. There was a low roaring rumble beneath their feet.

"Come closer!" Brother Elias shouted over the noise.

The other three moved next to him, holding their ground against the wind.

"The time has come!" the preacher shouted. "We must eat of the body, we must drink of the blood of power!" He looked at Gordon. "Give me your arm!"

Hesitantly, unsure of what the preacher was going to do, Gordon held out his arm. Brother Elias pushed up the sleeve of his shirt and drew the sharp edge of the remaining crucifix across Gordon's arm in a series of three quick slices.

Blood welled from the wounds, but Gordon felt nothing. His mind was shocked into numbness. He stared down at his bare arm, watching the rivers of red flow and grow.

Brother Elias raised the dried form of the fetus to his lips. He bit off the tiny head, chewing and swallowing it down before bending to Gordon's arm and licking clean the top cut, lapping up the blood. Gordon did not even flinch. He stared in shocked silence, feeling nothing. It was as if the entire ordeal were happening to someone else. When Brother Elias raised his head, Gordon could see that the top wound had completely disappeared.

"Now you!" the preacher shouted, nodding toward Jim. He held forward the remainder of the fetus's body.

The sheriff's arms and hands were shaking with fear and revulsion, but he found himself, almost against his will, bending down to take a bite of the tiny dried form. His mouth closed upon the upper torso of the unborn infant, and the torso snapped cleanly off. He could taste dust and dirt and mold. He found himself chewing.

"Drink!" Brother Elias commanded, guiding the sheriff's head toward one of the freely flowing cuts on Gordon's arm.

Jim opened his mouth and began licking the blood. He had prepared himself for the worst, but he found to his surprise that the blood had no taste at all. As he lapped it up, he felt a warm strength settle inside him. Beneath his tongue, Gordon's wound healed.

He straightened up, looking first at Gordon's blank face, then at the approving countenance of Brother Elias. His gaze shifted to Father Andrews, and his heart lurched in his chest. Next to the priest, wavering and unclear but becoming ever more distinct, was a familiar white human form. As he watched, the form came into focus, taking definite shape.

Don Wilson.

He stared at the boy, meeting his eyes, trying to make contact, but Don did not seem to see him. The sheriff glanced quickly back at Brother Elias, but the preacher only nodded silently.

Now Gordon was taking a bite of the fetus, chewing upon the dried dusty body. As he swallowed, a light came back into his eyes, his face once again became animated.

He followed the sheriff's gaze and saw the form of

the boy coming into focus. The boy was wearing the same clothes he had worn in Gordon's dream. His eyes snapped back to Brother Elias, but the preacher was already stepping toward Father Andrews.

"It's your turn!" Brother Elias shouted above the wind. "Hurry! We are almost out of time!"

The priest looked up. No. He could not. He had watched both Brother Elias and the sheriff participate in this sacrilegious inverse of the Eucharist. He had seen them act out this unholy ritual, and though he felt intuitively that Brother Elias knew what he was doing, he could not bring himself to follow suit. It felt wrong to him.

It felt evil.

A small hand gently grasped his own, slender fingers intertwining with his own larger thicker fingers, and he looked down to see a boy, not more than eleven or twelve, looking up at him. There was an innocent radiance in the youngster's face, and Father Andrews felt the negative resolve fade away within him. He glanced toward Gordon and the sheriff and was shocked to find them staring at the boy next to him. They saw him too!

But that was not possible. Even as he felt the boy's hand squeeze his own, he realized that the figure was not real.

"It is your turn," Brother Elias repeated.

Moving as if through water, hardly aware of what he was doing, allowing the gentle pull of the boy's hand to guide him forward, Father Andrews bent down to accept the last portion of the fetus's body. He opened his mouth to accept the small dried legs.

He licked the blood off Gordon's remaining wound.

The figure of the boy faded slowly from sight.

Brother Elias placed the final cross, the one he had used to cut Gordon's arm, into the ground at his feet next to the others. The earth lurched beneath them. "I must now confront the adversary!" he announced.

He gestured toward the ring of blood surrounding the field of crosses. "We are protected against any non-physical manifestations as long as we remain within the circle." He looked at Gordon and the sheriff. "But we are not protected against anything physical. The adversary knows this. So whatever it attacks us with will be real." He pointed toward the white crosses. "Shoot whatever comes up there. Shoot the hell out of it. You must protect us until the ritual is over or we will fail."

He bowed his head. "Let us pray."

There was a high-pitched shrieking, but they all ignored it, bowing their heads. The preacher recited the Lord's Prayer and the rest of them mouthed the words. Immediately after, with their heads still bowed, Brother Elias chanted a prayer that was harsh, guttural, and entirely inhuman. He raised his head and traced in the air before him a cross, a spiral, and a geometric shape.

Gordon looked at the preacher, whose eyes seemed to be filled with an unfamiliar emotion—Fear?

He pointed to the left side of the graveyard. "You station yourself there," he told Gordon. He spoke quickly, urgently. "You stay there," he told Jim, pointing to the opposite side.

Both men ran to their positions.

And the ground split open, the white crosses falling over.

"Jesus!" Gordon screamed.

Clawing its way up from the ground was a gigantic infant, easily as big as a large cow. Its skin was rotted and peeling, a disgusting bluish gray. Gordon could see exposed veins throbbing in its temples. A portion of its face had rotted away, leaving only skull. This was not one of the clearly supernatural creatures they had encountered at the dump. This was obviously a corpse that had been reanimated, a dead baby that had been allowed to nurture and grow in the ground underneath Milk Ranch Point for decades. Huge fingers, dripping with slime and dead skin, grasped the crumbling ground.

Jim aimed his rifle and shot the huge infant full in the face. The bullet passed through the monstrous head, sending shattered fragments of bone and skin flying. Black blood began to ooze from the wound.

Jim reloaded, aimed and fired again. And again. And again and again and again.

The huge creature fell, its head a shattered mass of pulpy flesh. The ground was littered with black blood.

Another huge infant pushed its way up from the ground on the far side of the graveyard and another crawled over the dead and bleeding body of the first.

Were these the babies who had been buried here? Jim wondered. He thought of his great-grandfather, Ezra Weldon, whom he had never met. Was this what had happened last time?

He loaded his rifle and fired again.

By this time, Gordon had regained his senses and was firing his own weapon at the monstrous creatures. They can be killed, he kept repeating to himself. They are real. They are physical beings. His first bullet missed, but the rest found their marks. The targets were too big not to hit.

Brother Elias and Father Andrews stood staring at each other as the ground erupted around them and the living corpses of the gigantic infants pushed their way to the surface. Hot wind whipped against their faces, bringing with it the rotten odor of decay. The priest closed his eyes as he felt an unwelcome and unfamiliar power pressing in on him, straining against his closed senses, trying to find a crack in the psychic block he had constructed in his mind.

"Open yourself!" Brother Elias commanded.

The priest closed himself off tight, protecting himself. The air around him was thick and heavy with the force of power. He could feel the evil closing in on him, and the monstrousness of it made everything he had ever felt before pale by comparison. He began to shake, feeling the pressure increase around him.

"Open yourself!" Brother Elias screamed.

My time is near, Father Andrews thought, recalling the verse from the Bible. I am ready to sacrifice myself. And then . . . *and then he was strong! His weak and vacillating will was bolstered by an infusion of iron determination; his numb and tired brain expanded instantly to encompass a knowledge vast and limitless yet perfectly ordered.*

And then he was drowning, fading, crushed and overwhelmed by the power of this new force, which drained away his being, sucking him into itself and growing stronger still. He heard himself cry out somewhere amidst this turmoil, his voice, his thought, shrinking, going, gone.

And then the power was no longer bodiless, no longer a disassociated will working imperfectly through other vessels out of necessity. Hot and burning, allknowing, strong with the forsaken lives of so many beings, the power was now free, now possessed of a form it could use, a form it could control perfectly and utterly. The power looked through seeing eyes, experienced through living senses, the world around it.

And the creatures opposing the power seemed suddenly so weak, so insignificant.

"BOW DOWN BEFORE YOUR NEW GOD."

The voice was so powerful, so awesome, that both Gordon and the sheriff turned to look. Even the monstrous babies crawling out of the fissured ground stalled for a second in their movements.

"I COMMAND YOU TO BOW DOWN BEFORE ME."

The voice was clearly that of Father Andrews, and it was obviously coming out of the priest's slack open mouth, but it was amplified beyond all possibility.

Brother Elias lunged forward and grabbed the

priest's shoulders, holding tight. He shoved his face right next to the priest's. At the top of his lungs, he screamed the alien words of the Ritual of Banishment, but even his powerful voice sounded small and impotent next to that of Father Andrews.

The priest's horrible laugh drowned out his chanting words. The noise was deafening, echoing across the hills and into the blackened sky.

"YOU HAVE NO POWER OVER ME."

Brother Elias spoke faster, the strange words tumbling out, as if he had only a certain amount of time in which to speak and that time was almost gone. ". . . The Lord our God," he screamed clearly in English, and then he was thrown away from the priest, his body tumbling back over itself until it landed against a large gray stone twenty feet away. He stood up, shook his head to clear it and immediately began chanting again, the inhuman words rushing out of his mouth at an auctioneer's pace. He walked toward the priest, hands and arms extended, his fingers tracing symbolic outlines in the air.

And Father Andrews began to change.

His body expanded outward, bloating, the skin pulling taut across his face and hands, his clothes ripping open.

"No!" Brother Elias screamed, and there was panic in his voice.

The hair on Father Andrews' head began streaming out, growing at the rate of several feet per second, reaching the ground. At first it was brownish blond, the color of the priest's natural hair, but it instantly darkened into jet. A distorted fist of bone punched its way through the priest's stomach. Two huge black eyes pushed the old eyes out, sending them sliding slimily down the taut fat cheeks. The priest's hands jerked off in a spray of blood, and two red whipcord arteries protruded through the newly made openings, thrashing blindly around. The legs split, divided, multiplied.

Brother Elias, still chanting madly, ran forward and grabbed the four gold crucifixes that were embedded in the ground before the metamorphosing body of Father Andrews.

The priest's body began to split down the center, streams of inky liquid blackness escaping through the torn opening.

"I AM GOD," a new voice said through Father Andrews' mouth as the head began to split apart.

And Brother Elias shoved the first crucifix into the center of what was left of the priest's body.

Pain and a sudden loss of vital energy. Awareness of a power equal to or greater than its own.

Comprehension.

Fear.

There was an audible rush of air as the cross withered and blackened. Father Andrews screamed in rage and agony, and both Jim and Gordon put their hands over their ears to block out the terrible noise.

The preacher shoved another cross into Father Andrews' distorted body, this one through the forehead. The body fell to the ground. Repeating over and over again the final words of the ritual, Brother Elias shoved the last two crucifixes into the priest's abdomen.

The power retreated back from whence it had come, its knowledge suddenly gone, its ambitions forgotten, its seemingly endless strength rapidly depleting. It pulled into itself. All that mattered now was survival.

Bolts of black energy erupted outward from the crosses, draining color from the surrounding earth and air. The crucifixes melted, their metal twisting into whirling spirals. The bolts of energy, growing increasingly weak, dissipated into the dark clouds above.

Two of the oversized infants were still moving, and Jim fired several rounds into each of them, killing them both. The bodies dissolved into the ground, leaving only a grayish slimy mulch.

The hot wind tapered off to nothing, and Gordon and the sheriff looked at each other, breathing deeply, their hearts pounding wildly in their chests. They said nothing as they moved across the broken ground toward the spot where Brother Elias lay unmoving in the dirt.

ELEVEN

Screaming crazily, the black figure of Dr. Waterston burst into flames. The charred skin flaked off, and in the second before the figure was engulfed entirely, Marina saw something shiny and white and wormlike.

The flame disappeared as quickly as it had come, and the fetus between her legs dropped the knife it was holding. It fell to its knees, as though it had suddenly lost what coordination it had.

All of the creatures in the kitchen were suddenly crawling around in dumb mindlessness, and Marina realized that, though she still could not move, she was safe.

She began to cry.

TWELVE

Brother Elias was just sitting up groggily as Jim and Gordon reached him. They helped him to his feet, each holding onto an arm as he stood unsteadily. The preacher smiled at them, a real smile, an open smile. "You did well," he said. "You both did well."

His smile faded as he stooped to look at the remains of Father Andrews. The hideous mutations that had torn apart the priest's body at the end had disappeared, reversing themselves, and the bloody remains, though mutilated, were undeniably human. The crosses had disintegrated completely. "If we had been here sooner, he would not have died," the preacher said. He gestured toward the bloody form before him. "We will carry his body to the truck and wrap it safely in the tarp," he said. "We will give him a Christian burial."

"Is that it?" Gordon asked. "Is it over?"

Brother Elias nodded. "It is over," he said. "This time."

Gordon looked around at the ground of Milk Ranch Point. Trees had been uprooted, grass and weeds flattened, rocks overturned. There were huge holes in the gaping earth. Only a few of the white crosses were still standing. Everything was covered with a sickly pale mulch. Gordon looked at his arm. There was no sign of any of the cuts. He could still taste a disgusting musty dryness in his mouth, however, and he spit. He looked over at the sheriff, and both of them smiled.

Above them, the sky was clearing. Silently, Brother Elias picked up Father Andrews' arms. Without being told, Jim and Gordon each grabbed one of his feet. They started down the hill toward the truck.

THIRTEEN

Gordon stood with Brother Elias in the crowded lumberyard of the sawmill, watching as teams of men shoveled the tiny dead bodies of hundreds of fetuses into the furnace of the smelter. It was late afternoon, but the sun was still high in the western sky. The men worked hard, using large flat sawdust shovels to remove the fetuses from the pickup trucks. The sheriff was standing on the stump of a log, coordinating the effort, telling the men exactly what to do. Several regular posse members as well as firemen and workers from the mill were helping to dispose of the bodies. Keith Beck stood nearby, taking photos for the newspaper and talking to various people, writing down their quotes in a small notebook.

He wondered what Beck would write.

Several dozen people stood outside the chain link fence of the sawmill, staring in. Many of the parents had taken their children home, not wanting them to view the horrible scene. Gordon looked out at the crowd. He could see Char Clifton pressed against the fence, and, next to him, Elsie Cavanaugh from the drugstore. Just like he had in his dream.

He looked over at Brother Elias. The preacher's

face was bandaged, but he did not look tired or worn out. There was a strange gleam in his eye. He fixed Gordon with his black gaze. " 'Just as the weeds are gathered and burned with fire, so it will be at the close of the age. The Son of man will send his angels, and they will gather out of his kingdom all causes of sin and all evildoers, and throw them into the furnace of fire.' Matthew 13:40."

Gordon shivered and turned back to the smelter. Black foul-smelling smoke billowed out of the single stack. Many of the workers were wearing surgical masks to protect themselves from the effects. Gordon glanced into the sky, half expecting the smoke to have coalesced into some type of coherent shape, but the black cloud was formless.

He looked at the pickup trucks filled with tiny bodies. He still did not know where all of the fetuses had come from. There seemed to be thousands of them. He found himself wondering how long it would take before all this happened again, and whether anyone then would remember this day. He watched the workers throwing the bodies into the fire, the sheriff shouting orders.

Toward evening, the smoke became so thick that all of the workers were forced to wear masks. Those who had no masks and all of the bystanders had to go home.

The sunset could not be seen for the smoke.

The black smoke hung over Randall for three days, like fog, until a long-overdue rainstorm washed it away.

It was another three days before all of the soot was cleaned off the streets.

EPILOGUE

ONE

Fall was coming. Temperatures were beginning to drop, and leaves on some of the trees were already starting to change color. Staring out the office window, Jim could see a small patch of orange and yellow on one of the trees lining Main Street. Farther to the north, near the sawmill, several trees were starting to change. The sheriff stared out at the town, thinking silently. It looked remarkably normal, amazingly untouched. There were no demolished buildings, no flattened homes. There was a large chunk of forest at the base of the Rim where the old landfill used to be that was now scorched and burned, but on the whole, the damage had been much less severe than he had expected. Most of Randall, in fact, had been cleaned up within a few days.

Of course, who knew what the long-range consequences would be?

Jim moved over to his desk and sat down heavily. He picked up the newspaper and threw it into the metal waste can near his feet. Eighty-five. The final death toll was eighty-five, counting the Selway family and the first two farmers. A lot of those had been self-induced or the result of panic, but a goodly chunk of them were not attributable to anything so rational. Deke Chandler had been torn apart, portions of his body switched. Three ranchers had been drowned in the blood of their farm animals. The coroner had found their lungs suffused with blood. Jeff Tilton and old lady Peltzer had been brutally stabbed to death. Tilton's face had been stabbed so repeatedly that it was unrecognizable.

He and the coroner had agreed to list the deaths as accidental.

Surprisingly, the TV stations in Phoenix and Flagstaff had mentioned the incidents only briefly. There had been a more thorough article in *The Arizona Republic,* but even that newspaper had glossed over the facts, instead laying its faith in a bizarre theory put forth by an uninvolved member of the state police. Only the Randall paper had told the real story, had gone into it with any depth. There had even been photos of the burnings on the front page.

The rumor was that Beck was trying to sell the story to the *National Enquirer.*

Jim smiled. He'd probably sell it. Those people ate up that shit.

Through the open window, the sheriff heard the pealing of the church bells, calling people for the noontime Sunday services. The staggered ringing carried clearly through the still, fresh air, and the sound was pleasant music to the sheriff's ears. He listened carefully, but he could not hear the tones of the Episcopal church bell.

Apparently, the bishop had not yet appointed another replacement.

The phone on his desk buzzed, and Jim picked up the receiver, punching the lighted button for line one. "Hello," he said. "Weldon speaking."

"Jim."

He softened at the sound of his wife's voice. "Hi, honey. What's up?"

"I was wondering if you were coming home for lunch. The kids're at Timmy Wharton's house, and we could have a nice private little get-together. Just me and you."

He smiled. "Sounds romantic."

"When will you be home?"

"I'll be there in ten minutes."

"Okay," she said. She paused. "I love you."

"I love you, too. Good-bye."

"Good-bye."

He hung up the phone, and his eye fell on the empty holster on the hat rack. Carl's. He would have to start advertising for a replacement soon. And replacements for Pete and Judson. Both had given him their notices. Both had also agreed to stay on until he could find new men. Pete, he knew, was planning to apply for a job at the post office. He wasn't sure what Judson had planned.

Jim stood up and grabbed his hat from the rack. He put it on and stepped out of his office, walking down the hall toward the front desk. He smiled and nodded at Rita, operating the switchboard. "Hold all my calls this afternoon, will you? I'm going to be gone the rest of the day."

Rita smiled. "Supervisor Jones is going to have your ass for this, you know. She's already mad at you."

"Fuck her," Jim said. He waved good-bye and stepped outside into the warm, fresh open air.

He got in his car and drove home.

TWO

Gordon and Marina sat next to each other on the couch, watching an old Fred Astaire movie on the new television Gordon had charged while they were in Phoenix. The old TV had been smashed. A commercial came on, and they turned to look at each other. They kissed.

She was getting prettier, Gordon thought. Maybe that old line about expectant mothers having a special glow was true. He reached for her hand and held it. He could feel the stitches in her palm.

They had not talked about what had happened. The subject was taboo, although Gordon was not sure why. They had not even decided not to discuss it, they simply did not mention it, although they had gone down to Phoenix for more tests.

All the tests had been normal.

Gordon looked down at Marina's slightly swelling abdomen. He wondered what their daughter would grow up to be.

The movie came back on, and Gordon turned toward the TV. They could afford the TV now. They could afford the baby. After Brad's death, ownership of the Pepsi franchise had reverted to Connie. But

Connie knew nothing about distribution or delivery, and she had hired Gordon on as manager or foreman—they weren't quite sure of the official title yet—at twice the salary. Marina would teach for a few months, but her students would have a permanent substitute for most of the year.

Gordon was still not entirely comfortable with what had happened. He still had a lot of questions, but no one seemed to have any answers. He and the sheriff had talked quite a bit, but the sheriff was just as much in the dark as he was.

God knew where Brother Elias had gone.

Perhaps that was why he had started the novel. Loose ends were tied up in novels, everything had an easy explanation, pieces fit together logically. There were reasons for why things happened.

Actually, he was fairly proud of himself. He had started the novel less than a week ago, and already he had forty pages done. Forty good pages. He had never written so fast or so well before, and he had hopes that the book might find a publisher.

It was a horror novel.

Fred Astaire was dancing in front of a long line of turret guns on a navy ship. Gordon put his head in Marina's lap. He felt good. Marina, he knew, was still having a lot of problems. She was depressed much of the time, and she was very worried about the baby, but that was understandable. Both of them were going to counseling now, and he had faith that they could work through their troubles. He pressed his ear to Marina's abdomen, and imagined he could hear, within her, the soft beating of another heart. He looked up at her. "How do you feel?" he asked.

She smiled. "I feel all right."

"All right? Just all right?"

Her smile grew wider. "Okay, then. Pretty good."

He kissed her stomach, and she ran her fingers through his hair. He kissed her again, his arm moving around her midsection. He grinned up at her. "Want me to kiss you somewhere else?"

She looked down on him, feigning innocence. "On my forehead?"

"Lower."

"On my lips?"

"One pair of lips."

She laughed and hit him on the head.

"Ow." He sat up, looked at her for a moment, then glanced at the TV. "It's a boring movie anyway."

"I like it. I want to find out what happens."

"Fred gets the girl and they all live happily ever after."

"The girl?"

"Okay, the woman."

Marina pretended to think for a moment, then stood up. She switched off the TV. "Come on," she said. She grabbed his hand.

They walked toward the bedroom.

THREE

The preacher stood next to the on-ramp of Black Canyon Highway, holding out his thumb, smiling. His suitcase, photo album, and a bundle of pamphlets lay at his feet. His black-bound Bible was clutched under his arm. Although it was fairly warm out, he was wearing a gray business suit, complete with jacket and tie.

He continued smiling, infinitely patient, his black eyes watching the road for approaching traffic.

Several cars and trucks passed him by before a tan Buick LeSabre, heading west toward Los Angeles, stopped to offer him a ride.